Akwaeke Emezi (they/them) is the author of the bestselling novel *You Made a Fool of Death with Your Beauty*, *New York Times* bestseller *The Death of Vivek Oji*, which was longlisted for the Dylan Thomas Prize; *Pet*, a finalist for the National Book Award for Young People's Literature; and *Freshwater*, which was named a *New York Times* Notable Book, longlisted for both the Wellcome Book Prize and the Women's Prize for Fiction and shortlisted for the PEN/Hemingway Award, the New York Public Library Young Lions Fiction Award, the Lambda Literary Award, and the Center for Fiction's First Novel Prize. Selected as a 5 Under 35 honoree by the National Book Foundation, they are based in liminal spaces.

Further praise for *Little Rot*:

'With an almost surreal narrative confronting societal decay and personal rebirth, Emezi's signature lyricism and profound character insights are on full display, creating an immersive and thought-provoking experience. *Little Rot* further cements Emezi's place as a master of blending the mystical with the everyday.' *Glamour*

'A dark thriller about corruption, told with beautiful style and a literary eye.' Nana Kwame Adjei-Brenyah

'[A] plot that ducks and dives with cinematic verve, gaining momentum and menace from a series of coincidence-fuelled twists . . . Emezi has a flair for descriptive exuberance, perfectly capturing the texture of this tainted world in which moral decay seeps into every fibre of life.' *Observer*

Little Rot

Akwaeke Emezi

faber

First published in the UK in 2024
by Faber & Faber Limited
The Bindery, 51 Hatton Garden,
London ECIN 8HN

First published in the USA in 2024
by Riverhead Books
An imprint of Penguin Random House LLC
penguinrandomhouse.com

This paperback edition first published in 2025

Printed and bound by CPI Group (UK) Ltd, Croydon, CRO 4YY

The second chapter of this book previously published as
"Femimo" in different form in SABLE LitMag (2014).

The right of Akwaeke Emezi to be identified as author
of this work has been asserted in accordance with Section 77
of the Copyright, Designs and Patents Act 1988

A CIP record for this book
is available from the British Library

ISBN 978-0-571-38282-8

MIX
Paper | Supporting
responsible forestry
FSC® C171272

Printed and bound in the UK on FSC® certified paper in line with our continuing
commitment to ethical business practices, sustainability and the environment.
For further information see faber.co.uk/environmental-policy

Our authorised representative in the EU for product safety is
Easy Access System Europe, Mustamäe tee 50, 10621 Tallinn, Estonia
gpsr.requests@easproject.com

2 4 6 8 10 9 7 5 3 1

*To those of us who cannot
help but look at true things.*

I'm just trying to look at something without blinking,
to see what it is like, or it could have been like, and how
that had something to do with the way we live now.

TONI MORRISON

one

The sun was setting in an oily splash of color, streaked blood in the sky under swollen clouds. A train circled the airport like a rusting tapeworm, lengths of loud metal dragging against old elevated tracks that the government could barely be bothered to maintain. Down on the ground, Aima looked up with nausea slicking greasily inside her. Metal screeched against metal as the train turned a corner, and she winced.

It had been years since she had stepped into one of those death traps; Kalu had insisted that a driver from his company shuttle her around since they had moved back home. She had thought she was blessed then, to have a boyfriend like him. He was generous, he adored her, and she was absolutely sure he'd never been unfaithful, which barely any other woman in the city could claim of their own partners.

None of that had mattered in the end. If there had ever once been anointing oil on Aima's head, it had long since dried up, leaving her faith unhappy and flaking.

From the cracked sidewalk, she stared at Kalu as he pulled her suitcase from the boot of his car, his shoulders strange under his shirt, his face warped. His hair was cut low and neat as always. A plane whined above them as it descended, the sound fanning through the hot air. Kalu's mouth was pressed into a stressed line. It looked out of place on his soft face—his mouth was always meant for easy smiles, his broad body for drowning embraces that Aima used to cherish. Her friends back in Texas had joked that Kalu was her personal teddy bear, somewhere safe and warm, someone who would never hurt her.

Now, he looked like a foreign place, and Aima wanted to tap him on the shoulder. He'd look up with those dark, dark eyes of his; and she would ask who he was exactly, what he was doing here, and what had happened to the man who had laughed with her in Houston and promised to never let her go. She didn't move, though; she just kept staring as a dry breeze blew the tips of her black braids across her back. Aima had loved him for four, almost five, years, and this morning, after she'd booked her tickets away from him, Kalu had refused to let the driver take her to the airport. He'd slid behind the wheel himself, and for the whole ride, Aima had pressed her forehead to the glass of the passenger window, her earphones locked into her ears.

Over the gospel music she was playing, she'd heard ghosts—snippets of his voice trying to get to her, timid and weak attempts at connection, tendrils dying in the air between them. It was all small talk, nothing she could hold with both hands, meaningless chatter that avoided the truth of what they had both become. So, when they pulled up to the curb of the airport and Kalu had reached out to touch her arm, Aima had shrugged him off and stepped out of the car without saying anything. If he wasn't going to talk about it, he didn't deserve to touch her.

Her dress whipped loosely around her legs as she stood next to the car, and she could feel the eyes of the uniformed men at the door moving over her. She wondered if they could see her thighs through the flowered chiffon—it was thin, and her skin was bare underneath. "You should wear a slip," her mother used to say. "Don't be indecent. God is watching you." But it was hot, and even though God had crawled His way into her life since she had come home, Aima didn't think He particularly cared about her clothing choices. With a body as full as hers, she'd been hearing people call her indecent since she was a child. She smoothed her hands down the front of her dress and waited as Kalu placed her suitcase on the ground beside her.

The terminal for international departures was full of people seeing others off, families gathered with their children darting through a forest of legs, gorged bags being unloaded from taxis, voices flapping and thickening the air. Aima wanted Kalu to drive away, but she knew he wouldn't leave until she was safely inside the building, as if someone was going to kidnap her from the pavement. As if another car was going to pull up, wheels smoking, arms and bodies leaping out to grab her and throw her inside and drive her off to a different kind of life, a secret part of the city, one that didn't involve Kalu. But there was nothing, nothing except traffic and voices and polluted air and ruined love and a cracked faith. Aima sighed and watched dully as Kalu extended the handle of her suitcase, pulling it up in two sure clicks.

"You don't have to go," he said, and she stared at him.

Two and a half hours in traffic coming down from the highland because there had been an accident on the South-South Bridge that squashed everyone into a single lane. There'd been blood on the road, a bus on its side, armed personnel guiding cars past. Two and a half hours, and it was now that Kalu had decided to find mouth. All that evasive small talk just to bring up the true thing when they were about to part.

Aima fixed her eyes on him and said nothing. His tone was an insult anyway. He'd made it too casual, as if he was presenting an informal option. He didn't want to sound like he was begging her. Pride. Another thing she didn't recognize in him. What other sins had he accumulated since they had come home? When had he become so set, so unwilling to be soft with her?

She stared at his face, at the instability of his eyes. Four years together, four years of his pupils dilating for her. She had seen those eyes in all their permutations—clear and bright, dim, narrowed, wet. Aima knew the forked wrinkles that crowded in the corners, the way they changed course like undecided rivers when he smiled, the swoop of his eyelashes falling as he laughed. It was amazing how strange his eyes looked now. You could be so intimate, so familiar with someone's skin and flesh and spirit, only to wake up one day and find that it had receded from you, suddenly, like a tide rushing back out into the sea, leaving you with dissolving foam and a damp heart.

"You don't have to go," he said again, the same way.

Aima knew she should ignore him, but to her regret, she was still soft. "What do you want me to do? Stay here? And do what?"

"What we've been doing," he answered. She knew he meant loving each other, but they'd already been over this.

"Wasting time? Living in sin?"

He flinched. "Please don't start that again; it's not true. We're not wasting time, and you didn't care about this living in sin nonsense until we came home."

Aima wiped a thin film of sweat from her forehead and sighed. It was humid beyond belief; New Lagos was in the middle of the rainy season. Of course Kalu didn't care. He was the man—he would get congratulated for getting her to live with and fuck him without having to marry her. She was the one considered to be a whore, a slut, a loose girl, easy, no morals. He didn't care that she'd woken up one morning and seen the sunlight break through the glass and something about the New Lagos dawn had woken God up in her heart. She had tried explaining it so many times, but he was hung up on the woman she used to be, and she was disappointed in the man he still was.

"I don't have energy for this, Kalu. Not again."

They'd been arguing for months and it was tiring, so tiring to fight for what was supposed to be love, allegedly love. It didn't feel like love anymore. Their relationship felt distorted, a mask of dissatisfaction or apathy that had fallen into the skin underneath, cannibalized it. Whatever it had been, if it had been love, that thing was gone, dead. Aima wrapped her hand around the handle of her suitcase and swiveled it to start entering the airport. If she didn't move, Kalu was just going to stand there and continue being the coward he'd recently decided to be. Before she could walk away, though, he came in for a hug.

"You can't just go like that, without saying goodbye."

Aima made a face and reached around him with one arm, going for a pat on his left shoulder, but Kalu wrapped her up as if nothing had changed for them. His palm was wide and gentle at the back of her head, and he buried his face in her neck, muffling his voice. "Please," he whispered. "I love you so much, baby."

Aima felt tears start up and it made her angry. He smelled like home. He smelled like a hundred sleepy mornings together, and it wasn't fair. As if she didn't love him. As if any of this was happening because they didn't *love* each other. He smelled like light, clean and bright and tearing through her. Aima squeezed her eyes tightly, refusing to cry in front of all these people.

"Love isn't enough, and you know it," she snapped, pulling herself away.

Her wheels clattered against the cement, and she didn't look back as she dragged her suitcase past the men at the door, ignoring their voices as they tried to get her attention. Once inside, she put her suitcase on the conveyor belt, through the X-ray machine; then she collected it from the other side and stood in the crush of people.

What was she supposed to do now? The counter for British Airways already had a long queue of people waiting to check in, heaping their bags on the scale and arguing with the airline employees about weight restrictions. Aima stood motionless and considered. She could get to the lounge, put her earphones back on, and listen to some music, pretend that none of this was actually happening. In three hours, she would be airborne and out of this damn place. The night would carry her away, and before sunrise, she would be in London.

Her phone buzzed and she glanced at the screen. Kalu. I love you so much. I am so sorry. Have a safe flight.

Aima wasn't sure why that pissed her off all over again. It should be fine that he gave up. It showed who he really was, and besides, she *wanted* him to give up, didn't she? If she was leaving, didn't that mean she wanted to be let go of? Her jaw clenched with a surge of rage. No, Kalu shouldn't have caved. She wasn't sure what he should have done other than be a different person who wanted something different, or wasn't afraid, or whatever, but he had definitely done the wrong thing. Aima shoved her phone into her handbag and turned left, walking to the Airtel booth, temper steaming off her. People stepped out of her way with curious glances at the set of her face. She recharged her phone credit, bought a new data plan, and went down to Arrivals, leaning her suitcase against her thigh to carry it down the stairs. Standing outside a snack stall, she took her phone back out and called Ijendu.

"Bebi gehl." Ijendu's voice sang over the line. "How far? Have you checked in yet?"

"Ije, I have a favor to ask, biko."

"No problem. What do you need?"

Aima hesitated, then jumped. "I don't want to take this flight. Is it all right if I come and stay with you? Just for a little bit?"

Ijendu whooped in her ear. "Ahn, of course, bebi! My house is your house. You don't even have to ask. So, you and Kalu are working it out, abi? I knew it. It's not possible to just have everything end like that, not for the two of you."

The rage hammered under her molars. "No, we're not working anything out. Unless he proposes, I'm not interested in whatever he has to say."

"Ah-ahn now. It's not by force, Aima. Let him propose on his own time. Men don't like it when you pressure them like that."

"I don't care what he likes. That's his own problem."

Ijendu tsked in her ear. "Babe, this your vex is much. The man loves you."

"Ije, please—"

"Okay, okay, sorry. Go and find your taxi. I'll be at the house."

Aima hung up and called an Uber. Eleven minutes. She sighed and sat down on her suitcase, trying not to put too much of her weight on it, hovering on the edge. She was good at that, trying not to put too much pressure on things, trying to fit into slivers of space, press herself against the edges so she wouldn't bother anyone. It was probably why Kalu was so shocked when she stopped doing it, when she looked around and thought—*Wait, I'm not happy like this*. When she'd told him what would make her happy, he'd acted like she'd asked him to kill his own mother. Maybe he'd thought she would go back to the edges and give him back the space to do whatever he wanted on his own time, but that's the problem with pressing yourself down too much, folding and folding when you're not really made of a material that's suitable for those kinds of creases. At some point, you just spring back up when you can't take another bending, not a single pleat more. And upon that, you spring back with force, and your momentum can be quite upsetting to people who didn't expect you to claim your space.

Aima had thought about folding back, of course; she knew how much easier everything would be if she just agreed with Kalu that, yes, there was no rush to get married and they didn't have to do things on the time line of anyone else; except that she wasn't anyone else. She *mattered* in this, and he'd acted like she didn't even have the common sense to think or decide or want things for herself, like she was just giving him an ultimatum because everyone else said it was somehow for them not to even be engaged yet. Something about that, how pliable he thought she was, had annoyed her to the point where she couldn't give way, not this time. And so here she was, suitcase packed and Kalu driving away after four whole years. Amazing.

Her phone rang and she picked it up, coordinating with the driver, who pulled up in a small but clean blue car. He made to get out of the driver's seat, but Aima waved him off and put her suitcase in the back seat herself, climbing in next to it.

"Mbano Estate?" the driver asked.

"Yes, thank you." Aima slid her earphones back into her ears and rested her forehead on the glass of the window again, watching the city reverse the way it had come less than an hour before. It was a thick city, especially in the lowland—brash and pungent, a hammering of colors and people. She tried not to focus on the burning sorrow in her chest, the despair that wouldn't even allow her to pray. She'd prayed before, for a love that would never leave her lonely. She'd gotten it in Kalu; she'd been safe in it for years, allowed herself to feel safe only for it all to be stripped away in the end. What kind of an answer to a prayer was that?

They were supposed to be together until old age claimed them. They'd both talked about forever, built a home together, made plans, and foolishly, she'd thought it was enough. Maybe this was all a lesson, that because she hadn't formalized it in God's house, that's why she wasn't getting her happy ending? Maybe she had been rash, careless to think that she didn't have to do things the right way. Maybe she should have known that if he didn't love God the way she did, then he couldn't have been the real answer to her prayers. This could have all been a false faith, and now her eyes were being torn open. If there was gratitude to give God for that clarity, that release from a lie, Aima couldn't quite find it in her to send it up. Right now, she didn't want to talk to God. All she had was a plate full of bitter silence.

There was no traffic in their direction, so the Uber reached Ijendu's house quickly, not even thirty minutes through the twisting roads that took them into the highland. Aima thanked the driver and unloaded without waiting for Ijendu's gateman to open the gate. As the car drove away, the gateman came out of the pedestrian door, the collar of his uniform stained with sweat.

"Ah, Aunty, it's you. Nnọọ."

He took the suitcase from her and she allowed it, following him into the compound. There were orange and lemon trees lining the walls, heavy with green fruit. Ijendu's mother was growing grapefruits and pomelos in the backyard—the woman could chatter on for hours about grafting and finger limes if you let her. The air was sweet from all the citrus, and Aima walked slowly to the back door, listening to the evening birds and the lack of the rest of the city.

Ijendu was in the kitchen with pink glasses perched on her nose, her long legs bare and brown under a pair of sleep shorts. She could've been a model if her parents had allowed it; she had the graceful limbs, the soaring neck, and a sculpted face that was almost painful to look at, she was so striking. Ever since they were girls together, Aima had always thought Ijendu looked a little inhuman in that high-fashion way. She was pulling a plate of jollof rice out of the microwave when Aima entered.

"Ah, perfect," Ijendu said. "I just finished warming your own." She handed Aima the plate and grabbed a jug of water, gesturing to the dining room with her head. "Bịa, ka anyị rie."

The room was decorated in typical rich Igbo ornateness—scalloped edges to the furniture, marble and gold, tufted and buttoned crimson upholstery. Two place settings had been laid out and Ijendu put Aima's plate down on one of them.

"I had them fry some fish for you instead of chicken," she said. She was keeping her voice light, but her eyes were soft and sympathetic.

"Daalụ." Aima sat down opposite her friend, trying not to let the kindness set off a wave of tears. The plate was sectioned into quadrants—rice, dodo, fish, and shredded cabbage in the name of salad.

"I'm glad you stayed," Ijendu said, cutting into her chicken thigh. "Even if it wasn't for him. I was already missing you. Besides, running away never fixes anything."

"What's there to fix?" Aima replied, poking at her food. She knew she sounded flat, but she couldn't help it. She'd moved home not for Kalu but *with* him. It was strange to suddenly be directionless now that she'd ended their relationship, like she'd turned into one of those women who ruined their own lives by centering it on a man. It hadn't felt like that at the time. It had felt like they were a unit, partners. She could already hear the voices calling her stupid for thinking like that without a ring, without actual commitment. What were words without a contract? What was a partnership without God's presence? She should have *protected* herself.

"Ah-ahn, don't be like that." Ijendu gave her a kind look. "Don't start repressing your feelings. These emotions are necessary! They're part of healing."

Aima rolled her eyes and stabbed her fish with her fork. "Emotions ko, feelings ni."

Ijendu snorted. "You know what? Let's not even discuss him for now. We need to distract you." She thought for a moment, then snapped her fingers, the sound echoing through the dining room. "Ah, I know! We already planned to go clubbing tonight, but now you're coming with us. Paffect. You can dance away your troubles."

"Coming with who? Your usual bad gehls?" Aima let her voice sound as mocking as she felt. She'd never bothered to hide how little she liked Ijendu's friends. It wasn't that she was a prude or anything, but she just wasn't on their level. The kind of things they liked to do left her uncomfortable—they were too free with themselves, with their bodies and what they put into them. She and Ijendu had known each other in secondary school, gone to Bible study together because their families went to the same church. When Aima's parents moved to London and Aima to the States, they never minded her returning to New Lagos without them because they knew Ijendu's family was there. The girls had essentially been sisters in Christ, but Ijendu had splintered off quietly into a secular decadence, something she and Aima never really talked about. It hadn't mattered; neither of them judged the other for her beliefs or lack thereof.

Ijendu gave Aima a look. "They're not that bad," she tried to say but couldn't make it through without smiling. "No, you're right, they are. They really are."

Aima laughed back. "It's no wahala; they're always entertaining." She pointed her knife at Ijendu. "But I swear, if one of them tries to start a fight again, I'm calling an Uber and leaving you there."

"Guy, Biola wasn't starting a fight, that bastard grabbed her ass."

"And then she broke a whole bottle on his head! Please." Aima raised her hands. "I'm just glad I wasn't near you people when that happened."

Ijendu grimaced. "I forgot about the bottle part, yeah. We can't go back to that club for a while."

"You see? Drama."

"Anyway, Biola's traveling; she won't even be coming out with us tonight."

Aima snorted. "We thank God." The phrase was flippant in her mouth, leaving sourness on the inside of her cheeks. What was there to actually thank God for? Half her things were still in Kalu's house—should she have made them get their own house together instead of moving into the one he had inherited from his family? Too late, too late—and the rest of her things were packed into one hasty suitcase and she had nowhere to live unless she went to

London and faced her mother's overt disappointment, her father's gentle confusion at how she kept making choices he didn't understand, just like when she'd chosen Texas over London. Aima had just wanted some air, some real space away from her family so she could figure herself out. She'd landed a cushy finance job there, but her parents still didn't get why she'd chosen somewhere like Houston when she could have had London. Even after Aima had met Kalu at a corporate mixer, even after they'd fallen in love and moved in together, her parents treated it like it was all a distraction from the life she was *supposed* to be living. Moving back to New Lagos had been the first thing that had made sense to them in a long time, and now Aima had fucked that up. She was going to be illegible to her parents again, and it would have hurt, but right now she was illegible to herself, and that hurt far more.

Ijendu's phone buzzed with a text message. She read it in a glance, cutting up plantain with the edge of her fork. "Okay, some of the girls are on their way."

Aima glanced at the time. It was still early in the evening. "Already?"

"We're all doing our makeup here."

"Oh, okay." Aima peeled some of her fish off its frail skeleton. "In that case, shouldn't they have come a few hours before? You people who need to bake and whatnot." She faked a grin as Ijendu cut her a side eye. Aima didn't wear makeup like that and she liked teasing Ijendu about it, a small reminder that they could be different and it could still be okay.

"I've already told you you're rude," Ijendu replied. "Biko, finish your food; let's go upstairs. The maid will clear the plates."

Ijendu's house had a marble staircase that clung and swooped dramatically against a curved wall and led to the upstairs parlor, which was upholstered in a deep plum velvet. Her bedroom was off to the side, large and lined with wardrobes, all filled to near bursting. Aima's suitcase had been tucked away neatly in a corner. She put her purse on top of it and plopped down on the bed, watching Ijendu throw open her closet doors to decide what she was going to wear later.

"I know you love those your platform heels," Aima interjected, trying to focus on anything other than the heartbreak crawling through her. "But if you're serious about dancing with me tonight, shey you know you have to wear something else—something you can actually move in."

Ijendu groaned. "Please don't ask me to kill my aesthetic in the name of practicality, Aima. I can't be going out in flats."

Aima rolled her eyes. "That's why the block heel was invented. Or the wedge. Or literally anything that isn't an actual stiletto."

Ijendu turned slowly to look at her, eyes wide with horror. "A *wedge*? It's only because you're sad that I won't slap you for even suggesting that. You that likes to wear sneakers to the club— remember how we had to beg that bouncer last time to let you in?"

"Beg ke? I had to bribe him."

Aima tried to ignore the mention of her sadness. Spotlighting it would make it balloon into a monstrosity she wouldn't be able to choke down.

Ijendu shrugged and turned back to her clothes. "That one is your own. We warned you, but you didn't want to hear word."

"But it's so stupid. What if I was . . . recovering from a surgery or something? Something where I couldn't wear heels."

"If you're recovering from a surgery, maybe you shouldn't be in the club in the first place."

Aima laughed. "Whatever. It's still wrong. Like how they wouldn't let us into the strip club that time because we didn't have a man with us." It had been her first time going to one, and she'd actually been rather relieved when they had to turn around and go back home.

Ijendu pulled out a silk peach dress. "That one pained me, I can't lie. I was thinking the whole day about how I was going to take that yellow Anambra stripper into the private room and do certain things to her. And they just blocked me like that. Wickedness." She held the dress against her and spun around to show Aima. "What do you think?" It was short, the hem hitting her upper thigh. Aima raised an eyebrow.

"I think you're not serious about dancing tonight if you're wearing that. Unless you're ready to expose yourself to everyone."

Ijendu winked. "Maybe I am."

Aima blushed and Ijendu laughed at how easy it was to scandalize her, then dove back into the wardrobe to try and find an empty hanger for the dress. As soon as she turned away, Aima let her face fall and stared over the edge of the bed at the carpet, the hurt in her chest quiet and solid, a drowning weight.

Friday, 10:05 PM

Ijendu's friends arrived in a flood of loud and raucous laughing, one of them connecting her phone to Ijendu's speakers as soon as she got in and blasting amapiano until it was beating against the walls. The girls moved around the room in an effortless cloud of perfume and powder, their gist overlapping, threaded with more laughter, delight bouncing off one another.

Aima smiled from the bed, now quiet as she watched them share space at Ijendu's vanity, their highlighted faces lined up in the large mirror. It felt as if they had their own world and she was a spy inside it, quietly witnessing, a visitor to a godless place, almost in a trance. Aima watched the stretch of sheer panties over hips and ass, the sway of breasts cupped in lace, their full lips as they slid small pills between them, the way their eyes dilated and hooded afterward. The whole thing was almost like boarding school again, that game of not letting anyone see the deliberately flimsy desire flitting about in her. Usually, she wouldn't even look at it, that secret and shameful want, but tonight was different. Everything was broken, which meant something was broken open. She was angry with God. She was going to play in the places she wasn't supposed to.

When they offered her a pill, Ijendu glanced over. She'd offered Aima things like that before, casually, open doors and windows in case Aima wanted to climb into that world or, at least, out of her own. Aima had always refused gently, and it had never been a thing. Ijendu offered portals and Aima said no, and that was just a fact of their friendship. But this night was different. Aima took the pill, and Ijendu smiled and blew her a kiss that said welcome and turned back to the mirror. Aima reached for her glass of juice balanced on the headboard and used it to swallow the pill. What did any of it matter anyway? She'd heard it could help make everything unreal, and that felt like exactly what she needed. Besides, she was with Ijendu; she'd be safe. The desire stretched out in her, her old confidante. She'd never told Kalu about it; there had never been a need. They'd thought they would be together forever and now he was gone, and she was free to think about different things, do different things since she didn't have a road to follow anymore.

The housekeeper came in and collected the clothes that needed to be ironed or steamed, returning them carefully draped on hangers. Aima watched as the girls crafted their faces, as they contoured their cheeks and noses. She held still when Ijendu came over and took her face in her hand, sweeping a liquid lipstick carefully over Aima's mouth. Her skin was buzzing from whatever the pill was. She hadn't even asked. A brief alarm shot through her, but she wiped it away—it didn't matter. Whatever happened would happen.

"You'll like this one," Ijendu said. "It's like black wine."

While the lipstick dried into a smooth matte, Aima brushed on mascara in the bathroom mirror and shaped her eyebrows with gel, hooking on gold earrings that dangled to her collarbone. There was a chance the earrings would be annoying once she started dancing, but with her hair up and her shoulders bare, they looked perfect. Out in the bedroom, one of the girls had lowered the music and started singing a song everyone knew from primary school days.

> Ijendu, nwe ndidi, i ga-alu di tomorrow / Ijendu, nwe ndidi,
>   i ga-alu di tomorrow
> I nwere powder te n'ihu / I nwere pancake itekwasa
> I nwere powder te n'ihu / I nwere pancake itekwasa

Aima came back into the room as the other girls were singing along and dancing in a circle around Ijendu, who was beating out the rhythm with a container of eyeshadow, tapping it against the headboard of her bed with one hand as she preened and pouted. When the song ended, everyone dissolved into laughter and someone turned the amapiano back up. Aima smiled, but she still felt so separate from them, so carved out, and not just because she was high. It was more like there was a picture she'd been cut out of and that cutout had been carried over and someone had propped it into this other picture and it was supposed to fit.

It was supposed to fit, but it didn't.

Saturday, 12:30 AM

The lounge had rattan armchairs set out on the balcony, with ankara cushions and curved backs, glass-topped tables scattered between them. This place served the best cocktails, complete with hot bartenders who spun bottles and flipped shakers while flirting outrageously with the girls. Aima took a few shots early on because she didn't want to stay in a funk all night. It would get too awkward; she would become a drag and no one wanted that. The girls were already skeptical about Ijendu's believer friend tagging along with them. Aima wanted to fit in, to be cool, to be a bad gehl just for one night. With the vodka raw and burning through her, she could feel her joints soften, her body begin a stretch into something languid. More of Ijendu's friends showed up and the group took up three small tables they had made a server push together. Aima crossed her ankles and stretched her feet in the comfortable gold block heels she had on, low enough that the other girls had made fun of them but high enough to flex her calves. She'd let Ijendu slather her legs in coconut oil so they were gleaming stretches, something you wanted to slide your hands or face on.

"I'm having lunch with my godfather tomorrow," Ijendu was saying. "Hoping he'll dash me some money. I did way too much shopping the other day and I want to take a quick trip to Milan, pick up some things there."

One of her friends laughed. "What do you mean 'dash you'? Your daddy is loaded! Besides, he loves to spoil you, don't pretend."

"She's not the only one he likes to spoil," another one chimed in. "Daddy O likes to spoil all his daughters in God." The table laughed and Ijendu laughed with them.

"Please, he has different kinds of daughters; I'm not one of those."

"That one is even better. You don't even have to do anything for the money."

Ijendu raised her glass in a toast. "We thank God," she said, her smile sharp and pretty. Aima knew Ijendu was fond of her godfather—he'd helped her out of a tough spot more than once, and there was nothing to do except laugh and shrug at the things he did, the girls he privately fucked and sponsored while still wearing his wife on his arm in public. All the married men in the city were like that, even the pastors. *Maybe I was lucky*, Aima thought. Maybe if she'd convinced Kalu to get married, he would've ended up like all the other men. A licking voice in her head asked, *What makes you think he wasn't like them already?* It dripped doubt in her memories, and Aima ordered another shot to wash it away.

She had been so confident that he was different, that she would've known, that she would've noticed something. Kalu never attended those secret parties that his oldest friend, Ahmed, threw all the time; he'd always told her she was more than enough, but now that her mind was loosening, Aima couldn't help but wonder if she was just being as foolish as the other women.

Look at Ijendu's own brother, Dike, for instance. He was back at their family house because his wife kicked him out for fucking their children's nanny. The man had twin boys, toddlers, but if you watched the way he moved through the day, you'd never know it. He'd settled into his old room as if he'd never left, but he still drove his shiny SUV, didn't wear a wedding ring, and even charged the hotel rooms he fucked in to his company credit card—expat perks, he'd joked to Ijendu. Half the women he was seeing didn't even know he lived in the city, let alone that he had a whole family in the highland. You could do *whatever* in New Lagos. No one needed to know; no one would notice. And the women accepted the futility—they just assumed that their husbands were sleeping around because that made it a little easier when they were proved right. Not a lot, but a little. Some of the wives slept around too, did their own; and somehow it all balanced out. Aima wondered if that was the kind of life she'd been insisting on without thinking about it. If that was the type of life Kalu had been trying to save them from.

The edges of her vision had gone porous. She needed to dance. "How long are we staying here?" she asked.

Ijendu slammed an empty shot glass on the table. "We move!" she answered, her eyes bright. The other girls whooped and dropped cash, probably too much for the bill, but they didn't care. They wound their way out of the lounge to the beat of whatever song was playing, glittering along the way.

The first club they hit up wasn't full enough, but they still bought drinks and Aima danced by the bar, green and blue strobe lights flashing over her skin. She could feel the colors—green was prickly, like small spikes brushing rhythmically against her. Blue was soft, like a hand made out of water. When they left half an hour later, Aima danced her way to the door and down the stairs and back into the car, leaving teal trails in the air. She was tired of thinking, and she didn't have to when her body was moving, so the solution was to just not be still for the rest of the night. The second club was much better, an excellent DJ and a sexy crowd. The girls got a table in the center of the club, on a raised platform roped off with red velvet and they ordered a few bottles. "Don't worry, I'm covering you," Ijendu said to her, and Aima kissed her cheek.

"Thank you, bebi."

Ijendu slapped her ass in return and laughed. "Oya, be dancing for me."

Aima smiled and let her eyes drift shut as she followed the music, braids swinging across her face, sweat beading down her spine. The music was molten silver rolling across her skin. Ijendu was dancing across from her in tight and controlled movements, not wanting to sweat too much. Aima lowered her waist, hovering above the floor, her hips snapping to the beat. She could feel people staring from the nearby tables (yellow stares, like the foam of dry sponges) and it fed her, a small performance. She was a mirror in front of a mirror, a looped reflection creating her own world. She spun in a circle, dropped her whole body to the beat, caught it on the next one, and alternated her shoulders on the way up. When she opened her eyes to glance at Ijendu, her friend was making mild circles with her hips and texting on her phone, a small frown blurring her forehead. Her nails were rose gold, matching her phone case, with tiny pearls curving against her cuticles. Aima closed her eyes again as the song started transitioning into the next one, letting the old beat go as she chased the new one underneath. She raised her arms, moving her hands and wrists, feeling the air-conditioned air push against her skin (lavender teeth scraping).

When she looked at Ijendu again, her friend was shoving the phone into her purse, her eyes locked somewhere else, occupied. Aima danced closer to her, trying to distract her from whatever was disturbing her. This was what they had come out for, after all—to stop thinking, to suspend the world outside and disappear into a beat, a song, colored smoke, and cocktails. Ijendu smiled and came back, sliding one leg between Aima's thighs, rolling her body back in a wave. Aima felt heat slide under her skin (pure red-hot, like the tip of a burning mosquito coil) but she just laughed and put a hand on Ijendu's hip, the peach silk riding up. They ignored the spiked interest of the men at the next table (cloying brown, like mud), who were leaning forward in their oversize sunglasses and velvet blazers.

Aima reached down for her vodka cranberry and Ijendu pulled out her phone again.

"Who are you texting sef?"

Ijendu kissed her teeth as she typed a quick message and put the phone away. "Nobody, just a friend disturbing me."

Aima pulled her close, her hand warm on the silk of Ijendu's back (this is what you do in a godless space, abi?). "At two in the morning? Sounds like a booty call." Her mouth was a blackberry stain against Ijendu's ear. "Let me know if you need to run off; I don't want to spoil your market." She didn't know where she was getting this courage from, but the world was a textured welt of colors and Ijendu was a warm clear amber, heated honey.

"There's no market, abeg," Ijendu replied, not pulling away. "I *wish* I had someone delivering early morning dick."

"You can always collect one of those guys and take him home." Aima tilted her head at the next table and Ijendu grimaced.

"God forbid! And you call yourself my friend." They laughed together, their heads touching, five different intoxications burning warm through them. Ijendu slid her arm around Aima's waist and put her mouth next to her ear. "Is this helping, love? You feel better about Kalu?"

In another world, Aima might have teared up at the care Ijendu was showing, but she was one pill and several drinks too deep into this one; she was an orphan of faith; she was climbing through a window and unsure of which worlds she was entering and which she was leaving behind. She let her hand slip down to Ijendu's ass and smiled a knife of a smile. "Do you want to help me feel better about Kalu?" she asked, her voice hard and playful, a bruised purple. It was only purple that could have made her do or say a thing like that, new world color, new madness, a dead God.

She expected Ijendu to push her hand away, to pull back, but her friend gave her a long look instead. They were both high, both drunk, but Aima could tell there was a pitch-black seriousness there, a barrel of tar. Ijendu raised an eyebrow. "Don't start something you can't finish," she said, her voice level and low between them. One of the other girls glanced over, saw Aima's hand still resting on the peached curve of Ijendu's ass, and immediately, she turned to the others and started whispering. Aima ignored her, too intrigued by the easy surety in Ijendu's voice. No one had told her unreal could feel so free.

"I asked you a question," she replied.

"I'm just making sure," Ijendu said.

Aima slid her hand along the silk till she met the skin of Ijendu's thigh, then she started sliding her hand underneath it. "Let me know when you feel I'm sure enough," she said. She felt wicked and it felt correct. Ijendu blushed and pulled away a little, but her eyes were laughing and bright.

"I'm calling the driver," she said.

Aima nodded and wondered what colors she would feel later when their skins were touching. One of the girls offered her another half a pill with gossip gleaming in her face, and Aima took it. It was a chance to spend the whole night chasing colors, falling into wonderland without a map. In that moment, she wanted nothing more than to be completely lost.

two

K alu had one of his drivers rent out a regular taxi to take him to the estate by the lagoon so no one would recognize the car. Security at the first gate waved it in with a flick of their torchlights, and Kalu felt invisible, masked in the yellow metal. The car seat was worn and frayed, a spring glinting through the ragged padding. It reminded Kalu of his childhood, before he'd left to plan a life away from home somewhere in an American suburb. Before his mother fell ill and turned into a muted and folded woman, thinning out until her fragility called Kalu home to take over the family's luxury car-service business. Every time she blessed him, her palms felt like spun paper about to flake gently over his scalp.

As his taxi pulled through the second gate, Kalu turned the invitation over in his hands, feeling out the weight of the heavy paper. His driver spun the steering wheel slowly and drove the taxi into a corner of the sprawling parking lot. Kalu handed him a fold of thousand-naira notes and he handed Kalu a mask in return—soft leather made in battered oxblood. Kalu held it against his face, and for a quick moment, it felt like another skin, almost like he wasn't the man Aima had walked away from yesterday, the man who had watched her crumple against a wall the week before, sobbing.

"You're never going to marry me!" she'd wailed, tears dragging her eyeliner down her heart-shaped face. "Four years of my life that I went and threw away on you! How do you think this looks in the eyes of God?"

Kalu had just watched her. He knew he was supposed to pick her up and hold her and tell her that of course he loved her, of course he would marry her—but the raw bitterleaf truth was that he simply didn't recognize who he was looking at. Aima sounded as if another woman's mouth had eaten hers, like a church had spat over her face. Finally, she stood up and wiped her face. She'd looked as beautiful as she always did—with her delicate wrists and soft arms, her hips flaring into lush curves, and her dimpled thighs he used to sink his teeth into.

"I'm going," she'd said. "Call me a taxi." She went upstairs and threw her things into a suitcase, drawers rattling and slamming as she packed. He'd run after her and held her, begged her to stay, and it had worked for a week. Then today he'd come home in the late afternoon and she was packed, about to call a car. Kalu had convinced her to let him take her to the airport, but he hadn't recognized himself when he had let her walk away. That feeling of being someone he didn't know had stayed with him since. Tonight, his plan was to forget about everything, including the way Aima hadn't even looked back.

The driver dangled a leg out of the car, striking a match to light one of his cigarettes. Kalu stepped out of the back seat and unbuttoned his jacket, the silk lining glinting a jealous green as he walked through the gleaming accumulation of cars. He was surrounded by residential prison blocks looming next to one another, dark units broken up by squares of blue and yellow light from the apartments. It was amazing how much people paid to live in projects like these. Kalu fastened the mask over his eyes as he climbed up the stairs, the leather sinking on his skin like a relieved breath.

The door was nothing, a smudged beige portal with half the number plate broken and missing. He knocked once, a lonely sound that seemed inadequate, then waited. There was a click from the lock and the hinges swung briefly, stopping at a crack. The doorkeeper's face showed through, covered in a heavy black veil of fine lace and thin gold thread, shining lines that Kalu followed with his eyes. His mask shielded his cheekbones but left his mouth open and vulnerable, one corner undecided, almost smiling in his nervousness. It had been a while since he had come to one of these parties. Kalu thought of the girl he'd just left, how she had smiled drowsily from a pillow that didn't belong to her. She was a random hookup he kept on deck, and he'd called her to meet him at his house as soon as he returned from the airport—it was his house now that Aima didn't want to live in it—before, it had been theirs.

"Your mouth is almost as expressive as your face," the girl had said, laughing when Kalu flinched from her hand. He had thought she could help distract him from the emptiness of his bed and chest, and she had, a little, before she started talking. "See," she said. "Like that. It just went tight. You don't like your face to be touched?"

Kalu almost told her that it was her hand he didn't like, that he used to let Aima run her fingers over every pore of his face in the cool mornings before the day kicked in. But he kissed her instead, ran his hands down her tight stomach, and washed his face after she left. Ahmed's invitation had been waiting on the kitchen table, humming softly in its scalloped gold, and it led Kalu here to this frayed welcome mat. The doorkeeper took his hand and pulled him into the apartment.

He knew the routine—turn off your cell phone and turn it in. Allow Thursday, the tall man with the milky eye, to pat you down. Give him your signed report from the approved doctor. The doorkeeper knelt and lifted Kalu's foot to unlace his shoe. Kalu flattened his palm against the wall to stop himself from falling and sighed. He already knew it was pointless to ask for explanations. You just showed up and went with whatever flow Ahmed had picked for that night. The first party had been eight years ago, and even though Ahmed and Kalu had known each other for long years before that, ever since they'd been inseparable in boarding school, Kalu could never predict what each party would look like. He made a mental note to ask Ahmed about the shoe thing later, but then he looked down at the veiled woman kneeling before him, her henna-stained fingers quick and deft with his laces, and something dark stirred in him. Kalu caught his breath. This was just the kind of thing Ahmed liked to do—awaken coiled desires you didn't even know you had. Kalu watched as she peeled his socks off his feet and he felt the beginnings of an erection as blood shifted in his body. Once he was barefoot, the doorkeeper unfolded to her full height and Kalu took a deep breath, stepping toward the weighted velvet curtains separating the foyer from the parlor and touching his new face to make sure it was still in place.

"Wait," said the doorkeeper, her voice winding out like soft ribbons from under the layers of gold-shot black. She lifted her veil just enough to uncover an unstained mouth so full that Kalu's throat went dry. When she raised herself up on tiptoe and pressed her lips to his, Kalu cupped her jaw lightly. Things slithered in him as her tongue flickered inside his mouth, the wet muscle depositing a damp pill before she pulled away. Kalu swallowed it obediently.

"What is it?" he asked.

"Something to help your mood," she replied. He reached for her veil and she slapped his hand away, the lace drowning out her mouth. "Not now." She pulled back the curtain to let him pass and Kalu stepped into the parlor, sweeping the scene with a practiced eye. *Ahmed, that hedonistic bastard!* He laughed softly to himself.

The apartment might have been something sterile and white when they gave Ahmed the keys, but it was sinuous now, a boudoir that cannibalized every room. The walls were deep blood orange and burnt mustard, lit by scrolled lanterns dropping from the ceiling on delicate chains. The heated light seeping out in dim streams made everyone's skin glow. And, Jesus Christ, there were skins— writhing, sweating, gleaming skins. People were pressed up against the walls, shirtless bodies crowding one another, teeth and fingers shining everywhere. Kalu's feet sank into a thick rug, and he smiled at the fabric soaking the floor, the embroidery on the floor cushions, the wine-tinted leather ottomans.

"You made it!" Ahmed appeared beside him, tall and dark, his gleaming teeth open under a chalk-white mask. His head was shaved, and together with the white caftan he had on, it made him look almost ascetic, nothing like the debauched ringmaster he really was. After Kalu had moved to America, Ahmed had left Nigeria as well and traveled almost nonstop. From London to Dubai to Cape Town to Melbourne to Nairobi, round and around. His voice sounded like nothing had stuck to it. The two men embraced, and

Ahmed clapped Kalu on the shoulder, gesturing around him. "Just like when we were in Casablanca, oui?"

"Hell yeah," said Kalu. "Looks just like it." That had been a wild stop, sixteen hours of Ahmed squeezing the city with long-fingered hands until juice ran down his arms. Kalu had followed him blindly, drunk and half-afraid, envious of the ease with which Ahmed touched life and it bent before him. "How's the party going so far?"

"No complaints." Ahmed kept his body relaxed and his mouth curved, but his slitted eyes raked over the room, as vigilant as his guards. In the city, Ahmed's careful reputation was that of an unserious playboy, someone people could underestimate until he severed their vital tendons and left them neatly fucked-up and floundering. Kalu had a lot of respect for his friend, and the two of them occasionally traded information on clients—Ahmed hiring Kalu's cars because those drivers could be deaf for him.

"Don't work too hard," said Kalu. "It's still a party, you know."

Ahmed laughed and grabbed his balls, thrusting forward slightly. "Oh, I know. I've been taken care of." He winked and Kalu bit back a smile. "That's the face of a man with too much weight between his legs," said Ahmed. "Go and take care of yourself, my friend."

Kalu laughed and looked out toward the balcony doors. A bloated moon hung low and swollen in the sky. Ahmed's hand gripped his arm, gold rings bracing the knuckles.

"Listen, Kalu," he said, his voice low. "Try and forget Aima, ehn? There are other beautiful people here tonight." He squeezed once, then left.

Kalu watched his friend's white caftan recede and tried to settle his shoulders. He was here for the night. Ahmed was right—there were other people and they were here, and he needed to leave Aima behind. Kalu stepped through the small crowd and went to the bar.

The bartender was a young man in a satin waistcoat, his face curiously exposed and his eyes wide as he mixed drinks and poured champagne with quick hands. It was clearly his first time at one of Ahmed's parties. Kalu almost wished he didn't look so excited. Ahmed liked to leave some of the staff barefaced, their identities unprotected. You're not important enough to be covered, it said, and if you open your mouth about what you see tonight, a mask won't save you anyway.

Kalu took a rum and Coke from the boy, sipping it as he looked over the buffet table. Half-shell oysters balanced on crushed ice and peppered snails curled around each other. There were meats and cheeses and fruits, skewered and roasted and raw. A large man in a deep-blue suit elbowed him aside to reach for the snails, strings from his gilt mask cutting into the flesh of his head. The mask was a mere formality—Kalu recognized his face easily, the man was a senator, a popular one. Sometimes Ahmed allowed politicians into his parties—he called them the money bodies—and they all seemed to smell like this man, clogged cologne and damp sweat. The senator was followed by a boy with a dancer's body wearing a bright feathered mask. Kalu moved aside for them and started heading for the balcony so he could look at the moon over the lagoon, let it settle the tides in him. He'd never been the type of man to gaze aimlessly into the sky, but two years of being back home had left him dreaming of flight and stars and levitation.

When he'd first returned, his mother had touched his face and told him plainly that she would like grandchildren. Before he could reply, she dropped her hand and changed the subject. That had always been her way, as gentle as a flame, only blistering afterward. Kalu had looked away, biting the inside of his cheek into a raised line. He had wanted to shout at her, to ask why it wasn't enough that he had come home, dragging his girlfriend all the way with him, but this was his mother and she was old, so Kalu held his peace. Months later, when he reached for a condom while in bed with Aima, she stopped his wrist with a soft pressure from her fingers.

"Would it truly be so terrible?" she whispered. "Let's see what God allows." Kalu stared at her in shock, at the woman who used to joke about him getting a vasectomy, and Aima quickly covered her question with a light laugh, taking the foil packet and tearing it open herself. "I'm just playing," she had said, but in that small space between her question and the delayed laugh, Kalu had started to see that he was losing her.

Inside the party, he passed a hand over his face as his eyes stung. This was no way to forget anything. The music filtered back into his ears, Bonobo sliding into Sutra, and two models sashayed past him arm in arm, their small breasts cupped in matching filigreed pearl, long weaves swaying down their backs. They were tipsy and giggling, flirting under thick eyelashes that stretched out from their golden masks, ruby lipstick framing pretty teeth. Kalu raised his glass to them and they burst into soft chattering giggles, glancing over their shoulders to appraise him. Perhaps later. They looked familiar. *They're probably sisters*, he thought. *Or lovers. Or both.* It was that kind of night, that kind of place.

The television was a black slab against the wall and a woman was dancing in front of it, a twisting collection of sinews and soft flesh. She moved privately—the way women move when they have stopped dancing for hungry men, a thing faithful to the music. It was beautiful and none of his business. Her hair was in long braids and someone had made her a lacquered ankara mask that draped over her face like wax. The low carved table in front of her was balancing towers of empty shot glasses and lines of coke. People were seated around her in a half moon, clapping in a steady rhythm as her hips snapped and snaked. A few of them were passing around a joint, frail smoke winging out as they threw their heads back to expose smooth necks. Kalu reached for the belonging he used to feel when he came to these things, but this time there was only a curious numbness. He felt imaginary.

The woman with braids was wearing half of a traditional out-fit, a tight printed skirt that clutched her thighs and sliced her ankles. Her top was gone. Her bra was triangular and white, more functional than sexy, covering her breasts wholly. It looked like something his mother would wear, something he'd seen dan-gling from the clothesline of his childhood. Aima would never have let something like that even touch her. The thought of her clawed its way back through his chest and Kalu stopped to catch a breath. He hadn't tried to stop her at the airport because the peace offering she wanted would sink him. They used to lie in bed when they lived together in Houston and make fun of friends who rushed to get married after three months.

"What will ninety days tell me about you?" Aima had asked, her breasts spilling over his hands. "See ehn, I want to know what kind of man I'll be looking at in ninety years."

"We won't live that long," Kalu had told her.

"Shun the unbeliever," she'd joked, and leaned in to kiss him. Her mouth had tasted immortal, so he believed her. After they had moved back home, to this city, Aima had changed so slowly that Kalu almost missed it until she was collapsing and God was in her every second breath and she was begging him for a ring and all he could do was wonder at the briny taste of desperation this city had put on her skin.

"We said we'd wait until we were both ready," he had said, and she looked like she could spit on him.

"It has been four *years*, Kalu! How much longer do you expect me to wait?" Each word had been a small and sour betrayal.

Kalu slid open the door to the balcony with Aima's voice reverberating in his head, and for a wild second, he thought she was the woman standing against the railing. Maybe Ahmed had kidnapped her before the flight took off and got her to come here. Maybe he took pity on Kalu's vast landscapes of pain and orchestrated a costumed reunion, a story that Ahmed would then tell at the wedding during his best man toast while Kalu stared at Aima and wondered how many children it would take on top of the ring to make her happy.

But it wasn't her. This woman was yellow like a firefly, her skin a window in the backless dress she was wearing. She half turned when Kalu stepped out to the balcony, a cigarette perched lightly between her fingers. Her nails were dark-red porcelain, curved and blinding, and the moon swung low over her head.

Kalu smiled politely. "I hope I'm not interrupting."

"Do you see anybody else out here?" Her mask was a smooth collection of blues with exaggerated cheekbones, and she'd painted her lips a deep pink. The color clashed with her nails. She offered the cigarette to Kalu as he leaned on the railing next to her, and he took it because the brightness of her mouth led him to think maybe he'd kiss her before the night was over. It would be better to smoke his own tongue instead of tasting it only on hers.

"I hate this city," the woman said, as if continuing an old conversation. "Don't you wish you had never come back sometimes?"

"How do you know I ever left?"

Her laugh was like a man's, low and swinging. "Ajebutter like you. See your head."

Kalu laughed and conceded. "It's not that bad, though. You just have to switch your mind over when you arrive."

It was the same line he always gave people, as if one simple mental readjustment when your plane hit the tarmac at the airport was enough to fortify against the things New Lagos would proceed to do to you, including but not limited to making your girlfriend unravel and leave you over a ring, or the lack of one. Some of Aima's friends had convinced her that Kalu wasn't serious because marriage wasn't on the table yet, that it was easy for him to talk about marrying her when they lived abroad but that once here he would want a quieter more respectable woman, a woman who behaved like a wife, not a girlfriend, a woman he could press between his palms like pounded yam until she became whatever shape he wanted. They told her that his mother would start to think there was something wrong with her and that eventually Kalu would leave her for a pounded-yam woman because they are easier, and this is Nigeria and is he not a man?

"It makes you complicit, you know?"

The woman was still talking. Kalu returned the cigarette and watched her blow smoke rings out to the sky. The moon was staring at them. Kalu's mouth was bitter with smoke, and he wondered why kissing her had crossed his mind, why he thought forgetting Aima would be possible tonight, and if the two were related.

"What makes you complicit?" he asked.

"This city. You think you'll never be a part of things you hate; you think you're protected somehow, like the rot won't ever get to you. Then you wake up one day and you're chest deep in it, watching some perverted gays at a random party in the highland."

Her bluntness surprised Kalu, but he followed her stare past the glass balcony doors to where the senator was leaning back on his elbows, forest-green cushions bolstering his sides and his belt half-undone. The man's face was sweating as the boy he'd brought sank to his knees and finished unbuckling the belt for him. Feathers from the boy's mask tickled the senator's potbelly and glitter marked out his spine as he bent his face over the man's crotch. Kalu looked away. He was open-minded, but watching men do things to each other was something else.

"Can you imagine?" Her lip curled up and her teeth clenched the cigarette filter as she stared at them. "I wasn't expecting that kind of nastiness here. Tufiakwa."

Kalu didn't know what to say. He wondered why she wasn't looking away if it disgusted her so much.

"Gays and pedophiles," she said. "They're everywhere."

Kalu glanced back at the senator, then tore his eyes away, looking up at the moon instead.

"It's a sex party," he said. "Not exactly the most conservative scene. Why would you be surprised to see gay people here? Isn't that the point—to come somewhere where you can enjoy without being judged?"

The woman looked at him properly for the first time.

"Some things shouldn't be indulged," she said. "Especially not in front of other people."

"Maybe that's the part they like," Kalu countered. She held his stare for a few seconds, then the muscles of her face rearranged in calculation. She dropped her cigarette and ground it into ash with the heel of her bare foot. Her smile was oily. Kalu decided she was fireproof.

"Do you like that kind of thing?" she asked, taking a few slippery steps toward him. Her dress was plunging, smooth cleavage presented like gourds on a tray. He hissed a breath instead of answering, her hand cupping and kneading at his crotch. "Doing things in front of people? It can be exciting. Maybe we can try it small. Someone from another apartment might see us."

Kalu thought about it, about her sinking before him, the metal whisper of his zipper and the hot wet of her mouth, spilling milky clouds over her face, over the sky of her mask. It wouldn't be the first time he'd done something like this at a party—it wouldn't even be the first balcony. Ahmed made it too easy. Once in his world, you could believe you were truly somewhere else, that the body rippling around you wasn't real, that none of this really counted.

"Why do you still invite me to these things?" Kalu had asked once, showering away another woman before heading home. "You know I have Aima."

Ahmed had laughed and slung him a towel. "You're an adult, Kalu. It's your choice and you're making it alone. Don't involve me. In fact, don't come if you don't like."

The fireproof woman kneaded Kalu into steel. He grabbed her wrist tightly and pulled her hand away.

"No." Too curt. He tried to soften it. "Thank you."

She snatched her hand back. "Suit yourself," she spat. "I'm sure that boy in there will be happy to service you once he's done with his oga. Or if you like children, I hear they're catering to that in one of the bedrooms." She was already sliding the door open when her last sentence clicked into place. Kalu reached out and grabbed her arm again.

"Wait, what did you just say?"

Even with her mask, the disgust on her face was palpable, a slimy green thing crawling out of her mouth.

"You fucking pervert," she said. "I should have known you were the type. God punish you."

She wrenched her arm away and slammed the door. Kalu curled his fingers over the metal of the railing, a dull panic climbing inside him. Why would she say there was a child here? *Why would a child be here?* The answers came faster than he wanted, news stories running and tripping up in his head, falling into jumbled heaps of fistulas and lacerations and girls bleeding from their grandfathers. But this was Ahmed's party, and he wouldn't. It was impossible. Kalu bent over, gasping in shallow breaths as words Aima once said to him lanced through his mind. She'd been disapproving of the work Ahmed did, the person he was underneath his rich family-money playboy exterior. "Is there anything Ahmed would not sell," she'd asked, "as long as it's for the right price?"

He threw the door open, pushing through the crowd, searching for the bedrooms. A cold premonition ran down his back, sticky like a cracked yolk. The pill was screaming in his blood and spinning his head. The senator was moaning obscenely, his shirt pushed up his chest and his hands locked behind the boy's head as he pumped his hips, feathers stroking his belly. Kalu felt a rush of sickness surge through him. *How old was that boy? Where was Ahmed?*

Someone was waving around that ugly white bra, and its owner was now stretched out across the table, a man and woman sucking on each of her nipples. Kalu found a small hallway and pushed open the first door, his heart erratic. The two models stared back at him from the bathroom, squatting in front of the toilet with thin white lines arranged on the closed lid.

"Sorry," he mumbled, closing the door as one of them wiped her nose, her eyes loose. How had he forgotten that the parties were like this? The next door opened into an empty office. The door after that was locked. Kalu smashed his shoulder into it and it slammed open with a splintering crack. A knot of men turned to look at him and a bouncer stepped in front of him, black-suited and blocking his view.

"You need a password for this room, sah."

The men had already lost interest in his maddened entry, turning back to whatever they were gathered around. Kalu let an American accent slide in, dragging a wide drunkard's smile onto his face. The pill cackled from behind his eyes.

"Hey, man, my bad; sorry about the door! I just heard this is where the party's at, you know?"

The bouncer looked coldly down at him, and Kalu searched through his memories for a detail—Ahmed on a beach with him in the Maldives, telling him a word that could get him through any door in his parties. "It's a master key," Ahmed had said, crystal-blue water stretching around them. "It opens everything. Especially legs." They'd laughed together, but Ahmed had given Kalu a careful look. "Just make sure it's a door you want to open," he'd warned, and Kalu had taken it seriously, hadn't tried to remember or ever use the key. He needed it now, though, desperately so, because if he didn't find out the truth behind that woman's comment, he would lose his mind.

"Gimme a second, bro," he fumbled. "I'm a little wasted, you know?"

The bouncer took an unfriendly step forward, crowding Kalu's space. "Turn around and go," he said. "Before we have to remove you by force."

Ahmed had spoken of darkness, shadows, and the eating of the light. You could go anywhere in the dark, enter any door, but then the dark could also enter you.

"*Husufi*," Kalu said, and the bouncer flinched, his eyes flaring with surprise. The man's body rearranged itself and his voice lowered into a deferential tone.

"Of course, sah." He stepped aside to let Kalu pass. "Don't worry about the door."

Kalu pushed his way through the small crowd gathered around what he could now see was the bed. The men were all older than him, much older, and there were no women there. Kalu stepped to the front, just by the foot of the bed.

There was a girl on the mattress.

All the sounds of the men talking and cheering faded into vague roars of static in his ears. The girl was a waif, tiny breasts and smooth skin everywhere. Her hands were handcuffed behind her back and her underwear was stuffed into her mouth. She looked maybe fourteen or fifteen and was lying on her side, crying. There was a naked man pumping into her like she was salvation, one of her legs draped over his shoulder as his hands pressed her down. Kalu tasted tears in his mouth and his hands stung with noise. His legs bent and uncoiled as he leapt on the bed and seized the man by the throat. The girl screamed behind her gag and the man's eyes swelled in surprise as Kalu tore him off her body, throwing him away from the bed. He tumbled to the floor, his penis slapping wetly against his stomach, too startled to be soft. Kalu stepped off the bed, intending to stomp on his testicles, to crush them like the balcony woman had ground her cigarette. The rage was almost a relief, the first pure thing he had felt in a long time.

The bouncer stepped through the other men and sunk his fist

efficiently into Kalu's side, right over his kidney, dropping him to the ground and dragging him out of the room. Kalu cried out and the rest of the men shouted in entitled outrage. Through the cluster of their sweaty, hungry bodies, Kalu saw the girl's wide eyes from where she lay toppled on the mattress. He thought he saw another man climb on the bed as the bouncer forced him out of the room, forearm pressed against Kalu's windpipe. He was quick and brutal, throwing Kalu into the empty office.

Kalu ricocheted off the desk and thudded down to the carpet, blinded in bright pain. The door slammed shut. He curled up on the floor, groaning and dry heaving. His mouth tasted like coppery nicotine, and he was high and hurting. What kind of man would he be in ninety years? A dead man, his kidney said back resentfully.

"Aima," he whispered to the air. "I was not a man who folded his hands and watched, Aima. Why couldn't you wait for a man like that?" Kalu sobbed against the carpet. He could feel the pill twisting his head. "I didn't bend, not even when it meant losing you. I had to stand for something."

He tried to think of her face, of the black wing-tipped lines above her eyes, the tart fullness of her lips, but the only face he could see was that girl's, the mucus from her nose and the thick tears clotting on her cheek. Kalu ripped off his mask and screamed into the rug as the door clicked open.

"Kalu, what the *fuck* did you do?"

Ahmed knelt beside him and pulled at his shoulder to turn him over. Kalu spat in his friend's face as soon as he saw it. It took a moment before Ahmed blinked and wiped saliva off his cheek, cleaning his hand on his white trousers, his eyes dropping in temperature.

The caftan from earlier was gone and his bare chest was slightly damp, a smudge of lipstick stamped on his neck.

"Fuck you," said Kalu. Ahmed stood up and waited for him to struggle to his feet, watching with a hard mouth.

"You're trying to fuck up my party?" he asked, once Kalu was more or less upright. "You can't assault my clients, Kalu! Just wait your fucking turn next time." He shook his head in disgust. "Fucking hell."

Kalu roared and rushed at him, his fist connecting with Ahmed's jaw smoothly, snapping his head to one side. Ahmed staggered and caught himself heavily against the edge of the desk.

"I don't fuck little girls, you sick bastard." Kalu was panting and it felt like everything in his eyes had burst. Ahmed massaged his jaw and looked up at his friend.

"Little girls? Did you just fucking *hit* me, Kalu?" He slid a finger inside his cheek and felt around. "You've gone mad. Completely mental. How much have you had to drink?"

"You have a *child* in there. You have a child *handcuffed* in there while men old enough to be her grandfather fuck her till she cries. *What the fuck is wrong with you?*" Just saying it out loud had turned his stomach and Kalu fought back the urge to vomit. He ran his sore hand over his face and turned away.

"Kalu." Ahmed was behind him, speaking slowly. "Listen to me. Listen. She's not a child."

"Fuck you, man." He was running out of venom, the horror coating him like a paralytic.

"I swear to God, Kalu. It's just a setup. The older men pay loads of money for that fantasy, I find a girl who looks like a child and I pay *her* loads of money to act it out with them. I keep one of my men there to stop them from going too far. It's clean. On my father's grave."

Kalu leaned his head against a bookcase and closed his eyes. "She was crying, Ahmed. Was that part of your setup?"

Ahmed sighed. "They like it like that. There's more money if she cries, if she acts like she doesn't want it. More money for her."

Kalu didn't want to believe him. It was too easy, a nice package of a story. "More money for you," he said.

"I'm a businessman, Kalu." Ahmed's voice spread like open palms, trying to soak and soften the brittleness. "You know that. Shit, *you're* a businessman. But for fuck's sake, I do not let people rape children at my parties! I don't *let* children into my parties. What kind of person do you think I am?"

Kalu's side was bruised badly, he could feel it pulsing. He rotated his neck till the wood of the shelf was pressed against his temple, so he could look at his friend. Ahmed's arms hung heavily, and the earlier sharpness of his face had given way to shadows under his eyes and fatigue in his mouth. The white chalk of his mask was scattered on the desk. Kalu couldn't tell if his friend was lying.

"You just let them 'pretend' they're raping children." Kalu didn't need any heat in his voice, the censure boiled out all on its own. It didn't make sense. This was New Lagos. Those men could find children so easily—why pay Ahmed for a farce? Did Ahmed believe Kalu was naïve enough to fall for this?

The lines by Ahmed's mouth took on sharp right angles and his voice was a strip of cowhide cracking in the air. "Would you rather they were actually out there doing it?"

Kalu didn't say anything. He wanted to tell Ahmed that he wasn't a savior, that any sins these men committed in here were just controlled versions of what they did somewhere else. Kalu wanted to ask him if the young girls in these men's homes were safe, if you could buy a child's consent, and if Ahmed knew the answers to these things or, failing that, if he could tell Kalu how much money had been enough to assassinate his curiosity. Instead, Kalu let his eyes close again and felt Ahmed's hand on his shoulder.

"You shouldn't have had to see it, Kalu. I'm so sorry. That was a private session for some very rich, very sick people. I wish you had stayed out with the main party, had some fun, unwound a little. I know you've been having a tough time of it with Aima leaving."

Kalu didn't plan to tell any of his other friends that Aima had left. He already knew how they'd react.

"Why can't you just marry the girl?" they'd say. "It's not as if you don't want to marry her eventually, so what difference does it make if you do it now?"

They had married old girlfriends who were due for a ring, married whomever they happened to be dating when they finished their degrees and got their jobs and the next step was to get married, so they did.

"At least you love her," they would say. "Marry her, jo. It won't change anything—you can continue having fun afterward. What's your problem?"

But Ahmed was different. He understood the small rebellion and what it had cost Kalu. He understood things Kalu didn't tell anyone else, like how he was struggling to hold on to who he was even as the city tried to strip him of it. Somehow, living here hadn't affected Ahmed the way it did other people.

"That's because they don't know their own dirtiness," he once told Kalu. "They come here and the rot grows like a weed inside them. Then it's a year later and they're surprised by what they've sunk to. Me, I started from the gutter, so I was prepared. There was nowhere left for me to sink to."

Women flocked to his playboy self, to his carnivorous charm and his incisive honesty, tumbling into his bed, some coy, some wild. He had girlfriends, one after the other although never at the same time, which was strange for this city.

The relationships all faltered and died anyway. "They don't believe I'm real," Ahmed said.

One of his exes used to email Kalu. "He scares me a little," she'd written. "It's like loving a snake who thinks it's a man and can't see it's a snake. The skin doesn't fit well."

Those stretches of being single were when Ahmed first threw his parties, and the invitations would find their way to Kalu no matter where he was. He woke up in a hotel in Dubai one December and found thick paper pressed under his breakfast plate. A small note was waiting inside his in-flight magazine on a plane to Amsterdam a few months after that, and a girl he spent a weekend with in Cape Town had whispered quick instructions before she threw on her clothes and left with a smirk. Ahmed had pawns everywhere; the whole thing was a joke to him, a playground.

Kalu had flown to Johannesburg for that murmured invitation, and Ahmed had stayed sober for the entire trip, even during the party. It was after a sour breakup with a woman he'd considered marrying and he was moody, an island of gray surrounded by his colorful guests.

"My women say they want me, but they're lying to themselves," he told Kalu, his mouth twisting. It was the first time Kalu had seen anything in the shade of bitter about him, so he just drank his wine and listened.

"They don't want a real person; they want someone pretending to be a real person, a character fitting himself to the role. They want me to follow the formula." Ahmed paused and gripped his friend's shoulder. He did this so often that Kalu's skin had placeholders for his fingers, shallow grooves waiting for Ahmed's hand. "Don't ever fall for the formula, Kalu. It's a bloody lie. We know better; we know to live outside it; we know how to live true."

There were times when Ahmed spoke as if he and Kalu were a unit, complicit in their own private freedom. It was true, they were a team; they had been ever since they were children at that boarding school. They had spent their last school holiday together, sharing a room in the family house in Kalu's hometown. It was night, all suffocating darkness and whining mosquitoes. The boys were sleeping on mats on the floor, and Kalu had been masturbating in the blackness that covered them, his hand repetitive and slick with saliva, his back turned to Ahmed. His orgasm was reluctant to arrive, and his forearm had started to ache, but Kalu gritted his teeth and tried to focus. When Ahmed sighed in exasperation and slid his hand over his friend's hip bone, Kalu's heart screamed into a shocked halt. He stopped moving. Ahmed tugged on his side until Kalu rolled over and lay on his back, staring into the darkness and forgetting to breathe.

"Relax," Ahmed whispered, and his wet hand replaced Kalu's, stroking and coaxing. Kalu's heartbeat resumed like a stampede, and he wondered if he should stop what was happening, but then Ahmed flicked with his thumb and slammed his hand to the base and Kalu stopped thinking completely. His body was moving in unplanned ways, a rocking pelvis and a searching hand that reached inside Ahmed's trousers and found him hard and hotter than white iron. The sound Ahmed made in response to his touch was like an animal in the sweating night, and when he gasped Kalu's name,

Kalu had a fresh understanding of what power could be held in a palm. His forearm forgot that it was ever tired and his ears wanted to hear Ahmed say it again and again, so he moved his hand faster and faster and so did Ahmed and he said Kalu's name over and over and Kalu wanted to say his name too but it was a seed stuck in his throat and Ahmed said his name; he said his name until the brightness washed the insides of their eyes as they climaxed. In that moment, Ahmed made a monopoly of him. When Kalu finally managed to crack his voice open, his friend was already turning away.

"Go to sleep, brother."

They never spoke of it or the stiffened stains of it, but it was there, a pearled bond. The boys, now men, knew pieces of each other that no one else did. In the twenty years that followed, no man ever gasped Kalu's name again, let alone with all that surrender in his voice.

In the raging silence of the office, Kalu's brain staggered against his skull, and Ahmed's hand on his shoulder felt like a brand.

"How old is she?" Kalu asked, his throat dusty.

"What?"

"How old is the girl you hired?" He made his voice more solid, less like a shadow. Ahmed sighed and stepped back.

"Kalu, come on—"

"Tell me!" Kalu was shouting now, shouting at the books that lined the shelves of the office because he didn't want to look at Ahmed's face, didn't want to shout into his eyes or let the volume of his voice bruise his cheeks.

"She's seventeen," Ahmed said, sounding tired.

Kalu laughed, lacking the energy to cry. It hurt to be right. "Those men are in there fucking a seventeen-year-old girl and you're telling me she's not a child?"

"Because she's not legally eighteen? Where do you think you are, Kalu?"

Ahmed had no bile in what he was saying, just a weariness from even having to debate the topic. Kalu could hear it and it infuriated him. He turned so Ahmed could see him, see the contempt seething under his skin, the way it was molding his face.

"I don't know, Ahmed. Tell me where I am, because I seem to be standing in front of a man who lets a girl get raped under his roof because his palm got greased enough, like a fucking pimp. Is that where I am?" Kalu knew he was going too far, but he was losing everyone already. He felt so betrayed—he just didn't care anymore.

Ahmed's face went blank. "Okay, so tell me, Kalu, which part of what you saw actually surprised you? Is this setup really so impossible to believe?" His voice was silk now, dragging and collecting filth. "Tell me you've never wondered if they really do feel tighter the younger they are. Tell me I was wrong about you just wanting a turn."

Kalu winced. Ahmed knew the soft places to aim his barbs at. "You're just a fucking pimp. Selling a child—how the fuck do you live with yourself?"

"This isn't fucking *America*, brother, where they hide the ugly things they do." Ahmed was snarling now, his lip curled, his teeth striking. "You can't walk in here and judge my business by your fucking standards just because I'm not pretending. She's a prostitute, Kalu. She was spreading her legs and having abortions before she was fourteen, and if she wasn't here tonight, she'd be doing this somewhere else. I give her more fucking money than she'll see in two years, and my people take her to a clinic to get checkups because if she goes alone no one will agree to see her. I put a fucking bodyguard there to make sure she doesn't get hurt, and all she has to do is put on an act so these bastards can get off on their fantasies. I do more for that girl than you and your self-righteous bullshit ever will."

Ahmed stepped forward and his eyes glittered. "You're a client just like those men—you come under my roof, fuck my women, and then think you can lecture me because you walked in on her? She's *lucky*, Kalu. She works for me. What about the other ones, the ones you don't see because your windows are tinted when your car drives past them? They get ripped apart and beaten into a bloody pulp, but what the fuck do you care? You don't see it, so it doesn't happen? Don't fucking come at me. I'm a businessman. I hire whores who are old enough to fuck and I take fucking good care of them!"

Kalu felt the air on the wetness of his face before he realized he was crying. "She's still a fucking kid, man. Don't you see that?" His voice was breaking, and if it was any other man standing before him, he would be humiliated, but it was Ahmed. "She's still a kid."

Ahmed stared for a minute, then turned away, cursing in a stream of words, a hand pressed to his head. Kalu sat down heavily in a swivel chair, dropped his face into his hands, and wept. Ahmed crouched before him and leaned his forehead against Kalu's. Kalu knew his friend wouldn't apologize—after all, no one had forced Kalu here. He came in alone, by his own free will. He did this to himself.

"You shouldn't be here," said Ahmed. "You know I've always welcomed you to my parties but . . . this is the gutter. And it's ugly and we're ugly inside it. You don't belong here."

He stayed like that, balanced against Kalu and breathing his air. Kalu felt like the sky had fallen except he was the sky and also the ground it landed on and the fractured air in between. He pulled back from Ahmed and tied his mask back over his face, the leather pressing against dried salt as he stood up from the chair. Ahmed quietly put his chalk face over his real one and they left the party so quickly that Kalu barely saw anything, just a glimpse of the bartender watching him with a tracker's eye, Ahmed's hand settled again in the grooves of his shoulder. Thursday with the milked eye helped Kalu put on his shoes and the doorkeeper hovered anxiously.

"What happened?" she asked Ahmed. Her lace was blurred in Kalu's eyes. "Was he drugged?"

She leaned toward Ahmed's body and Kalu almost laughed. He could tell that she loved him just from that.

"Saidat, back off. I don't have time for this," snapped Ahmed. The girl shrank back from the serrated razor of his voice, and Kalu wanted to console her, to tell her that Ahmed was just worried, that he was always sharp when worried. You should notice these things, Kalu wanted to say, but his tongue felt like foam expanding in his mouth. You should notice these things if you love him.

Ahmed draped his arm over Kalu's shoulder. "Come, let's go," he said. They took the stairs one at a time and slowly made their way to the glowing pinprick of Kalu's driver. Ahmed laid Kalu down in the back seat, arranging him so he was half sitting up. The driver started the car and Ahmed took Kalu's face in his hands, sighing.

"You have to get your shit together. Call Aima tomorrow after she's landed. You hear? Stop trying to prove this senseless point. We all surrender on some level. Call her."

He patted Kalu's cheek gently and closed the door, stepping back as the taxi pulled past. Kalu tried to breathe as Ahmed's silhouette blended with the night. He thought of Aima, of every time he'd touched a woman who was not her only to come home afterward and kiss her cheek, dropping a lie on the bone behind her ear. Is this not Nigeria and was he not a man just like those men in the locked room?

He lay in the back seat like a corpse as the car drove through the gates. The security guards lifted the metal bar quickly, as if they wanted the smell of damp fear and shame gone from their estate. Kalu willed his ribs to stay together, to hold his lungs in deep breaths.

When the taxi drove past the women who walked the night, he closed his eyes.

three

Ahmed ground his teeth together as he watched Kalu's car pull away. The mild tremor in his left hand started up again, just a whisper, and he wrapped his fingers into a fist to stop it. Anger was coughing up his throat from the bottom of his lungs.

A car entered the parking lot, pulling past him toward its allotted space as the woman inside stared out, a strange look passing over her face. Ahmed frowned back, then realized he was the one standing out in the night, shirtless and with a bone-white mask over his face. He turned and went back into the building, jogging softly up the stairs and pausing when he reached the flat in front of the cracked number plate. Saidat was going to open the door, and Ahmed knew she'd be upset about how he had spoken to her on his way out. When she first started working for him, he'd found her innocence endearing. He usually didn't fuck young girls—they were too emotional, showing their hands and their hearts with no control, but Saidat was achingly sweet, enthusiastic, simple. It made up for her age. His hand was still shaking though, and his lungs were still full of rage, so if she expected tenderness tonight, she was going to have to wait.

Saidat opened the door after the first knock, sweeping her veil off her face and stepping into the doorway. She braced her hand against the frame and looked up at Ahmed with wide and pained eyes.

"Is everything all right?"

Ahmed forced a smile from beneath the edge of his mask. "Everything's fine. Let's get back to work."

Saidat's jaw set. "Don't lie to me, Ahmed. Something is wrong. What happened to your friend?"

Ahmed's smile ended. Kalu's jaw was under his hand again, Kalu's forehead against his as his friend wept into his air.

"Not now, Saidat," he said, gently pushing past her to enter the foyer.

"Ahmed, please—"

"I said, not now!" His voice raised to a snarl and Thursday glanced over, his blind eye rolling unsteadily. Ahmed caught his other eye and Thursday dropped his stare, turning away. Saidat's silence was choked. Ahmed turned around as she closed the door and dropped the veil back over her face. Usually, he would play the part of caring; he'd hold her, kiss her, make her feel better. But this was not a good night for him.

"Leave me alone tonight," he said. "You hear?"

Saidat nodded, her shoulders small and scared. He couldn't decide if that made him want to hold her or shake her until her head snapped off.

"Good," he said instead, slipping off his shoes and entering the parlor. Saidat would probably avoid him for a week or two as she sulked until the fright wore off. It was better like that; they both needed the space.

Once inside, Ahmed stood and looked over the scene sprawling before his eyes, breathing in the soaked air pungent with sweat and fluids. Every time, every party, this centered him. Distill people down to their basic needs and desires, and it would smell like this—salty and ripe. Most of the time, in other spaces, Ahmed could feel how false they were, with all their layers, masks, pretenses. But not at his parties. Here, he never had to wonder if the world he was seeing was real. It was always true; it was the one truth he could be sure of.

A loud groan cut over the writhing mass of sound that filled the room, moans mixed with music. Ahmed looked over to see the senator shudder as he emptied himself into the boy he'd brought with him, the dancer folded over and holding his ankles. It was interesting that he'd stayed out in the main room. Ahmed watched the man pull out, gasping for air, the boy twirling quickly to his knees to clean him off, his head bobbing dutifully. What a picture that would make if anyone's phone was allowed into the space. The gossip blogs would go wild over it, and that was why it couldn't ever happen, why these parties were designed to protect the guests no matter who they were or what they did. Ahmed was their guardian for as long as they were in his world.

He leaned against the wall and watched the party rut its way deeper into the night. The Balogun sisters were at the bar, arguing softly, dressed as usual in matching lingerie from their line. The younger one, Timi, broke away from her sister and walked up to him with two glasses of wine, pearls clutching her breasts, all thin arms and sharp collarbone.

"Hello, stranger," she said, offering one of the glasses.

Ahmed took it and bent to kiss her cheek. "Enjoying the party? I haven't seen you and Bola here in a while."

She shrugged. "Traveling. Busy with our line. The autumn collection needs to be ready soon."

He nodded and sipped the wine, staring at her breasts. It was amazing how full they were even though the girls kept their bodies as hungry as if they still worked on runways.

"It's lovely, though," Timi noted, looking around. "The place looks beautiful."

He scoffed. "You should see it in the morning."

She tilted her head. "Don't kill the mood. Aren't you having fun?"

Ahmed touched his thumb to the edge of her mouth and dropped his voice. "I'd like to." He was bored, antsy, looking for trouble. He almost didn't mean it.

Timi's eyes widened and her lips parted in surprise. On instinct, Ahmed slid his thumb into her mouth and over her lower teeth, tugging slightly, just to see how she'd react. She inhaled sharply and didn't look away.

He smiled. This was going to be fun.

Timi didn't resist when he took her hand and led her out of the main room, the sound of her heels drowning in the carpets. When they passed her sister at the bar, Bola hissed and Ahmed winked at her. He'd taken her to Cape Town the year before for a weekend away. It felt like a slight accomplishment, to check her sister off the list of people he'd wanted and hadn't got. On another night, maybe he wouldn't have been so blatant, but there was an anger still inside him and Ahmed felt like making a small destruction. One of his guards stepped up to him as he was walking past with Timi.

"What is it?" said Ahmed. The guard cleared his throat and

glanced at Timi, reluctant to speak. Ahmed turned to her and kissed her hand. "Give me a moment, love."

Timi smiled and sauntered off to the side.

"Sorry to disturb you, oga. They are finished in the other room."

"And?"

"The girl is waiting in the office, sah." He jerked his head toward the door behind him. Ahmed's irritation spiked at the thought of the girl. It wasn't her fault Kalu had reacted the way he did, but still. He blew air out of his nostrils sharply.

"All right. I'm coming." Turning to Timi, he smiled and spread his palms open. "Business is calling, darling."

She pouted and jutted out a hip. "How long is it going to take?"

Eager. She was so eager. Ahmed almost wanted to push her down to the carpets right then and there, but he chained the impulse. "Shouldn't be too long," he said. "Would you like to wait for me?"

Her face brightened and she nodded. Ahmed snapped his fingers at the guard.

"Sah," the man responded, almost at attention.

"Escort her to the spare room." As Timi walked off down the corridor, Ahmed stared at her ass curving out from all the pearl. *That Balogun body*, he thought. *Fuck.*

He had to take a deep breath before opening the office door, refusing to think about Kalu, his friend's saliva wet on his face, the anger Kalu's sobs had built in him. The room was fully lit this time, and the girl was standing by the bookcase, running her fingers over the spines of the books. She was wearing a T-shirt that was slightly too big and hung off her shoulders, dark skinny jeans, and open yellow sandals. Her hair was short and she'd twisted it out, but the past few hours of getting fucked had messed it up. Small beads of water clung to the nape of her neck.

"You took a shower," Ahmed said, unthinking. She turned around, startled. Her eyes were liquid, her lashes heavy and thick. She lifted a hand to the dampness of her neck and lowered her eyes.

"I remembered," she said softly. She spoke with a slight Igbo accent, a low voice, weighted like a handful of ripe udara. Ahmed could hear hard seeds inside, black and shiny under her tongue. She remembered? He was blank for a moment, then it came back, the first time he'd met her, when Aunty Promise introduced her at his office in Section One. The girl had come by keke and the sun had been oppressive, the traffic mutinous. By the time she entered the room, she smelled sour and rank. Aunty Promise didn't seem to even notice although she had come by driver in an air-conditioned car and reeked of strong vanilla, from the pearls wound around her neck to the lace wrapped around her body. Perhaps that blocked her to every other scent. Ahmed had been pissed.

"This is the girl you have for me?" He was annoyed that she was late, that she smelled, that this preening woman trying to market her hadn't thought of even handing her a stick of deodorant. He was irritated by her thinness, her long fingers, her lost eyes, that she looked like exactly what his clients wanted, small and defenseless and like his little nieces. Surrounded by the glass and metal of his office, the wide white monied spaces, the girl's presence was a distortion in the air.

"Stand up well!" Aunty Promise snapped at her before smiling widely at Ahmed. "Is she not okay? She resembles a small girl, ba?" The girl straightened her back and twisted her hands in front of the worn dress she was wearing. She looked maybe fifteen but could pass for younger by her height, barely breasted and clear skinned, all good things. Pimples were too old. "I can get someone younger if you want, but that one will be proper small girl—"

"I don't want that," Ahmed interrupted. He was irritated to be dealing with her in the first place, but there had been a last-minute request and all his other suppliers were booked in advance.

Aunty Promise spread her palms. "Eh hehn. That is what I am saying. This one is perfect."

"How old is she?"

"Nineteen."

He swiveled in his chair and looked at the girl full on. Nineteen, like hell. She flicked a glance up at him and her eyes were briefly sharp, no longer lost.

"What's your name?" he asked.

"Machi," she said.

"How old are you?"

"I said nineteen na!" Aunty Promise interjected.

"Promise." Ahmed didn't look at her. The air cringed around her head. "I'm speaking to the girl." Machi looked over at the vanilla woman, nervous now. "How old are you?"

"Nineteen," she mumbled. *All right*, he thought. *Leave some lies alone.*

"Do you know you smell?"

She winced. "No, sah."

"Well, you do. My clients won't like that."

"We can handle that, oga. No wahala." Aunty Promise was radiating assurance.

Ahmed cocked his head and looked her over. "Have her show up ahead of time," he said to the madam.

"No problem, Alhaji."

He waved a hand. "That's all for now, Promise. We'll talk later."

She rose up from her seat in a cloud of fragrance and smiled again, then gestured for the girl to follow her as she left.

"No, leave the girl. I want to talk to her."

Aunty Promise was instantly wary. "Ah-ahn, Alhaji. Why now? You fit talk to me about anything wey concern her."

"Promise, unless you're the one planning to take off your clothes, you really don't need to be a part of this conversation."

A quick fury flared briefly through the madam's yellowed and powdered skin, but she left and closed the door behind her. Ahmed turned back to the girl, who was standing motionless except for her twisting fingers.

"You can sit down," he said. She shook her head, a tiny arc. He leaned back and took a good look at her from the fluffed cornrows to the dusty feet and the rubber slippers. "How old are you? And don't lie again, I don't have the energy."

Her hands stopped moving. "Seventeen next month."

"All right. I won't tell your aunty that you told me that."

She mumbled something under her breath.

"Speak up!"

"She's not my aunty." He got another sharp glance from her.

"Well," he said slowly. "I guess she's not, is she?" The girl didn't say anything, fingers working again at each other.

"How long have you been working for her?"

A shrug. "Since last year."

"And you know what this job is about?"

She nodded.

"You're all right with that?"

The look she gave him was sudden, scorching, contemptuous. As quickly as it blazed, she killed it and dropped her head.

"Yes, sah." Her voice was taut, and Ahmed knew it had been a stupid question. This was her job. It wasn't her first time, and even when the party was over and the men drained, it wouldn't be her

last. He had let her go shortly after that; there wasn't much more to
say. Now she was standing in this other office, her face tired and
clean. He was grateful; he didn't know what state the men had left
her in, and it was easier not to think of what she'd probably looked
like by the time they were done, thick gobs of white congealing like
cooling pap over her eyes and nose and mouth and cheeks and—

"Alhaji?"

Ahmed started at her voice.

"Are you all right?"

You know what? he thought. *Fuck you, Kalu.*

"I'm fine. How are you?" Clumsy. She looked at him like he was
confused. Ahmed sat on the desk and took off his mask, staring
back at her.

"Erm . . ." She seemed uncertain and he almost felt bad. Aunty
Promise probably never asked her anything so foolish afterward.
How are you, now that those old men have finished filling you up,
now that you've completed the task your body was rented out for?
The girl wrapped her thin arms around her torso and shifted on her
feet before looking up at him.

"I'm tired."

"Of course. Where do you live? One of the drivers can drop you."

"Fishing Bay. It's better if I take a water taxi."

Ahmed kept staring at her, wondering which driver he was planning to send her with anyway and why he'd suggested it. He usually just let the women find their own way home. Highest, he'd
have Thursday put them in a taxi. But Kalu was still with him,
crying in this same office over this same girl. Or himself, or Aima,
who knew? The guard had told Ahmed what he'd done. "Like a
madman, sah," he'd said, "the way he just threw that man on the
floor like a bag of rice." She was so damn thin. He didn't want to

put her in a taxi. He knew he was pissed at Kalu for a lot of reasons, but still, putting this girl into a car and sending her out into the night, into the emptiness, somehow it was disturbing him. Kalu had wanted her safe. Ahmed knew that didn't exist, but what close approximation could he reach, at least for Kalu, for her?

"I don't want you on the water at this time," he found himself saying. "My driver will take you to my house for the night and drop you in the morning."

To his surprise, she winced. "Oga, please." Her voice unspun like a fraying thread. "I'm tired."

Oh, fucking *hell*. She wasn't being professional, and he didn't know what to do. She was so obviously a child, it was easier to pretend they were adults when they wore professional masks instead of breaking down in front of him.

"Machi."

She blinked in surprise when he used her name, and the tears dotted her lashes like crystals.

"Wallahi, it's not like that." Ahmed grimaced and stood from the desk, walking over to the window, passing his hand over his face. *What a fucking night.* He turned to her, to the suspicion and fear warbling under her skin.

"I'm not going to touch you. No one is going to touch you. The driver is just going to take you to the guest room where you can sleep, all right?"

She shuddered out a breath he hadn't realized she was holding and nodded tearily, giving in. She really did look so young, so fucking young. He wasn't sure she believed a damn thing he'd said. Ahmed walked to the door and called one of the guards.

"Go and call Thursday for me." He saluted and left. Ahmed clicked the door closed and thought of Timi in the spare room, waiting, probably getting pissed off. Balogun women were not known for their patience. She'd have to wait a little more, though; he wasn't done with what he now thought of as Kalu's complication, this girl he felt he owed something more than money.

"How much does Promise pay you?" he asked. The girl sat down in one of the armchairs and drew her legs up under her, then shrugged. The air conditioner whirred quietly next to her.

"She never tell me yet. Maybe 40k, 50k."

Ahmed stopped moving. "What?"

"Full night."

He could still feel the grime of Kalu's anger on the walls, swirling into the heat of his own, and now it was all boiling into a greasy hot ball under his chest. The price he'd settled on with Aunty Promise was maybe ten, fifteen times that, for a few hours, not the whole damn night. Fuck. He wouldn't even have used the woman to find the girl except that a small girl was in shockingly high demand and she was an unexpected late addition to the party.

"Okay," he said. "That's not the correct amount. But we can handle it in the morning."

"And you want me to sleep in your house." She sounded suspicious, and even Ahmed had to admit, his reasoning was a little shaky on that one. He just didn't feel like watching her get swallowed into a thick city night, especially out on the black water. Still, these ashawo-saving feelings were new for him. Maybe it was her age, her frailty, her fucking eyes. He hadn't watched anything they'd done to her. He never watched when it involved girls this young, girls he pretended weren't still children. He rolled his neck around and listened to it crack. *Whatever.* He was Ahmed Soyoye. He could do whatever he wanted whether it made sense or not.

"Yes," he told her. The door opened and Thursday entered, his hands resting easily beside his thighs. "Good, you're here," said Ahmed. "Take her to the house and show her the guest room. She'll be staying there tonight." Thursday raised an eyebrow but nodded, and Ahmed turned to her. "Okay, go with him. I'll see you in the morning."

The girl untucked her legs and followed Thursday obediently. Ahmed wondered what on earth had made him say he would see her in the morning. For what? Pancakes? He laughed at how idiotic he was being. *There's a Balogun waiting,* he told himself, *and this is what you're filling your head with?* He held his mask up over his face, not bothering to tie it, and left the office for the spare room.

Inside, the bed was made and the lights dimmed. Ahmed could make out Timi's form posed in the pillows. He smiled and placed his mask on a dresser. She wriggled off the bed to slide her slim hands over his shoulders.

"I missed you," she murmured, pressing her body against his back and kissing his neck—what a convincing liar she was. Ahmed braced his hands against the dresser and squeezed the wood until his fingers felt more solid. Timi dropped slow kisses down his spine, and he felt the gold of her mask scrape against his skin.

"Take off your mask." His voice was flat, tamped down with effort. She pulled back and he turned to watch her untie the ribbons and pull it off her face, smiling crookedly at him. She ran a hand over her hair and flirted heavily with her eyes. Ahmed didn't smile back. Instead, he let his eyes travel the long length of her body, the smooth of her legs and the pearled lingerie she had on. "Take off everything."

She giggled and took a step back. "No."

His hand tremored. "I don't have time for games, Timi." Dimly, in the back of his head, Ahmed knew he was too volatile to even be in a room with this girl. *You should leave*, he told himself. *Before you hurt her.*

Timi laughed softly and took another teasing step backward. She was playing with him, as if he was a thing to be played with. With a quick stride, Ahmed was against her, wrenching a fistful of her hair so her neck arched back and her face tilted up toward him. He lifted his other hand and placed it on her throat, tracing her larynx with slight pressure from his thumb. Her eyes stayed hooded, amused. She was nothing like her sister.

"Do what I say," he warned her.

"Why don't you make me?" she replied, almost too quietly. A quick deep ache shot through Ahmed's chest and he cupped her cheek in his hand, pressing the side of his face to hers, closing his eyes. He pressed on her face till he could feel her teeth against his fingers through her flesh. She giggled through her restrained mouth, her laugh low and cunning. "I thought so," she whispered, her tongue thick from his hand. "I know your type."

Ahmed released her and stepped back. He couldn't afford to do this with a Balogun. He had other women for this. "I don't think this is a good idea, Timi. You should go."

Timi put her hands on her hips. "Now you're afraid?" she challenged.

He looked at her and laughed. *These innocents.* "You don't know what you're asking for, Timi."

"I think I do," she answered, stepping closer. "You want me to say it?" She stood on tiptoe and released a stream of words into his ear, things that made his pulse slam noisily against every blood vessel in his body. When she stepped back, she drank in the look on his face and grinned. "Do you still want me to go?"

Ahmed stared at her. "Are you sure? I don't want to hurt you."

They both knew the second sentence was a lie, but he needed to be clear.

Timi spread her arms out, presenting herself. She was tall and glowing, an idol waiting to be broken. "Yes."

Ahmed closed his eyes and tasted the word on his tongue. *Salvation in the strangest place*, he thought. He opened his eyes. "Remove everything you're wearing," he ordered. Timi lifted her chin by a fraction and looked him in the eye.

"No," she said.

The force of his hand against her face knocked her to the ground, her body hitting the side of the mattress as she fell. Ahmed looked down at her. "I said remove everything. Or I'll tear it off you, and I don't think you'd like that—it looks expensive."

Timi touched her cheek gingerly but stood up and unfastened her bra, letting it slide off her arms and fall in front of her. Ahmed sat down in a carved chair by the window and watched her shimmy the panties past her hips. The lagoon was a black hole outside the building. She left her heels on and pushed her long hair over her shoulders so it wouldn't cover her up. He stared at the dip in her collarbone and his hands were calm.

"Beautiful," he said softly. "Turn around." She obeyed, lifting her hair so he could see the notations of her scapulae, the small bumps of her spine, and the flare into her hips. Her waist was tiny. "Good girl. Back again." She faced him and smoothed her hands over the sides of her thighs nervously.

"Come to me," he told her. She took a small step forward and he raised his hand to stop her. "Not like that." He gestured and watched the heat rise to her face as she knelt and dropped her palms to the carpet, crawling to him slowly. It nearly broke his heart, how beautiful she looked. She didn't stop until she was between his thighs, kneeling up and untying the knot of his trousers, reaching in and filling her mouth with him. Ahmed hissed in air between his teeth and let his head drop back against the wood. He slid his hand into her hair, cupping the back of her head and urging her deeper.

"Jesus Christ, Timi. Your father should never let you out of the house." She looked up with mischief in her eyes and he slapped her bulging cheek lightly. "I don't know whether to charge him more or give him a discount when he comes to the next Abuja party." She choked in laughter and he pushed a little harder, just enough to make her start gagging, her eyes tearing up. Machi's face flared up in his mind and he dragged Timi off immediately, breathing hard. His hands were in fine shocks, but he wasn't going soft. He didn't want to think about it, so he dragged Timi to the bed, threw her on it, and did things to her for a long time, coaxing out sounds from her throat that kept his people away from the door. Afterward, when he was just a slick reminder in her mouth, cavities, and skin, they lay breathing hard in their sweat and she lit a cigarette, the flame a crackle as she inhaled.

"That was . . . intense," she said. "Was that all for me or were you thinking of someone else?"

Kalu's moon of a face against his, his breath on Ahmed's skin, young hardness in his hand. *Fuck.*

"All for you, love." Ahmed's body stayed relaxed; he knew better than to let tenseness translate.

"I'm flattered." She giggled.

He tried to keep his hand from trembling as he stroked her skin and dozed off.

Saturday, 5:54 AM

Ahmed woke to a flurry of short knocks on the door. He broke away from Timi and stumbled to open it, still naked and bleary. The bouncer from the first bedroom was there, unmoved in the face of Ahmed's naked scattering.

"Sorry to disturb you, oga. They are finished in the main room."

Ahmed exhaled and leaned against the doorframe. It must've been almost sunrise.

"All right. I'm coming." The bouncer nodded and left as Ahmed shut the door and turned to look at Timi's body sprawled over the bed. He thought about waking her up to kick her out, but then he decided it would be far more interesting if Bola found her like that. His trousers were a crumpled white spill on the floor; he shook them out and pulled them on, then slipped out of the room and went down the corridor. Halfway down, he saw Bola striding toward him, her legs lithe and warm. He almost missed them. She slapped him as soon as she was close enough.

"You fucking bastard! I came to get Timi and your fucking touts wouldn't let me pass."

"That's their job," he reminded her mildly.

"Where's my sister?" she demanded.

"In my bed. Follow the smell of pussy." He caught her hand in midair. "Bola."

She sucked her teeth loudly, drawing it out like okro. "I don't even know why she would fuck you."

"Maybe because you told her how big I am." This time, she slapped him too quickly for him to stop her.

"Fuck's sake, Bola!"

She tossed her hair and stalked off. He watched her ass leave and it mellowed the burn of her slap. Thursday faded into his peripheral vision.

"What's the time?" Ahmed asked.

"Six," Thursday said.

"Fuck." He stepped into the parlor and looked at the carcass of the party. It had been picked apart and smelled like it.

"The cleaners are on their way," Thursday told him.

"Good." Ahmed couldn't wait to put the whole place behind him; he'd burn it down if he could, particularly the office, particularly the memory of Kalu, especially Machi's small tucked body. Speaking of. "Is the girl asleep?"

Thursday scoffed. "That girl is not going to wake up until afternoon."

"Good. We're going to Ruqaiyyah's house."

Thursday's gone eye rolled towards him. "It was a full moon last night."

The bouncer came up with Ahmed's caftan crumpled in his hand. Ahmed took it and pulled it over his head. "I know. Let's go."

Thursday followed him out of the apartment, down the stairs. "I dropped Saidat at her house."

Ahmed had forgotten about her. "Good." There was some guilt. "How was she?" He got a look in reply.

"Are you sure?" Thursday asked drily.

Ahmed thought about it. "No, you're right. I don't really want to know." Thursday climbed into the driver's seat of the black Defender and Ahmed sat on the passenger side, earning a tired look from him.

"You know it looks bad when you sit in front."

"Oh, I don't care, Thursday. It's fucking six in the morning.

Who's going to see?" Ahmed reclined his seat back as they drove out of the parking lot through the gates, then patted his pockets. "Where did I leave my phone?" Thursday reached inside his jacket and passed it to him. The phone was a dark weight of glass in Ahmed's hand. He turned it on and it sang, alerts rolling and buzzing down the screen. The latest was from Timi.

Not very nice to just leave me in bed like that, she'd sent, just a few minutes ago. Bola was pissed.

She'll get over it, he typed back. And I'm not nice.

Where are you? she asked.

Work.

Already?

Such is life.

Was that a one-night thing? Just so I know.

Ahmed smiled. He liked them direct. What do you want? he replied.

More nights like that. You nko?

I want to give you what you want. Let me call you when I get back.

Okay. Where are you going?

He paused. Thursday was entering Crescent. They were nearing Ruqaiyyah's house. *What the fuck am I thinking?*

Still in the highland. Talk later.

He turned off his phone. Thursday wound down his window and exchanged a few low words with the security officers, then the gate slid open. Ruqaiyyah's car was parked against the wall, but there were no other cars there. She used a limo service for her parties, not Kalu's because Ahmed had told her not to involve him.

They drove past the main house to the guesthouse in the back and Thursday killed the engine, then leaned his seat back. Ahmed sat for a minute before unbuckling his seat belt, wondering if this was really what he wanted to do. He hadn't been thinking about it; it had been a reflex to come here, an escape when everything else felt like walls, when even Timi hadn't been enough for whatever irritation was scraping inside him. The front door opened and Ruqaiyyah stepped out. She'd dyed her hair blue since the last time Ahmed had seen her, and it was in short bright twists sticking out of her head, her eyes black, her mouth a faded red under her doorframe. When she leaned forward, the white dress she was wearing hung away from her body, shadows milling about on her chest.

"Who's there?" she called out. The car sat in the pale light of morning, and Ahmed sat inside of it, his hand trembling. Ruqaiyyah walked out into the driveway, her feet bare against the gravel. She wasn't afraid, Ahmed realized, probably because she recognized his car. As she reached his window, Thursday wound it down from the driver's side, exposing Ahmed's face to her. Ruqaiyyah was tall, like a swaying palm tree, and she leaned both her arms on the ledge of his window, pushing her face close to his.

"So you finally found your way here," she said.

Ahmed nodded and his car door clicked as Thursday unlocked it. Ruqaiyyah took the handle and opened it, then reached in and wrapped her hand around his trembling one. Her skin was cool, and Ahmed flinched at her touch. She tightened her hand on his and tugged on it.

"It's all right," she said. "Come inside."

He swung his legs out of the car without looking back at Thursday, and Ruqaiyyah shut the door behind him.

"When should I come back?" asked Thursday through the open window.

"When we call you," she answered. He started the car again as Ruqaiyyah led Ahmed into the house. Faint strains of highlife wound out of the open door as they walked through it, and Ahmed felt his hand relax inside the curve of Ruqaiyyah's skin. She'd been inviting him to her guesthouse every full moon for the past year and a half. Regularly. With no impatience when he didn't reply, when he replied and said he couldn't make it, when he said he would come, then canceled at the last minute or never canceled at all, just didn't show up. And now he was here, sweat dry on his skin and under his arms, his throat tight. He would've felt alone if it wasn't for her hand that refused to release his. The door closed and Ahmed blinked, clearing his eyes for a morning that he knew was about to feel like a never-ending night.

four

Ijendu's mouth was a copper cave, a soft terror.

Aima reeled from her kiss, spinning in the back seat of the car as their entangled limbs slid over the dark leather. Ijendu's driver, Godwin, didn't even look into the rearview mirror. Briefly, Aima wondered how many other times this had happened, how many times her best friend had fastened her teeth to another woman's neck and sucked on the skin there. Enough that Godwin knew not to blink. Did she care? Ijendu's teeth were small bones scraping silver across her throat, and Aima closed her eyes to watch pinwheels burst behind her eyelids. No one had told her that godless places could feel like this. It felt like she had twenty hands, and Ijendu's warm flesh was under all of them, the peach silk of her dress crumpled, shoved up and aside, a thigh thrown across Aima, a rocking hip bone.

The car took a turn with speed and the girls spilled against one of the doors, giggling as their shoes fell off. Ayra Starr was playing over the radio, loud and aggressive and sexy. Ijendu pressed her palm to the ceiling of the car and looked down at Aima.

"Are you okay?" she asked.

Aima wasn't sure if she could form words with her tongue, but she reached between Ijendu's thighs and hooked the lace of her thong to one side, then sank two fingers into her up to the second knuckle (What color was lava? What texture?). She watched as her best friend gasped and threw her head back, stretch of dark brown neck, golden with body shimmer. Ijendu rocked against her hand and moaned loudly as the car pulled up in front of her house. Its windows were tinted, so at least the gateman wouldn't be able to see what was happening inside. Aima wondered if Ijendu even cared. She was acting as if they were alone, as if the driver was unreal. It was an easy story for Aima to fall into, this unchecked reckless behavior, this open wantonness. Whatever restraints she usually wore bound tightly against her, they were broken open, loosened, almost as loose as she was. She'd been drunk before but never this drunk, never high, never this drunk and high. How could the world be a place? Maybe the driver was a man with spooned-out eyes and perforated eardrums, driving only by memory of how the road felt under the tires of the car, by the vibrations that passed along into the seat and steering wheel. Maybe that was why Ijendu didn't care that her dress had fallen away to show the demi bra she was wearing underneath, that it was rucked up to show her ass and its rhythm as she ground against Aima (shards of bubblegum) even as the car pulled through the gate.

It was only when they parked that Aima saw Godwin look into the mirror. She wondered what his view was—Ijendu's hair tossed against the headrest of his seat, her back like a symphony of hungry muscles? She was almost naked, the peach dress rearranged into a wash of silk around her waist. Aima reached her hands around, meaning to pull the dress down and cover Ijendu, especially now that the driver's eyes were cool and unmoving in the glass (black water). When her hands brushed against the soft skin of Ijendu's ass, Aima felt an unexpected and harsh desire to grab the flesh, seize it in her fingers, spread Ijendu open for the glass and the black water. Instead, she caressed it for a brief moment before tugging down the peach silk like a curtain. Godwin met Aima's eyes briefly in the mirror, his gaze as flat as a lizard's, then he spoke, addressing Ijendu.

"We've reached, ma."

Ijendu giggled and flipped her hair as she twisted her torso around to look at him. "Thank you, Godwin." He nodded and turned off the car, slipping out of it like a ghost. Ijendu slid off Aima like an otter (oil-slick purple), spilling back into the owner's corner and re-arranging her dress to cover her bra. Her cleavage still strained against the silk, and Aima wanted to lean forward and drag her tongue against the curve of it. Ijendu smiled at her. "Inside," she said, every syllable crushed with promise. "Leave the shoes."

They clambered out of the car, unsteady and holding hands, then snuck into the house on tiptoe with stifled giggles.

"Let's not wake Dike them," Ijendu whispered, as they climbed up the stairs and spun into her room, two warm bodies, planets orbiting into a collision. Aima felt a brief frisson of worry now that they were truly alone, now that it wasn't a room of strangers and strobe lights or a rectangle of glass filled with blackwater eyes. It was just her and Ijendu, who was wriggling off the dress, leaving it in a puddle on the carpet, reaching her hands behind her back to unhook the bra. Aima paused, wondering if she was sinking too deep into something that would decimate her, but in that moment of hesitation, the half pill she'd taken before they left the club kicked in—a sweet and vicious riptide of iridescent bells and velvet orange. She sighed and spun around to float onto the bed. Ijendu looked down at her, naked except for her thong, and laughed.

"So, who's going to take off your own clothes?" she asked, putting her hands on her hips. Aima stared up at her, following the curve of her belly up to her breasts and the clenched darkness of her nipples.

"You're so beautiful," she said, her words sliding into each other a little.

Ijendu smiled and jumped on the bed, straddling Aima and putting her face a breath away so she could look down at her. "So are you." She brushed a few of Aima's braids off her forehead, and there was a glimmer of memory, of Kalu's hand doing the same thing in a different time, a different real. There was no space for him in this one, so the memory stuttered, became confused, and gave up, flew away. Aima was floating miles above her sadness; it had no chance of capturing her, locking her in its gutters. Ijendu was made of butterfly wings. "I always wondered about this," Ijendu said, and Aima reached up a hand to touch her cheek (butter-yellow satin).

"Stop talking," Aima whispered, and she didn't say it very well; she meant stop because Ijendu's words were too loud and real, too much of thought and not enough of blind feelings. But the way she said it sounded overloaded with desire, so Ijendu didn't notice. She started to pull off the black shorts Aima had on, and together they helped her shimmy out of the gold blouse she was wearing, dragging scraps of lace down each other's thighs until there was nothing between them but air, and soon, not even that, just wetness and heat and mouths, and Aima fell into the patterned wilderness spilling out of her mind and it was wonderland.

Saturday, 5:15 AM

Ijendu was asleep, her body scattered in the sheets and blankets, her hair strewn over her face. Aima had been lying next to her, eyes closed but still with a world whirling inside them. She could feel her pulse blooming in the side of her head and a slow pressure on her bladder that had her swing her feet off the bed and pad quietly to the bathroom. Ijendu snored behind her, light and peaceful rumblings. The air felt thick, as if she was pushing through it, and when she sat down to pee, it felt like the whole room was slowly but certainly rotating counterclockwise. Her body was sticky in places, wet in others, dried fluids plastered to her skin.

Aima ran the shower as hot as it would go and tied her braids up with shaky hands, then stood under the scalding fall of water and rubbed at her skin. She was too tired to find the soap or a washcloth, and the feel of her palm making circles as steam raised off her arms was almost soothing, almost another place to fall into. Eventually, the water started to cool, so Aima turned it off and climbed out, wrapping herself in a towel. She stood on the bathroom tile for a few minutes, trying to think, trying to hold on to images of the last hour or two, what had happened in the bed with Ijendu, but everything kept slipping. When she reached for Kalu, he slipped away too. There was only her and the bathroom tile, her body that had done things, and the way her nerves felt tight and gritty, enough to counterbalance her exhaustion.

Aima halfway dried herself and pulled on an extra-large T-shirt that was hanging behind the bathroom door. The cotton clung to her body as she walked through the bedroom quietly and slipped out of the door, then down the stairs to the kitchen, looking for some water. The lights hissed briefly when she turned them on, and the refrigerator hummed in a corner, metal and shiny and cool. Aima rested her forehead against it for a moment before wrenching the door open—everything felt thicker and heavier than it had any right to. She poured out a glass of water from a pitcher, then stood leaning on a counter as she drank, feeling the cold worm of it wriggle down her throat. The kitchen window opened out to the back verandah, and Aima noticed there was someone standing out there smoking, a red dot glowing in front of the person's face. Curious, she opened the back door and stepped out, the warm night air swirling around her legs. Ijendu's brother, Dike, turned quickly, but his surprise faded once he saw it was her.

"Oh, it's you," she said. Dike was wearing basketball shorts and a white singlet, his muscles leaping out from under it. He was smoking a joint and sitting on the concrete verandah railing next to a row of hibiscus bushes.

"It's just me o," he replied. "Who else were you expecting?"

Aima shrugged. "I wasn't expecting anyone. I thought everyone would be asleep."

Dike cut his eyes at her. "With the kind of noise you and my sister were making? Are you serious?"

Embarrassment flooded Aima and blood rose heavily into her face. "I don't know what you're talking about," she said, her hand tightening around her glass.

Dike snorted and took a pull of his joint, blowing out the smoke in an unhurried stream before closing his eyes and undulating his body in a mocking simulation, moaning as he mimicked their voices. "Oh God, oh fuck, yes, yes, yes! Don't stop, oh God!" He stopped and looked back at Aima. "Or that wasn't you two? That was someone else in her room?"

It took everything Aima had not to throw her glass of water at him, shame and rage billowing through her. "That's what you do in your free time?" she asked, rolling contempt out through her voice. "Listen to your little sister have sex?"

He grimaced and spat over the railing. "You think I want to hear that nonsense? I was minding my own business and trying to sleep. No one told the two of you to be that fucking loud. Or to even bring that back to the house in the first place; other people live here too. You couldn't find a hotel or what?"

Aima looked down at the floor, at her feet against it, not knowing what to say. Dike turned slightly toward her, his curiosity engaged.

"And I didn't know you were a lesbian, for that matter. Weren't you with that your boyfriend, Kalu? Or have you and Ijendu been doing this behind his back from since?" He took another pull and shrugged. "No judgment, I'm just impressed. You never struck me as that type."

"Kalu and I broke up." Her voice was flat. The sentence she was saying didn't feel like it weighed anything—it would have to be real to do that.

Dike whistled. "It's a lie," he said. "You two were the kind to get married, na."

Aima barked out a short laugh. "Well, Kalu would disagree with you on that."

"Ah, I see." He paused, then nodded. "It's a shame. Anyone can tell you're the type they should marry."

Aima frowned, annoyed. "As opposed to what type?"

Dike shrugged. "Some women are good as friends, you can party with them, you can fuck them. They're fun, but they're not the type you have children with or put in your house."

"And I'm that type?" Aima wanted to cut him with the edge in her voice, but Dike just looked her up and down.

"Are you really this girl? Partying with Ijendu and those her friends?" He leaned forward and fixed his eyes on her. "You know I remember when we all used to go to Sunday school together? And I remember when Ijendu changed, and I remember that you didn't. You may have gone to the States and moved in with your boyfriend without marrying him, but I know your type, Aima. You don't judge people like my sister—probably because you're a real Christian, not like all these people pretending—but you don't join them either. And maybe because that idiot didn't want to marry you, you're trying this out." He tilted his head and the smoke from his dying joint obscured his face for a moment. "In which case, clap for yourself, because you really committed to it. Fucking my sister like that under her parents' roof? You no dey fear. In fact, I hail you."

"You don't know me," Aima hissed, her heart stampeding with fury.

Dike sucked his teeth. "Abeg. I've known you since we were small, Aima. You don't lie; you can't even swear properly." He shook his head. "I just hope Ijendu didn't think any of what you people were doing was serious."

Aima slammed her glass down on the nearest surface. "I don't have to stand here and listen to your bullshit."

"No, no, it's okay." He stubbed out the joint on the cement and hopped off the railing. "I'm going inside anyway." Aima glared at him as he walked past, but then he stopped right next to her, his breath against her face. "You're wearing my shirt, you know." He took a long slow look at her body. "And with nothing underneath sef."

Dike smirked and paused, as if to give her time to say something, but Aima was frozen, holding her breath under the looming interest of his proximity. She could almost feel how much his hands wanted to move on her, how he was holding them back, pressing against her with nothing more than presence and promise. "Maybe you're more this girl than you think," he said. "There's nothing wrong with that."

Still, she said nothing. He was close enough that she could feel his body heat and his shoulder bumped gently against hers. Dike bent his head so he could whisper in her ear—unnecessarily, since there was no one else around to hear them. "If you want to come and give me back my shirt, you know where my room is." He stroked her braids with one hand even as she flinched. "I can make you shout louder than my sister can."

When she didn't respond, he chuckled and walked away, leaving her out in the night.

Saturday, 10:34 AM

A wave of terrible nausea woke Aima up, bile surging up her throat, a sickness that had her rolling off the sofa she'd been sleeping on and stumbling to the nearest bathroom. She fell to her knees and slammed up the toilet seat, clutching the porcelain edge as she vomited, her abs cramping, her throat involuntary, her mouth bitter. It lasted for a while, the seizing convulsions, the chunky thickness coming up from her stomach. She kept spitting and retching, trying to clear the vomit from her throat, its taste from her mouth. Her head was pounding and everything hurt. Beyond the body, down to the membrane shrink-wrapping her heart, pulling tighter.

Draped over the toilet, her skin clammy with sweat, Aima started crying. The stench of her vomit wafted back into her face. It had splattered all over the inside of the toilet bowl and over the edge of it in some places, streaks of rotten yellow. She reached up and flushed, recoiling from the whirlpool, then tore off some toilet paper to wipe the splashes, flushed again, used more toilet paper to wipe her mouth and some of her tears, but the crying wouldn't stop. It hurt so much. There was no pill cloud to cushion it, no drink to wash it away, only the husk of a body that had done things she was ashamed of. Aima curled up on the floor and tried to swallow her sobs before they mutated into screams, before anyone heard. Her spine convulsed with grief—how had she lost Kalu? How was she still in the city and he was out there somewhere but apart from her, and they weren't together and they didn't have a home anymore because she'd thrown herself out of it and he'd allowed her to go, to leave without him; he hadn't even cared. After all this time, he hadn't stopped her. It was like she didn't matter, like he already knew how he would live his life without her in it, easily. How could she be nothing to him? She had loved him so much, so much, and he didn't stop her. They had moved home together and *he didn't stop her.*

The hurt turned Aima into a knot, her knees by her face, tears pooling on the tile below her. She couldn't bear to relive all the fights that had sprung up like weeds choking out their love; there had been so many, and somehow they had all led to this. It wasn't supposed to end this way. He didn't even know she was in the city. She was probably a ghost to him by now. He hadn't even texted to see if she'd arrived safely in London, that other her that was meant to be going to her parents' house there. Maybe he'd gone and found some girl to be with for the night; maybe he was still asleep in a new lover's house, in her bed.

What, said a voice in her head, *like you did? Claimed to love him, then immediately went and slept with your best friend?* Aima buried her face in her hands and muffled a scream against her palms.

What had she gone and done? All those feelings she'd had from since, she wasn't meant to have acted on them. It wasn't that she thought they were wrong or sinful; she had no problem with gay or lesbian people, but it just . . . it just wasn't her. It wasn't right to just have sex like that, anyhow, especially the way she had done it, with alcohol and pills and—Aima gasped for air, hyperventilating as she remembered groping Ijendu in the club, fooling around with her in the car. Godwin had been watching! Shame roared through Aima, clamoring and insistent. She had acted like someone who didn't respect herself—what kind of woman allowed the driver to watch her do things like that? Only someone with no decency.

It had been different with Kalu, they were going to get married, they had a home together. Even so, she would never, never in a thousand years have behaved like that with him. What had entered her head? And Dike had heard them, then felt like he could invite her into bed because—well, at that point, why not? She had made it clear what type of girl she was, the kind who would do shameless things like that; why wouldn't he feel that he could fuck her too, forget his wife and children, that she was worth the same as any other random girl he took to his hotel rooms. You are what you do, and look at what she had done. In just one night. It was only right that she should feel like this in the morning. There were conse- quences to living like that; it was as if her own body was punishing her. *You should have been obedient*, it was saying. *You should have lived the way God wants you to, not like this. Not like someone who doesn't know they belong to the Most High. You know better; you should have done* better.

Aima rolled her body over till she was on her knees again, then bent over and rested her forehead on the ground, spreading her palms against the floor. "Please," she whispered. "Please, Father, forgive me. I don't know what I was doing, but this isn't me; this isn't who I want to be." She hadn't prayed like this in a long time, a heart crying out to God.

After she had moved to Houston, it had felt like God wasn't as loud in America as He'd been in New Lagos, like His voice was muted. One Sunday of missing church had turned into weeks, and by the time she'd met Kalu, Aima had felt like a different person, someone who didn't need God standing in a corner of her bedroom. Prayer had become a private thing, and her old dreams of having a partner she could pray with now seemed foolish, unrealistic. Kalu was a good man even if he wasn't a godly one. It had felt like more than enough, and Aima kept God tucked in her heart, not in the front of her tongue, not in the rooms of the apartment she and Kalu rented downtown. It was only after they had moved back to New Lagos that Aima realized she had been hiding God from her partner, that she had been pretending to be someone else. Kalu had never known her before, not like Ijendu did, and once Aima was home, God was loud again, spilling out of strangers' mouths. Aima had *remembered* who she was, and she had let Kalu see it, and it had ruined them.

She let out a fractured sob and the crack went into her voice. "I didn't mean to stray this far from You. I don't want to become lost; I don't want to be this person. I want to be back in your Light; please show me the way. Please, Lord. Please forgive me."

The bathroom floor was cool against the pulse pounding in her head, and Aima stretched out her body, lining up her legs next to the bathtub, pushing the floor rug out of the way. She wanted the tile pressed against her thighs, her stomach, her chest. To be prostrate. It felt right.

"Please, I'm begging You. Help me. Help me. I'm so sorry, I don't want to be this. Please, Father Lord, forgive me."

She kept whispering against the tile, residue of sickness in the air and on her tongue, salt slipping from her eyes over and over, packing prayers into the grout.

five

S ouraya never slept well.

She was used to it by now; she had become friends with the night. It wasn't even a struggle anymore. She had a hanging chair out on the balcony of her apartment in Kuala Lumpur, where she would sit and spin, her ankles catching the dark air of midnight. She smoked out there often, thin delicate joints, and she played old music that encouraged melancholy and, specifically, homesickness. Aṣa's first album. Nneka. Plantashun Boiz, the slow ones. She hadn't been home in years, even though some of her clients were Nigerian too. She'd been to many other places though. Dubai. London. Bahia. Paris. Berlin. Cape Town. Tokyo. Cities and nighttime skylines that blurred into a shimmering row of meaningless lights. So many balconies. Each place smelled different, she remembered that much. Her favorites were wherever she was near the water—Seychelles, Langkawi, Negril. That clean taste of salt in the air. Souraya would slip out of bed (the men never woke up, never noticed) and stand out in the breeze, her eyes closed, her tired body swaying. She was always tired, perhaps from not sleeping, perhaps from not eating enough, even when she smoked. In the mornings, the men would open bleary eyes to find her wrapped in a silk robe, her hair tousled and falling down her back, her mouth like crushed rosebuds. Morning light made her look like an angel; they were always enchanted. They sent her bank transfers and extravagant gifts. She hoarded the money and resold the gifts, but only after taking careful photographs of them for her Instagram account. Some of the men didn't like that.

"Why must you show everything on there?" one of them complained. Souraya suspected he was one of the lazy ones who duplicated gifts—buying the same thing for her and his wife or, more likely, for the other girls he saw. She wasn't the type to throw tantrums over it, but another girl might. Souraya had a few hundred thousand followers, and several of them were girls in the same line of work as she was, their cover professions written in their bios next to the emojis and handles for their Snapchat accounts. Hers said she was a personal shopper and stylist, and on some days, that was actually true. One of her clients, an international attorney from Türkiye, did pay Souraya to go shopping for the both of them.

"But don't buy me the things you wear," the lawyer said, her eyes crinkling. "I'm too old for all of that." She was one of Souraya's favorite clients, likable and generous and pleasant to sleep with. For most of the others, the money and gifts compensated for the tedium of having to deal with them. Souraya worked in bursts, a few months of traveling, then she would vanish, returning to KL and her hanging chair, only working if someone worthwhile was in town. She lost many clients because of this, but the ones she kept were intrigued by the unpredictability of her availability, her flakiness covered with mystique; they hungered for her in her absences and devoured her when she emerged.

It was during one of her months off that her friend Ola asked her to come back home with her. They were eating at a small vegan restaurant downstairs at Megamall, and when she heard the request, Souraya stared at Ola as if the girl had gone mad.

"Sorry," she said. "But you want me to do what?"

"Tchw! Don't give me that look." Ola swirled her noodles around in their broth with a porcelain spoon and tucked some of her hair behind her ear. It was long and gleaming black, reaching down to her hips. Last month it had been red and curly—Souraya should've known that the change likely meant a new job. And it wasn't uncommon for one of them to accompany the other, but *there*?

"Come on. You know I haven't been home in ages," she said.

"You mean home as in Naij in general or home as in New Lagos itself?" Ola replied.

Souraya dropped her eyes. She didn't like talking about home or people trying to trace where she'd grown up before she got out. Honestly, she'd never thought she'd go back. The world was such a big place once you escaped. "You know I was raised more in the East," she said. "And you know I don't want to discuss it."

Ola sighed. "Fine! This girl and your mystery. No one is asking you to go back to your father's village. Just come and stay with me small. I have a big client in the city, and usually he travels and flies me out, but this time he has . . . work." She was suddenly vague, but Souraya had no interest in pushing.

"I don't know, Ola," she started saying, but her friend jumped back in.

"Oh, come on, Sou! I already told him I won't come without a friend, so he's agreed to book us a suite each at the Signature. You literally don't have to do anything other than relax next door to me. It's like a holiday!" Souraya hesitated and Ola made a wise play. "Sleep on it, okay? I know it's been a while since you took yourself on a holiday, habibti, you're always saving, saving, I don't know for what. I can gist you more about it tomorrow if you're interested." She glanced at her watch and swore. "Fuck, I'm supposed to meet someone; I have to find my driver." She shoved a wad of noodles into her mouth, grabbed her purse, and blew a kiss to Souraya as she left, scarves and perfume flurrying in the air around her. "Call you tomorrow, darling!"

Souraya sat there and looked at the roti on her plate. She tore off a piece and dipped it into the bowl of curry, then chewed it perfunctorily. The thought of returning home burned in her chest like pepper. It was true that the city wasn't home, not really; she'd spent only a year or two there before she left but still. There are some places that you swear you'll never go back to because the space itself has become inseparable from the time; the there is the same as the then and you don't know how to deal with the space if it's inside a different slot of time. This was the whole of Nigeria for Souraya ever since her father went back to Lebanon, leaving her and her mother behind as if they were nothing, inconsequential items that didn't fit into his suitcase. When her mother got a chance to get married, her new husband didn't want a half-caste bastard in his house, so she shipped Souraya off to extended family in New Lagos. Nothing was the same after that, and Souraya ran away, disappeared into the city and never saw her family again. She had her reasons for not returning.

When Ola called her the next day, it was to tell the story of how a client's wife had found some of his text messages and had started bombarding her on WhatsApp with accusations and curses.

"Can you imagine? She was there telling me I was going to be barren for life, that my womb had been poisoned, and I just laughed and told her I never had one in the first place!" Ola's laugh gurgled through the phone. "She was so confused; she didn't know what to say again. Started calling me abnormal, so I blocked her. It was getting annoying." She kissed her teeth. "These wives just don't know what to do when they find out their husbands are fucking a trans woman, you know?"

"Not just that, they also think the worst thing that can happen to a woman is not giving birth to children." Souraya spun in her hanging chair, her headset snaking white from her ears.

"Ugh. For what? So, we can end up like them, trapped in some fat bastard's house? God forbid."

"Don't mind them. You're the embodiment of a kind of freedom they can't even begin to dream of."

"Abi! They can't be angry at themselves, so they decide to come and vex with me. Abeg. Carry go."

Souraya stared out at her skyline. "I'll come with you," she said, switching tracks.

Ola paused on the other end. "Back home? Are you serious?"

"Why not. Just make sure your guy doesn't disturb me. And tell him I need some pocket money to entertain myself while he's busy with you."

Ola laughed. "That one is no problem, forget. Thank you, thank you so much! I was going to ask Liza, but trust me, I wasn't looking forward to it."

"Didn't she try and steal that your investor guy when you all went to Sydney?"

"Can you imagine. And she still denies it till today."

"I can't believe you're even still talking to her."

Ola made a resigned sound. "We still have to look out for each other. But I warned her I would throw acid on her face if she tried that nonsense again. She won't be that stupid."

"Inshallah."

Ola laughed. "Okay, let me go and call this man and tell him to wire me the money."

"Who is he again?"

"As if you know anyone there. Don't worry yourself. You won't have to meet him."

Souraya wasn't surprised by Ola's evasion; it wasn't rare for girls to try and poach men off each other, so the less you knew, the safer it was.

"As long as I get my first-class ticket, bebi."

"Of course, habibti. Before nko. Catch you later." Ola hung up and Souraya's music automatically turned itself back on. She leaned back and let it center in her skull, loud and engulfing.

Friday, 8:04 PM

Two weeks later, she was listening to the same song as she unpacked her bags in her hotel suite in Lagos, arranging her face serums and creams in the bathroom, turning them so she could see all the labels neatly in a row. Ola was next door, cooing at her guy over the phone, probably throwing dresses all over the place as she tried to decide what to wear for dinner that night.

"He can't wait to see me," she'd told Souraya, giggling. "It's as if he's starving for me. They spend so much money when they're in that state. I almost said we should have dinner tomorrow instead, but he would have gotten so angry if I said that."

Ola's eyes were bright and Souraya knew her well enough to

understand that for her friend anger blurred with passion the same way she'd forgive—or even encourage—jealousy and paranoia. Dangerous games. Souraya had warned her before, it was a man like that who could kill you and call it love. Ola didn't want to hear it, so she let it go. It wasn't Souraya's job to save anyone other than herself, and she was already wondering if it had been a bad idea to come home. The voices were getting to her; everyone sounded so goddamn familiar, like an uncle from a childhood long gone, like a recurring cousin, a resentful stepfather. She'd put in her earphones as soon as she was alone, trying to replace the sounds with something more neutral, like a flurry of strings, the breaking of air over a violin, a cracked voice. It wasn't really helping.

Souraya sat heavily on the bed, kicked off her black Nikes, and curled up on the huge white duvet, drawing her knees into her chest, her forearms softly scraping against the leather and mesh of her overpriced leggings. Perhaps she could stay in here the entire time and not have to venture out. Order room service for a week. Watch a series of shitty movies or, better yet, Nigerian reality TV, which Ola assured her was a worthwhile and absolutely hilarious option. The bed was swallowing her up. She knew she needed to shower but she couldn't quite move, not yet.

There was a knock on her door, and it took Souraya a few moments before she could gather the energy to raise her head, let alone roll off the bed to answer it. As soon as she unlocked it, Ola pushed past her and came swirling into the room, draping herself dramatically across the bed. Her dress was frilled and silk and butterscotch, a slit running almost up to her hip.

"Can you imagine, that bastard just canceled our dinner!" Ola propped herself up on an elbow and her cleavage deepened. Souraya closed the door and sat on the lounge sofa.

"On the first night? That's weird."

"He's just lucky I hadn't started doing all my makeup. Do you know how angry I would be if I had done all of that for nothing?"

"What did he say was his reason?"

Ola flopped back down. "Guy, I don't even know. He said he had a party to go to and he didn't realize it was tonight."

"Are you serious? He canceled you for a party?"

Ola peeked out from the elbow she'd covered her face with. "Well. It was a very exclusive party."

"And so? You came all this way!"

Souraya watched her friend sigh and sit up on her elbows, biting her lower lip, teeth scraping against silky lipstick. "It was a sex party," Ola said. "The kind you have to wait months to get into."

"Oh, I see." Souraya shrugged. "Why didn't you start with that? And why couldn't he just take you with him?"

"Abeg. Why would I want to go to something like that with him? I tried it once, you know, in London, actually."

Souraya started tying up her hair. "And?"

"And trust me, they're overrated. If I already have to deal with one fat hairy man sweating all over me, I'm not interested in watching six of them sweat all over other people." She made a face and sat all the way up, her dress falling open around her thigh. "So, what are we going to do tonight instead?"

"Which kind 'we'? I'm going to sleep, jo. I'm jet-lagged as fuck."

Ola groaned as she got up and flounced to the door. "You're so boring sometimes, Souraya!"

"I promise we'll go out once I've caught up on my sleep. Promise." She smiled convincingly as Ola blew her a kiss and closed the suite door behind her, and once she was alone again, Souraya had to fight the urge to just sink back into the bed. It was too easy to miss days, even weeks, like that. She knew from experience. So, she stripped off her clothes instead and stood under the hot water of her shower until the fog blocked her reflection completely.

Saturday, 10:02 AM

Souraya stayed in her pajamas after she woke up, cocooned in duvet and pillows, watching Netflix on the hotel flat screen until she got hungry enough to stir herself. She ordered room service—an English breakfast, baked beans and mushrooms and tomatoes and toast and bacon. Fresh orange juice. Sitting in the fluffed white of the bed with the tray in front of her, she took a picture of her legs and the food, then fell on her back, holding her phone above her as she quickly edited the image to fit her Instagram grid. The white was good, as was the glossy brown of her legs, touched with amber. A thin gold chain was clasped around her ankle, catching the sunlight streaming in. She'd pulled back the blackout curtains in her room just to take the picture; sometimes bulbs didn't quite give the kind of lighting she wanted. Indulging for breakfast, she typed. The city is already spoiling me. She threw in a few emojis and bit her lip before tagging her location as New Lagos and hitting share. There. It was done; she was officially back. Ola would have to help her take some bikini pictures later, either by the pool or at a private beach.

By the time she finished her breakfast, the post had a few thousand likes. Souraya scrolled quickly through the comments. The account was to help very specific clients find her, that was it. A red notification in the corner let her know she had messages, but she didn't want to look at them just yet. They would be full of people in the city who wanted to meet up with her—some legit potential, others delusional and hopeful, men she would never look at, not even once, talk less of twice. She didn't feel like sifting through all the muck quite yet. As she was putting her tray out in the corridor (she couldn't stand seeing dirty plates around her), Ola walked out of her room in her robe, her hair wrapped in a towel.

"Oh, good, you're awake." She brushed past Souraya and went into her bathroom. "Where's your lotion? Can you believe I forgot mine? I refuse to use hotel lotion, no matter how fancy they claim it is."

Souraya closed the door. "It's on the sink."

Ola was already naked, squeezing out lotion into her palm. "He wants to meet for lunch. I would invite you since he's technically hosting you, but he sounded really angry, so I'm not sure today is the best day."

"What, at you?"

"No, no." Ola bent over and worked the lotion into her legs. "It sounded like something happened at the party. He didn't want to talk about it on the phone. Was just snapping at me that I should be ready to meet him."

"Hmm. Are you sure you want to meet him when he's like this? Maybe he should cool down first."

Ola looked up with a grin. "Are you mad? I like them hot, abeg. It makes the sex so much better. They want to work out their energy instead of just lying there and watching me do all the work."

"Well, you know the drill. Be careful."

"It's the bed that should be careful. You know, once he was having me stay at this fancy guesthouse and we broke the bed there. And then they gave us a new room and we broke that bed too!" Ola burst out laughing and Souraya couldn't help but join her.

"Sounds like those guesthouse people needed a better carpenter."

"You're such a hater." Ola flicked her towel at her before wrapping it back around herself. "Well, let me go and finish getting ready. What are you going to do today, habibti? Please don't tell me that you're staying inside; I don't even want to hear that one."

"No, no, I'm going to get ready and probably go get lunch somewhere. Where's a good place?"

"There's this fancy Asian restaurant that I think just opened. Let me text you the name when I find it. You're going to go alone?" Ola was already making a face. Souraya rolled her eyes.

"I'll find someone to go with."

"Please tell me you know someone here at least. It would be too pathetic otherwise, you going by yourself."

"I know a few people. Some artists from online, a few of the girls. Besides, I'm sure if I just enter my inbox, I can find someone there."

"Wow, it's not that serious." Ola laughed. "Go with someone you know, so you guys can catch up."

"Actually, you know what? I do think I know someone." Souraya was surprised she'd forgotten about him. "We met months ago, at a braai in Joburg. Ridiculously good-looking guy. Didn't try to sleep with me. I think that's what got my attention."

"Are you sure he's not gay?"

Souraya rolled her eyes again. "Yes, Ola, I'm sure. The chemistry was insane, and he even asked for my number and everything, but he seemed, I don't know, restrained? Maybe he had a girlfriend." It was a half-truth, but she didn't need to tell Ola everything.

"And he lives in New Lagos?"

"Yeah, he was just in SA for work, he said. Told me we should link up when next I was here, so I figured I'd be seeing him—"

"Never," Ola said.

"Exactly."

"Well, we thank God."

Souraya pushed her friend gently, laughing. "Shut up."

"Do you have a picture of him?"

"I think he found me on Facebook; let me check his profile."

"I don't even know why you have an account on there. No one actually uses it."

"I like to look normal somewhere. Okay, look." Souraya tilted her phone to show Ola the picture.

"Oh, shit. This guy is fine! Does he have money?"

"For sure. He's not the flashy type, but he has. If you saw his clothes, his shoes, everything. Very understated, very expensive."

"Ooh, I like that type. Usually, they want to show off all their money on you. Perfect." Ola kept flicking through his pictures. "You should definitely hit him up. You have his number?" Souraya nodded. "Then just send him a message and be like, you're taking me out to lunch today. Pick me up in an hour." They laughed and Souraya snatched her phone back.

"I'm actually going to send that," she said, typing in it. "I want to see how sharp he is."

"Let's hope he has sense. Text me when he replies. I have to go, can't be running late." Ola kissed Souraya's cheek. "Start getting ready, sha. You're going out with or without him."

"Yes, ma." Souraya closed the door again and finished typing out the text. She'd kept it almost verbatim. You're taking me out to lunch. You can choose the place. 2PM. The Signature.

She hesitated before sending it—the encounter with this man in Joburg had been more than a brief encounter, more than an afternoon flirtation. She'd forgotten he lived here, to be honest, and it hadn't mattered, not when she thought she'd never be back. He'd be stunned to get that message from her, but Souraya also knew he would drop whatever he was doing to see her. Not because he wanted anything from her but because of Joburg, because of everything that had happened there. Or maybe he had changed, maybe he'd turned into one of those men who chafed at the tone she used in her text, who wanted to be difficult, as if it proved anything or did anything. Souraya smiled to herself and sent the text. It was always fun to see how people would react; a quick way of weeding out those who weren't serious, those who wouldn't be able to afford her or keep up with her, those who didn't understand the game or thought they could implement their own kind of game. That's not how it worked. The world was too big; there were too many people in it to waste time with the useless ones. Souraya wanted to see which one he would be.

She turned on her speaker and started playing some music, tossing the phone on the bed. She was in no hurry to see if he'd reply or to text him again even if he did. Either he would be there in an hour or he wouldn't. Her day was going to continue regardless. She danced to Kah-Lo as she went through her clothes, trying to pick something to wear, tossing dresses onto the bed. They fluttered down in a cacophony of color, green and marigold, rust, red, smooth cream and bright blue. Everything, she knew, would look good against her skin. She picked up her phone again just to look at her Instagram grid to see if there was a recent color she'd used that she could repeat, pulling the grid a little tighter together. Blue. From a shot of her against a brilliant sky, the post right before the breakfast post. Perfect. She fished out the blue dress and held it up against herself in the mirror, glass stretching from ceiling to floor. It would stop midway down her thighs and it had sheer sleeves banded with tiny intricate buttons at the wrist, hand-embroidered cream flowers trailing along the bodice. Like most of her dresses, it was made of silk. Souraya loved dresses, especially light and wispy ones. They made her feel a breath away from naked; they rode up so deliciously when she walked or sat, and she lived for the feeling of someone else's hand sliding underneath the hem, slipping up her thigh. One of her clients liked to drive like that, her legs against the leather of his car seat, his hand falling into her as he broke speed limits and pushed her dress up to her hips.

"Your skin is an even finer silk than the fabric," he'd told her, taking his eyes off the road for a few dangerous minutes just so he could look at her as he said it. He never let her wear anything under the dresses.

But this was a normal lunch, she reminded herself, pulling out some underwear. *Behave yourself.* She showered again, this time a quick one with cold water just to wake her skin and senses up, then let her face air dry before patting in a toner, which doubled as an essence, made from maple tree sap. After that would be a serum, then her face cream and sunblock. She was lotioning her body when her phone buzzed, jarring the music playback. He had texted back, just a simple line. I'll be there.

Souraya smiled and texted Ola. He replied. Said he'll be there.

Lol! Nothing else?

Nope.

I like him already. Look extra hot so you can just scatter his head one time.

Souraya glanced at her face in the mirror and tried to see it as he would, with all these years in between. She still had skin as smooth as a mask, carved cheekbones, the same mouth that he'd begged for in Joburg. She texted Ola back.

Before nko?

She was brushing her hair when Ola's reply came in and didn't read it until she was done with her moisturizing routine and about to start putting on her makeup when she picked up the phone to change the playlist. Her friend had filled the message with admiring emojis. I trust you! Madam the madam!

Souraya smiled and didn't text back.

six

Kalu stumbled back into his flat with his head still reeling, his key unsteady in the lock, the door swinging like a loose jawbone. The corners were buzzing in the dark. He fumbled his hand against a wall until he found the light switch and hit it, making the bulbs crackle before they popped into brightness.

The whole place felt wrong without Aima, unfamiliar, half-orphaned. His stomach was uneasy, clenching and twisting—he couldn't tell if he wanted to vomit or needed to eat. When was the last time he had even eaten? Sometime the afternoon before? A salmon wrap from the neighborhood cafe with a green juice. Before he'd taken his love to the airport and given up on her. Kalu slumped into an armchair and let his spine sink into the upholstery. Maybe it could swallow him. His stomach did a particularly unpleasant twist, sidetracking his mind—*I should eat something*, he thought, then held on to the thought ferociously, grateful for its clarity. A decision. Something to do.

The fridge had leftovers in it, jollof and beans, cold soup, and a green packet of moi moi. His mother insisted on sending food over with her chef all the time, as if he or Aima didn't know how to cook. By the time things started cracking apart with Aima, she had decided that his mother was doing it to poke at her, to say in quiet honey-coated ways that Aima didn't even know how to take care of her son. Kalu had tried to convince her that his mother wasn't thinking that, wasn't saying it in carefully layered Tupperware containers filled with fried rice and chicken stew, but Aima wouldn't listen. At some point, she wouldn't even touch the food herself, leaving it for Kalu. "After all," she said, "you're the one she's making it for, not me." Mealtimes became strained and Kalu started eating out more, grabbing quick bites on the go. The evenings when they'd sit at the table together faded out of their calendar, and Kalu kept moving, kept avoiding until she was gone.

Plantain. He could fry plantain. Yes. A decision.

But first, something to drink. He opened a cabinet and poured himself a water glass full of vodka, then pulled out a bunch of plantains from his pantry. They were still firm and yellow, only a few brown patches forming on the skin, not too soft yet. He and Aima used to argue about this all the time. She wanted them overripe, almost like mush, soaking up oil when fried. Disgusting. One more thing he wouldn't have to deal with anymore. Overripe, oversweet, almost spoiled. Maybe their love was like that, just spoiling from being kept on a shelf for too long. Kalu chopped off the ends, squeezing that bit of raw plantain into his mouth and chewing, washing it down with vodka as he skinned the rest of it, cutting it into diagonal slices.

The one thing Aima had converted him to was frying them in coconut oil instead of groundnut oil and using as little as possible, so he poured out a restrained puddle in the middle of the frying pan and watched it, hovering his palm over the spreading clearness until he could feel the heat on his skin. When the oil was hot enough, before it started smoking, he slid in the slices, whipping his fingers back as they sizzled, avoiding the splatter. He watched the slices turn golden with a detached concentration, emptying his mind of everything else except the changing color on their flesh, the creases of the paper towels he was folding to soak up the oil when they were done, the smooth ceramic of the dinner plate as he brought it down from the shelf.

If he thought about each step, then he wouldn't think about the night, or about the man he'd thrown to the floor, or about Ahmed's face close to his, his breath like a breeze. That last image intruded, forcing its way into his kitchen, reflecting off the steel countertops. Kalu shook his head, emptied and refilled his glass, then pierced the pieces of plantain with a golden fork, part of a set Aima had insisted on buying. The oil hissed as he flipped the slices, and Kalu tried not to think about the girl at the party. If he thought about her, then he'd have to think of all the other girls, the ones he didn't know, the ones Ahmed had thrown so callously in his face. And if he thought about that, if he let all that potential pain and fear and horror creep into his head, Kalu was fairly sure that he would go mad. Had he even saved the one girl? Had he even done anything worth doing? Once they threw him out of the room, what had happened? Everything must have continued; he was nothing, just a hiccup in the night, a speed bump that they crushed down into the rest of the road. He strained the plantain out from the oil, emptying the slices onto the paper towels, then grinding pink sea salt over them. Another of Aima's stamps on his life. It was strange to have a life that was his, just his now, no longer shared. The hurt was like a monster wave frozen in the moment before it crested and breaks, just waiting and threatening with its shadow.

Kalu ate the plantain while it was still hot, standing up in the kitchen with his hip against the counter and the oil searing his tongue. He tossed the plate into the sink when he was done, hard enough that it chipped off a corner, and turned off the kitchen light, grabbing the bottle of vodka as he stalked into the bedroom. He was getting angry again and he didn't know why. It hadn't even been twenty-four hours since Aima had left. Left, can you imagine? Thrown away all their years together as if it was nothing. He pulled out his phone and texted her best friend, Ijendu.

Did Aima land safely?

He'd thought Aima would have texted him herself when she arrived but if she didn't want to, that was her problem. At least someone would tell her that he was asking around, since she had gone and turned them into strangers, relying on secondhand news. He wasn't expecting Ijendu to reply—it was almost two in the morning—but his phone vibrated almost immediately.

Go to sleep, Kalu. Aima is fine.

Kalu looked at his phone and thought about the empty kingdom that was their bed. I can't sleep, he replied. Why are you awake?

I was talking to her.

So she had texted Ijendu but didn't want to text him. The pain that lanced through his chest was fine-tuned and sharp, a precise laser. Maybe talking through Ijendu was the best way to talk to her. Tell her I miss her.

He could see the bubble that showed she was typing, but Ijendu's reply was slow to come.

No.

Please. Kalu paused, then sent another text. Come over. I fried plantain. Maybe they could hang out. Maybe she'd tell him more, like what Aima had said, how she was feeling, if she really hated him, why she didn't even look back when she walked away. He almost added the truth, that he didn't want to be lonely, but that seemed too much, too desperate.

Ijendu didn't text back for long minutes. Kalu left the bedroom and wandered into the living room, then sat on his couch staring at his phone screen, sipping from the bottle and touching the screen occasionally to stop it from falling asleep. Ijendu probably thought he was hitting on her, trying to get her over so he could get her into bed. As if he'd be that stupid, to try it with his girlfriend's best friend. His ex-girlfriend's best friend. He wanted to text again, to clarify, but then he imagined—what if she did come over, what if she wrapped her arms around him and said she was so sorry this was happening, that he didn't deserve any of it. What if, because he couldn't sleep, she agreed to cuddle for a little bit, just as a friend, just hold him small so he wouldn't feel alone in the empty kingdom. What if, when they were in bed, their bodies just found each other, maybe in what started as an embrace of comfort, but the heat of their skin and his brokenhearted breath and, and, and. His phone buzzed and he looked at the text from her. It wasn't insulting him, like he'd half expected. In fact, Ijendu sounded like Aima, just tired of his nonsense.

Go to sleep, Kalu, she'd said.

Rage flared up through his chest. Kalu hissed and threw his phone before he knew what he was doing, his arm uncoiling with all his force. It smashed against the wall with an ominous crunch, but Kalu couldn't bring himself to care. He toppled over to lie on the couch, his feet dangling off the edge. The rooms of the flat were too quiet, just the hum of the air conditioner crawling against the walls. His head felt clouded and clashing. He closed his eyes and pressed the heels of his hands into them, as if he could squash them, pop them like rotten grapes. In the blackness behind his eyelids, he saw Ahmed in that same room where they'd kept their childhood secrets; except they weren't children anymore, they were grown, they were now, and Ahmed's whipcord body was pressed over Kalu's, his hand crushed between them, skin stretched against skin. Kalu ripped his hands from his face with a growl and leapt to his feet.

This flat was going to drive him mad either with Ahmed or Aima or that girl, they were all going to take turns haunting him, he could already feel it. And if they were showing up like this when he was awake, then how could he even risk falling asleep? Kalu wasn't in the mood to find out. He was exhausted, so tired that the bones of his face ached, but he couldn't stay there and go gradually mad. He had to get out, go somewhere, so he grabbed the bottle and his keys, cash still in his pockets, and he left, with no direction, no destination, chased by ghosts of alive people.

Saturday, 2:45 AM

There had been a brief moment outside his building when Kalu paused, wondering if he should take his car and go for a drive, but then he turned away and continued on foot. There was a way he wanted to disappear into the night, into the city. Become the nobody he felt like. The security guards looked at him curiously as he left through the pedestrian gate, surprised to see him without his car, just walking out wearing slippers, vodka bottle dangling from his fingers. Usually, Kalu would smile through his car window and exchange a few words, pleasant and empty, but this time his face was set and struggling, so they murmured quiet greetings and let him pass without anything more.

It was an unnatural time of the night to be out on foot. Kalu could feel their concern like an oil slick against his back, but he ignored it and walked down the road under sputtering streetlights. He kept like this for a while, meaningless turns until he was walking by one of the main roads and he heard the trains roaring overhead. He looked up as the wave of noise washed over him, rumbling vibrations scraping through the air. When was the last time he'd been on the train?

Kalu turned and walked toward the nearest station. He didn't have any tokens, so he fed hundred-naira notes into the token machine and a handful of them clattered out, stamped round steel with serrated edges. He counted out three and pocketed the rest, then dropped the fare into the slot and pushed through the turnstile. The station attendant watched him from behind a pane of greasy plastic, eating shawarma as his bloodshot eyes slid over Kalu and his too-expensive-to-be-here clothes. Kalu could feel the stare; it felt like everyone had been staring at him all day, and he could feel their eyes as surely as touches; they were intrusive and uncomfortable, and he wanted it to stop. He had a moment of imagining himself snapping, screaming and circling nothing, shouting for everyone to stop looking at him. What kind of madness. *It was probably my imagination*, he thought, skirting a haggard man sitting on the floor fixing shoes with deft fingers. The client waited on a nearby stool, his big toe poking out from the hole in his socks. They both glanced at Kalu, then back at the shoe and its flapping sole. *No one is interested*, Kalu told himself, as he tried to ignore the moment of their looks. *No one cares. You're not that important.* He unscrewed the cap of the bottle and took a long burning drink. It was like an eraser, wide swathes of hot numbness spreading through him.

The platform for the train heading to the lowland was halfway empty, an odd populace dispersed and waiting. There was a woman with about five Ghana Must Go bags gathered tightly around her legs, as if she was afraid someone would try to snatch one of them away. The bags were swollen, though, so full that Kalu wondered how she could carry them all herself, let alone how a thief could expect to get far with that kind of weight. The sleeves of the woman's blouse were folded back, showing her corded arms, small scars scattered all over them. Kalu didn't dare look at her very long; there was a strange and desperate sharpness in the air around her. He went to lean against a pillar, fatigue weaving into his body as he tried to ignore the acrid smell of urine from its base.

Three young boys were jostling in a corner of the platform, half-playing, half-angry, a seesaw unsure of which side it should settle on. They were a tangle of brown limbs and loud voices; everyone else on the platform was ignoring them, giving them a bubble of space to wrestle themselves out in, unravel one another in aggressive intimacy. A series of beeps sounded out over the loudspeaker, signaling that the train was approaching the station. Kalu stood back from the draft of hot air as it pulled in, graffiti swirling over its metal. The doors chimed and jerked open, and he and the rest of the odd nighttime populace entered the train cars.

It was cleaner than he expected, than he remembered. The scarred woman blocked the doorway with one of her bags, heaving the others in one after the other—either she was stronger than she looked or the bags weren't as heavy as Kalu had thought. The doors complained as they tried to close a few times before she moved the last one into the car and sat with the bags crowded around her, a loyal flock. Kalu made his way to the other end of the car and stood in a corner, sipping and leaning against a pole as the train left the station, rocking gently from side to side. A garbled announcement came over the speaker in pidgin, amputated with static. No one paid attention to it.

The train stopped at the next station, but no one entered or left the car Kalu was in. Three stations later, the woman blocked the door again and lifted her bags out of the train, shoving them onto the platform. Kalu wondered who she was and what the bags had been carrying, which train she was transferring to as she sat with her load and became smaller and smaller in the distance. The train car smelled like crayfish and sickly sweet Ribena in a sticky patch under his slipper. He scraped it against an edge, and the door between train cars opened, the three boys from the platform spilling in, quieter now. They seemed tired, pouring into seats next to one another, their bodies at ease with their own nearness. It made Kalu think of Ahmed again, the easy closeness of childhood, how it was stretched and fraying now. The train braked and shuddered to a stop. A young man got on, his shirt carelessly buttoned, chest gleaming briefly under the weak bulbs of the train car. There was something familiar about him, but Kalu was hyperaware of how heavy stares could be, and he didn't want to weigh this stranger with one of his. He looked at the floor instead and tried to sneak quick looks when he thought the man wouldn't be able to see, but his eyes were clumsy, and when he glanced up, the stranger was staring straight at him. Kalu wrenched his gaze away, but it was too late.

The man walked down the length of the train car, holding on to the poles for balance as the floor bucked beneath their feet. He stopped a few seats away from Kalu before speaking.

"I know you," he said.

Kalu didn't look up. He wasn't supposed to be recognizable; he was trying to be invisible and he didn't want any wahala. "I doubt," he answered. "It must be another person."

The stranger snapped his fingers. "You're that madman from the party in the highland."

That made Kalu snap his head up. "What?"

"Yes, the one who jumped on the pastor."

Distracted, Kalu frowned even as he studied the man's face, trying to place him. The bottle in his hand was nearly empty. "Pastor?"

The stranger leaned in. "Is it that you're still drunk? Or high?" He pulled back and clicked his tongue. "Stupid of you to be on this train if that's the case. Heading in the wrong direction sef."

It felt like a dream, like a warped wonderland mistake, this whole conversation. The man laughed at Kalu's confusion.

"You're surprised I recognized you without your mask? It's not that hard."

He smiled and the memory clicked into Kalu's head—that smile, a hand passing a glass to him, the bartender from the party. His eyes widened and the bartender laughed again.

"You've remembered," he said.

It was strange, how he'd seemed like a boy at the party, young and innocent, and Kalu had pitied him. But now, in the train, his whole body was arranged differently, flush with confidence, comfortable in the early morning strangeness of the moving metal worm. Did he look taller? Older? How had he morphed like this?

The train took a turn and Kalu stumbled, off balance, while the bartender merely swayed, his body rippling, his hand wrapped around the pole, his eyes on Kalu.

"You no dey fear," the man noted. "Walking around by yourself, on the train? You get liver die."

"Why should I be afraid?"

"After what you did?" He whistled. "If I were you, I would be inside my house with soldiers outside the door." Kalu blinked and the bartender looked at him, then made a low sound of surprise. "Oh, you don't know yet."

"I don't know what?" Kalu felt thickened, slow, stupid. None of this was making sense.

The man took a step closer and lowered his voice. "Did you think nothing was going to happen to you after you tried to beat up a whole pastor? A whole Daddy O upon that?"

It took Kalu a few seconds. "Okinosho?!"

The bartender hit him on the arm. "Shut up!" He looked around the train. "Of all people, you should be careful saying his name."

It wasn't possible. The man in the room couldn't have been Okinosho. Not the most powerful religious leader in the city. Kalu laughed. It was impossible. Everyone knew Okinosho was a power-drunk charlatan, everyone except his millions of followers around the world. He was too rich, too dangerous, too big. He *couldn't* have been the man in the room.

The bartender watched Kalu laugh and pity crossed his face. "You're really mad," he said. "Chai. It's a pity he's going to kill you."

Kalu's laughter cut off. "He's going to what?"

The train was slowing. The bartender turned toward the doors. "He's put out an offer. As soon as he left the party. Whoever brings him your body, or if it's too heavy, just your head is okay. Twenty million naira." He looked Kalu over. "I won't tell anyone I saw you, but it's better you go back to your house, I'm warning you. Twenty million is a lot of money. It's only a matter of time before they find you."

"Wait," Kalu said, as the train pulled to a stop. "Who told you all of this?" He tried to grab the man's sleeve but the doors opened and the bartender twisted away from him.

"Hapụ m aka, dead man. It's bad luck." He dusted his shirt, standing on the platform as the doors started to close and Kalu stared, frozen, too shocked to move. A brief softness passed over the man's face. "God protect you," he added, shaking his head as he turned away.

"Wait!" The train began to move and Kalu ran down the car, searching through the windows as he shouted. "Wait! How do you know!"

The bartender was walking away, then a tall man stepped out of the shadows and greeted him. Kalu watched as they shared a quick embrace, as the station light caught the milky white of Thursday's eye, as Thursday draped an arm around the other man's shoulders and they walked away. The train plunged into a tunnel, throwing Kalu into darkness. His heart was erratic, thudding, terrified.

He had attacked Okinosho.

The bartender was right, he needed to get home, get to safety. He needed to talk to Ahmed. Kalu patted down his pockets, searching for his phone, his pulse doubling once he realized he'd left home without it. *Shit, shit, shit.* He forced himself to breathe, looking around the car. *No one on this train is going to kill you*, he told himself. *Just get home.*

Run.

He downed the rest of the bottle and tossed it to the floor. As soon as the doors opened, he dashed out of the train and tore through the station. There was a row of taxis parked outside, the drivers asleep, their feet hanging out of the windows, seats reclined. Kalu banged on the bonnet of the nearest one.

"Bros! Wake up!"

The driver startled awake and started to curse immediately, but Kalu had pulled out thousand-naira bills from his pocket and shoved them in the man's face. "Highland. Now now." The driver paused for a negligible second before he nodded, took the money, and started the car, sleep draining away. Kalu entered the back seat and lay on it. No one could see him if he was flat like this, pressed against the questionable upholstery, lying like an already dead man. He was more drunk than he'd realized; the ceiling of the car was rolling. He closed his eyes and was surprised when his body started shutting down, dripping into a doze. The bartender was probably lying. Probably just wanted to see him piss himself, be that scared. Everything was probably fine. He'd call Ahmed and see if Okinosho was really even a client at the party.

He gave the driver some more money when they reached his compound, prompting shocked thanks from the man, then Kalu stumbled up the stairs and through his front door. His phone was lying on the floor under the dent in the wall from when he'd thrown it. The screen was a web of fine cracks, and it stayed black even when Kalu tried to turn it on. He groaned and went to the bedroom, plugging it in next to the bed. Maybe it was just dead and he could use it after it charged. He had time now that he was home and safe and the bartender was probably lying and everything would be fine once he got to talk to Ahmed.

Kalu lay on the bed and passed out.

Saturday, 10:30 AM

The dreams started frantic, a heap of Ghana Must Go bags burying Kalu, vodka pouring into his eyes, garbled train announce-
ments in Hausa. The dream images trailed into nothingness, then
burst up later, pictures of the girl at the party, her body trembling.

Kalu woke up with a gasp, shudders quaking through his bones,
sweat in the pool of his neck. Hours had dripped past and it was
morning, the next day lumbering slowly through his windows. He
sat up and looked for his phone. It had fallen from the bedside table
and his fingers scrabbled against the carpet to pick it up. The screen
lit up underneath the web of cracks and Kalu sighed with relief as
he called Ahmed from speed dial. Ahmed would be awake by now;
the party would be over. He could ask him what happened to the
girl and Ahmed would tell him the bartender's story was a lie, that
Okinosho wasn't even at the party, that the man in the room had
been a nobody. Kalu could go to Ahmed's house and let Thursday
make yam and eggs, and they would eat it in the dining room and
play Obongjayar's latest album while they smoked and the day
would continue and the night would be just a dream, a dream that
didn't mean anything, something stuck in the darkness where it
belonged.

His head was splitting open. When he dialed, Ahmed's phone
rang for so long that Kalu thought he wasn't going to pick up his
call. But then it went through and the sounds Kalu heard were
cloyed, muffled.

"Hello?" Kalu said, his voice hoarse with dawn. "Ahmed? Are
you there?"

Someone laughed as if from a distance. A man. Kalu knew it was
not Ahmed; he knew his friend's voice too well. The laugh was low,

intimate, flirting. Kalu ended the call quickly. His stomach was churning again, sick with apprehension, and his shirt was sticking to his skin.

"Fuck," he said, dropping the phone and putting his head in his hands. Why was there a man there? Why had that laugh—no. No, he was asking stupid questions and he knew it. He lay back down on the sofa and stared at the ceiling.

So. Ahmed was with a man.

Kalu exhaled and tried to decide what to do next, if he should call back, why the thought of his friend with another—with a man—was making him sicker to the stomach than the vodka had. The whole night on the train didn't seem real. Maybe he hadn't even seen the bartender. Maybe it was a hallucination. Especially the part about Thursday picking the bartender up? That was definitely some kind of dream. Everything was fine. No one was coming to find him in his house.

Kalu went back to sleep.

seven

Y ou look like shit," Ruqaiyyah said.

Ahmed sighed and smoothed down the terrible creases of his caftan. "I know. It was a long night."

"And yet you came."

They were standing just outside her doorway, having a quick smoke before going in. Outside the pool of the security light, Ahmed couldn't see Ruqaiyyah's face and he was grateful for it. She was someone who saw him too easily, which was unfamiliar and uncomfortable. They'd met at one of his parties years ago, a New Year's thing in Zanzibar. She'd walked around the whole night wearing a thickheaded strap-on, rolling condoms on and off it, fucking whoever however, always with the same amused smirk on her face. Ahmed had made eye contact unexpectedly—he'd been sitting back on his heels, knees pressed into a bed, his head thrown back against a wall and his eyes closed while a girl with a full veil draped the fabric over his hips and gave him a blowjob under it, her hennaed hands stroking in swirls of orange and black. Years later, he would describe the veil to Saidat and have her wear it, but back then, the girl moaned around him and Ahmed had opened his eyes to see Ruqaiyyah behind the girl, sliding in her strap. The girl began to thrust back on it and Ruqaiyyah grinned at Ahmed, watching as the rhythm of the girl's mouth changed on him.

"Remix," she'd said, and laughed from her throat.

They became friends in the next hour as they discovered a mutual desire to inflict pleasure, a good-natured competitiveness that left the veiled girl with useless legs and exhausted lungs. Ruqaiyyah made it clear that she had no interest in Ahmed other than as a partner in crime, and they would have been closer, done more things together, if it wasn't for what happened at the end of the trip when they were lying naked on a beach the morning before their flights.

"I can't believe we never met in Nigeria," Ruqaiyyah had said. "Both of us living in New Lagos, just to come all this way and meet like this."

The surf washed gently up their legs, and Ahmed thought about the sand against his skin, particles against pores, a solid compaction that still washed with water. "I'm thinking of doing one of my parties there," he said. "Back home."

"Ah, I've been thinking the same thing! Except I want to make it a queer party." She reached out and smacked his shoulder lightly. "We should work together."

Ahmed frowned and turned his head toward her, squinting against the early sun. "What do you mean? You want to do one of my parties with me?"

Ruqaiyyah laughed. "No, keep your own parties. I mean, since you're the one with all the party experience, maybe you can help me host mine. For the queers, by the queers, you know?" She managed to say the word "queer" with a small sour twist that somehow acknowledged how it could be an arrow with a disgust-poisoned tip even while reclaiming it in her mouth. The way it cut Ahmed was between the ribs, like a betrayal.

His voice was slow as he propped himself up on his elbows. "Why would I host that with you?"

Ruqaiyyah yawned and rolled on her stomach, folding her arms under her head. "Why not?"

"Why not get a gay guy to do it?"

There was a pause as Ruqaiyyah stared at him. She laughed, but Ahmed didn't move his face so she cut it short. "Wait, are you serious?" she said.

"Yes, I'm fucking serious. Why are you asking me?"

Ruqaiyyah sat up, her breasts swaying gently, her voice careful. "I'm not sure exactly what conversation we're having right now, I can't lie."

Ahmed sat up as well. "I think it's pretty fucking clear what conversation we're having," he said. He knew he sounded defensive, but he couldn't help how easily the irritation was slipping off his tongue. It wasn't her assumption that annoyed him, it was the way she was continuing with it, looking at him as if he was a child trying to get away with a blatant lie, as if she knew him better than his own words were claiming. It felt like a violation, like she was reaching deep inside him and holding something and saying, *This is you; you are only this,* when his own voice had never even gone there. He wanted her to back down.

She wasn't that type of woman. "Wait, so you're trying to tell me you're straight?"

Ahmed had cocked his head to one side. "As opposed to?" He knew it was fucked-up the way he was saying it, but he didn't care.

Ruqaiyyah finally seemed to be getting the hint. "Okay o," she said. "If you want to behave like that."

He relented a little. "Why would you think I was gay?"

"I didn't say that. I know you like women too."

The irritation spiked again in him. "Too? Are you serious?"

Ruqaiyyah shrugged. "I don't know what you're getting annoyed for. It's such a terrible thing to be mistaken as anything other than straight? Okay, sorry, Alhaji. Ma binu."

"You know what? You're an asshole," he'd said, clambering to his feet, wet sand mapping out on him.

"And you're a coward, so whatever," she'd replied, lying back down. Ahmed hadn't looked back as he walked away, and they didn't speak again until they were back in the city, months later, when she walked up and stood beside him at a Lady Donli concert.

"I was an asshole," she said. "Sorry."

They hadn't looked at each other. "It's all right," Ahmed had replied. "Forget it happened."

Ruqaiyyah had put her hand on his arm, and he covered it with his. A brief moment, then she pulled away and left. They remained friendly afterward; she came to some of his parties, and once in a while, they'd have lunch and she'd ask for advice about running hers. It took her a while to set it up, but she spent the time planning, and once it kicked off, she ran it with an even tighter leash than Ahmed ran his. "I allow some straight men there, for some of the girls. Some of the men end up not being so straight, but overall, they're the type who won't freak out at seeing some gay shit. You should come. We could have some fun."

"I'll think about it," he'd said, wondering if she'd just said the bit about straight men to placate him. She shot him a WhatsApp message about the party every month and he had never taken her up on the offer. He hadn't held on to the beach in Zanzibar, truly. There was nothing in Ahmed that held space for unfamiliar wants—he thought of himself as simple, his desires as simple if sometimes a little strong. There would only be a reason to hold what she said on the beach against Ruqaiyyah if something in him thought that there was truth in her assumption, and since there wasn't (anything in him or truth), he didn't.

Still. He didn't go to her party. He didn't know why, and he didn't think about it past that. Now, standing outside her door, bracing for the moment when he would enter it, he swore at Kalu under his breath. Something was broken inside him, a seal perhaps, a key in a lock after swinging open a door. No, that was wrong.

"I wasn't closeted," he said, looking down at the cigarette in his hand.

Ruqaiyyah glanced at him. "Okay?" She didn't sound confused, and he loved her a little in the moment for that, for knowing exactly what he was talking about, for not being surprised that he'd brought it up.

"I'm just saying. Everyone thinks it's something being repressed, but maybe it just . . . wasn't there. Or was there and faded."

She turned slightly toward him. "And then came back?"

Ahmed lifted the cigarette and dragged on it.

"Is that why you're here?" she asked.

He leaned his head back against the wall and was silent for a while. "It's been a long night," he finally said, and there was surrender under his words.

Ruqaiyyah heard it and nodded. "Well, there's no point hiding outside here. If you're coming in, then come in." Her blue twists were shifting darkness in the night. She stretched a hand out to Ahmed. He tossed the cigarette to the floor and ground it out, then took her hand, feeling her cool fingers wrap around his.

"Take off your shoes," she said. He slid them off just outside the door.

Walking in with her felt like the third, maybe the fourth, world of that night. There had been his party before Kalu arrived, every moment within the office, an attempt at a reset with Timi—a failed one—then now this, another attempt, maybe one that would scrub his inside skin of the things that were clinging to it. Or maybe it was a stupid plan, maybe coming here was just going to layer more things onto him and make him so heavy that he would fold, crash under new and unexpected skins. He blinked as they entered the house—it was so different from his own setup. Here everything was gauzed, white sheer curtains like a maze everywhere. The lighting was cool and blue, the whole thing was like a dream, shadows moving between the hanging ghosts, music curling through the air.

"Oh, wow," he said. "This is . . . different."

"Not what you were expecting, ehn?" Ruqaiyyah smiled and passed him a plate.

Ahmed looked down at the arrangement of delicate desserts, complete with fine-spun chocolate and sugar pearls. "What's this?"

She grinned. "Edibles."

He picked up one, powdered sugar sliding smoothly on his fingertips, and raised an eyebrow. "It's a bit over the top, isn't it?"

"Abeg. Everything is an experience here." She spread out her arms and spun, reminding him a little of himself, ringmaster things. "You want common brownies? Go somewhere else."

Ahmed shrugged and bit into the sphere. Coconut and cardamom burst in a swirl in his mouth and his eyes widened. "Oh, shit." He looked down at the dessert. "That tastes fucking amazing."

Ruqaiyyah laughed. "I know. We've got a wonderful pastry chef. Come, there's someone I want you to meet."

They wound their way through the maze, and Ahmed could hear sounds leaking out under the music from blurred corners of the room, moans and gasps and steady frictions. She led him to a back room where a bar was set up, chrome and shiny, a tall man who had to be a model with those cheekbones mixing the drinks. There were a few people sitting there, talking quietly—it looked like a scene from somewhere else.

"Okay," Ruqaiyyah said, leaning close to Ahmed. "You see that one on the far end? In the orange shirt?"

Ahmed looked down the bar at the man she was talking about. He was young. Tall and skinny, corded arms coming out of a retro orange T-shirt, jeans, Converse high tops, short locs falling over his face, dark skin. "He looks familiar."

"Ah, you've probably seen him on TV. That one is not important. The thing about seeing people here is that they also see you here; so do me, I do you."

"I can't remember his name at the moment." The man was handsome enough, there was some ill-fitting elegance around him, like he'd dragged it on and not quite taken the time to make sure it was his size but was wearing it anyway.

"That's not important either. I think you two would get along."

Ahmed laughed shortly. "You think I'll like him? Matchmaking now?"

"Oh, no. I think you'll dislike him quite a bit. Most people do. He tries too hard." Ruqaiyyah shrugged. "Actors, you know. Always fighting that their raging inadequacy."

Ahmed liked that they weren't pretending he was at her party for anything else other than what he was there for. "So why do you think we'd get along?"

Ruqaiyyah took a drink someone handed her, an inch of amber liquid with clattering ice cubes. "I've known him for a while, you know. He has this desperation he tries to hide, and when he's with women, it makes him try to be dominant, try to be the kind of man he wishes he was, with the kind of power he wishes he had. But at the end of the day, he's just looking for validation."

"Like everyone else."

"Like everyone else, yes. But when he's with men, he's earnest. Eager to please. He wants to be pleasing and even though his actual personality is . . . very far from that, he's learned how to be pleasing in . . . other ways."

Ahmed's mind ran a quick reel of how many ways desperation could please him. "Ah," he said. "I see."

Ruqaiyyah was watching his face. "Yes, I think you do. Should I introduce you two?"

"Let me get a drink first."

"Have mine."

He threw it into the back of his throat, the whiskey burning a short and fierce light, then handed the glass back to her. "All right."

Ruqaiyyah hid a small smile. "Come on then."

The actor was telling a story when they came up, his long hands gesticulating in the blue light, his voice deep and amused. He broke it off when he saw Ruqaiyyah and came up to kiss her cheek. "Ruky-bebi! Where have you been all night? I've been dying to have a drink with you."

"Out and about, taking care of business, luring new people in. This is Ahmed."

The actor looked him up and down, slowly and blatantly. Ahmed stared coolly back. "Nice to meet you," the actor said, offering his hand. "Seun."

"Pleasure." Ahmed felt the actor press down on his hand as he kept eye contact, and he almost smiled. It was so typical, these little power plays, these little tests, like he wanted to find out where Ahmed fell in the hierarchy. Men like Seun always had one, a map that dictated how they moved through the world, who was useful, who they should defer to, who they could safely ignore. It was a stupid game, one that he didn't usually play, but this wasn't a usual place and if there was a game to be played, Ahmed would, as he always did, win. He gently ground the bones of the actor's hand together, keeping their eyes locked so he could watch the frisson of pain that shot across Seun's face and then, of course, inevitably, the dilation of desire in his pupils. These games were almost too fucking easy sometimes.

Ruqaiyyah smiled. "I'll leave you to it," she said, and turned to order another drink.

"Let's go somewhere quieter," Ahmed said. He was ignoring everyone else at the bar and he could see that Seun was flustered by the singularity of his attention.

He was trying to play it cool, though, keep that elegant skin on. "No wahala. It's your first time here, right?"

"It's your first time seeing me here," Ahmed replied, this time letting his smile show, a I-see-what-you're-looking-for type of thing. Seun smiled back, looking a little embarrassed.

"Well, I have a room that I like here, and I think it's available."

"Lead the way," said Ahmed, leaning back and watching as Seun stepped past him, long limbs articulating smoothly. He had a beautiful body, Ahmed had to concede, if an average face. A nice mouth.

He followed Seun through the sheer clouds. There were trays of edibles set around and Seun picked a small tart off one of them.

"Have you had these?" he asked. "They pack quite a punch after a while."

"I had one earlier."

Seun stopped and turned. "Have another," he said, reaching his hand out to Ahmed's mouth, a broken tart in his fingers. The curd was a pale yellow.

"Lemon?" Ahmed let Seun place it between his lips, fingers brushing his skin.

"Mango, actually."

"It's good."

"Here, you have a crumb on your face." Seun lifted his hand and brushed beside Ahmed's mouth, startling when Ahmed grabbed his wrist and held it tightly.

"The room," he said. He was losing patience with the little flirtations; he had things to peel off the inside of his skin, and if this boy wanted to help with the peeling, then fine, but get to it. Seun got that small thrilled look on his face, the one people got when they mistook his desire to be about them, like he was eager to be with them. Sometimes Ahmed let them believe that. Other times, while holding them down, bodies twisted, he whispered in their ears that they could be anybody, that they were just a thing, a place for him to be. Some of them came then. He wanted to say that to Seun, but maybe later when they knew each other a little better.

The room was lit differently, a pale rose. All these damn pastels, cooling off the walls and the bed and the armchairs. When Seun took off his shirt and the light hit his chest, though, Ahmed didn't mind. There were things the color did to the boy's skin, a surreal cast to everything; it was exactly how Ahmed felt inside.

He watched Seun unbuckle his belt, the hiss of leather passing through loops. He could've taken off his jeans and left the belt in, but when he passed the belt to Ahmed casually, as if he was just giving him something to hold, Ahmed took it, acknowledging that it could be—it *would* be useful. He folded it and put it aside.

Seun unzipped the jeans and pushed them down his hips. He wasn't wearing underwear and he was already aroused. Ahmed stood and watched him lever the denim down his legs and off his feet. When the undressing was complete, Seun stood with his hands on his hips. His partial erection was large, heavy. Ahmed understood why he'd stripped immediately—showing what he had to offer, believing it to be of worth enough to bypass any other vetting someone might want to do of him or who he was or what he had to offer.

"Well?" Seun said, smirking.

Ahmed sat down in one of the armchairs and crossed his ankle on his knee. "Why do you come here?" he asked.

Seun dropped his arms, thrown by the response but trying not to show it. "Well, Ruqaiyyah is discreet, you know. That's always number one. Especially for someone like me, who's on TV, who's high-profile. I have to be careful about what kind of social life I have; last thing I want is to be some sordid gist on the gossip blogs, you know?" He was starting to ramble. Ahmed sat quietly and listened. "Everywhere I go, there are cameras, whether it's red carpet or being at an event, at a restaurant, and people just bringing out their phones, wanting selfies with me, shit like that. And it's irritating sometimes, but it's the price of fame, you know? I remind myself; this is my life! This is just my life!" He spread out his arms, as if power was sweeping from them, then smoothed his palms down his torso. "So, yeah, that's why I come here. For some privacy. Where I don't have to be in celebrity mode."

"This is you as yourself?"

Seun touched his penis absently. "I didn't say that. This is me as . . . who I am here and now. Why are you here?"

Ahmed watched the boy stroke himself and didn't answer.

Seun began to do it with more purpose. "You know you're looking rough," he said. "Your clothes are rumpled; you look as if you haven't slept in days."

"I haven't slept in days."

Seun stepped closer. "So why are you here?"

Ahmed sighed and stood up, pulling off his caftan. "Kneel down," he said, his voice businesslike.

"Excuse me?"

Ahmed slid his hands against his own skull, cracked his neck, and took account of the things inside his skin. "I said, kneel the fuck down."

The boy blinked, then did as he was told, slowly, one knee after the other. His casual arrogance was wavering in the air around him. Ahmed found himself looking forward to smashing it into indecipherable pieces. He untied the drawstring of his trousers and walked toward the bowing hunger in Seun's face, and just like that, the peeling began.

Saturday, 10:33 AM

Ahmed was asleep again when the phone rang. He fumbled for it and it danced through his fingers, his vision blurred, the ringtone stopping. Seun slid an arm across his chest and laughed, his voice drunk with satisfaction. Ahmed pressed the buttons on the side of his phone to decline the call, not bothering to look at the screen, then tossed it aside.

"Want to go again?" Seun asked.

What Ahmed wanted to do was to shower. There were too many bodies sticking to him. Seun reached down and Ahmed pushed his wrist away.

"Maybe another time," he said, swinging his legs off the bed. There was a brief knock on the door, and it opened to show Ruqaiy-yah's face.

"Your driver is here, Ahmed."

"Thanks, love."

She nodded and left, and he pulled on his trousers while Seun watched, pouting.

"Seriously, you can't spare another fifteen minutes?"

Ahmed picked up his caftan but didn't bother putting it on.

"Come onnnnnn . . ." Seun rolled on his back and looked up, his voice whiney and dragging.

"Don't sulk," Ahmed snapped. "You sound like a little bitch."

"*What?*"

Ahmed paused at the door, ignoring the look on Seun's face. "I had fun. Take care." He closed the door behind him, and just like that, everything beyond it, both past and present, was gone. The sheer curtains were still floating throughout the house; he drifted through them and out the front door, entering the back seat of the car.

"Good morning," Thursday said.

Ahmed grunted in reply as the engine started and the car pulled out of the compound. "Any updates?" he asked, not wanting to look at his phone just yet.

Thursday clicked his tongue. "A few." His voice was tight and it should have been a warning, but Ahmed was distracted. They were headed back to Ahmed's house, and he thought of Machi as he stared out of the window.

"Is the girl still asleep?"

"I took her home."

Ahmed frowned and looked at Thursday in the rearview mirror. "You did what?"

"I said, I took her home."

"When did I tell you to do that?" He met Thursday's eye and got a twisted half smile back.

"You didn't tell me anything. She woke up, she wanted to go home, I took her home. Or were you planning on keeping her locked up in your house?"

Blood heated Ahmed's face. "Of course not. I just wanted to talk to her."

Thursday's mouth tightened. "Look, boss, there was no need. It's better that you leave the girl alone, no matter what that your friend said."

"I wasn't trying to—"

"Ahmed." A moment of silence held in the glass of the mirror as the road went by. "She's not your business. Leave it alone."

Ahmed bit the inside of his cheek and looked out of the window. "What else?" he asked, his voice tight.

"We might have a bigger problem." Thursday was cautious . . . he was never cautious, not with Ahmed, not after all this time and the things they had done together. Ahmed felt foreboding creep across the back of his neck like a glob of saliva crawling sideways.

"Jesus fucking Christ." He closed his eyes briefly. "How big?"

Thursday tilted his head from side to side and made a vague but ominous sound. "Possibly monumental."

Ahmed pressed his fingers to the bridge of his nose. The air-conditioning was pouring over his bare chest. "Okay, tell me."

"The client Kalu attacked—"

"I told them to refund his booking payment and give him the next few parties for free. That wasn't enough?"

"It was Okinosho."

The foreboding on Ahmed's neck stabbed into his spine. "No fucking way."

Thursday sighed. "I know."

"That's impossible. He's a high-alert client. I would have been informed immediately."

"Emmanuel was afraid to tell you. He thought he could resolve it himself and it wouldn't have to leave the room."

"He's a fucking bouncer! He's not paid to *think*." Ahmed reached for his phone and started scrolling through his contacts. "Fuck! I have to call Okinosho."

"I already spoke to him and conveyed your apologies. He was joking about it, said it's fine, that there's always a useless somebody at these parties. As long as it never happens again."

Ahmed snorted. "That man is a petty lying snake. Do you believe him?"

"I believe he's not holding you responsible, which is a small miracle, by the way."

There was a weight in whatever Thursday wasn't saying, and Ahmed put his phone down, staring into his second's face through the mirror. "What's the problem then?"

Thursday grimaced. "There are rumors that he's put a hit out on Kalu."

The air around Ahmed screamed with silence. He couldn't form words, and Thursday glanced back at him with concern.

"Relax, boss. It's just rumors. I'm seeing if I can get them confirmed. We started hearing it early this morning, just back-channel things, but it's sounding like it could be serious money."

Ahmed groaned and dropped his head back on the seat. "You have *got* to be fucking kidding me."

Thursday shrugged. "Okinosho's a powerful man. He can't allow anyone to treat him like that and get away with it."

"Jesus, it's not as if his fucking reputation is on the line. Who would know about it?"

Thursday gave him a don't-be-stupid look. "Everyone else who was in that room. And even if they weren't there, he himself would know. That's all that matters to him."

"Shit. *Shit.*" Ahmed tried to think, but his mind was too scattered. "Have you told Kalu?"

"There's no need, not until we can confirm it."

"Good. Don't say anything. We have to think of how to handle this."

"If it's true, I'm not sure we can stop it. Do you know how many people will be looking for Kalu?"

"Fuck. I hope it's not true." Even as he said it, Ahmed could taste the futility of the statement. Outsourcing Kalu's killing sounded like just the kind of thing a man like Okinosho would do to salvage his thrown pride. He pressed the heels of his hands against his eyes. "Try and get a confirmation as soon as you can."

Thursday nodded as they pulled into Ahmed's compound.

"What did you do with the bouncer?" Ahmed hated loose ends and bad employees with almost equal fervor.

"Broke his jaw," Thursday replied. "By the time it heals, maybe he'll learn how to open his fucking mouth when he should."

Ahmed nodded in approval as they stepped out of the car. He

placed a hand on Thursday's shoulder and squeezed in gratitude. "I don't know what I would do without you."

"It's not in this lifetime that you'll find out," Thursday replied, opening the front door and following Ahmed into the kitchen. Ahmed could feel the other man's loyalty like a warm cloud pressed against his skin.

It had been like this ever since Ahmed had driven past a car accident eight years ago and jumped out of his car to help an elderly woman who was wandering by the crash with blood soaking her headscarf. He'd taken her to the hospital and paid her bills, visited her every day because something kept commanding him not to leave her alone, and three days later, when the man with the milky eye had shown up searching for his mother, wild with fear and grief, Ahmed had been the one to take him by the shoulders and tell him she was fine, that she was safe. Thursday had looked through him, and for one of the very few times in his life, Ahmed had felt a frisson of fear skirt the edge of his mind as he realized he was looking into a darkness that could mirror his. Thursday had become his second only because the man had no desire to be first, to be up front and shiny when he could be the whispering terror in the dark instead. It suited both of them well.

Thursday opened the fridge. "I'll make some food. Will you eat?"

Ahmed started heading upstairs as the stove clicked on. "Yeah, thanks. And some coffee." His house was much like his office, large windows and stretches of white space he'd tried to build into a calming emptiness. Outside, he was always being buffeted by the volume other people created, their loud wants, their colors, their noise. Ahmed wanted to come home to clarity, something stark and clean, somewhere he could think. Nothingness echoed through his rooms and he found it peaceful. He started running a shower, then took off his trousers, tossing them into a laundry hamper. His phone chimed and he glanced at the screen. A WhatsApp message.

You're taking me out to lunch. You can choose the place. 2PM. The Signature.

Ahmed frowned and read the message again, then clicked on the person's profile picture to see who it was. He recognized the girl immediately. *Souraya.* His chest caught. Souraya was a person from another world, another time line. He would've doubted the profile picture, but it was impossible to forget the chilling symmetry of her face—as if it wasn't real, as if she herself wasn't real. It was impossible to forget anything about her; Ahmed had spent years trying.

He blinked and looked at the picture again just to make sure. He'd never thought she'd show up outside of Johannesburg—that he'd ever see her again, in fact. Not after the promises that were made. *What was she doing here? How long had she been around?* His memory wanted to peel back to those weeks in Joburg, to all that had happened, but he fought it. There was too much else going on now and he couldn't afford to sink into the past. Yet, as much as he tried, Ahmed couldn't help but remember how her hand had felt in his, how low her voice ran.

He read the text message again. So, she was in town. A thin thrill went through him, the simple cut of an almost forgotten desire. A small alarm was ringing in the back of his head, warning him that there were only so many places he could run. Timi. Seun. Now this? He ignored it.

I'll be there, he texted back.

The first time he'd met her at some braai in an acquaintance's backyard, Ahmed had stared at her mouth as Souraya introduced herself, at the slow parting of her lips as she listened, the flicker of tongue inside. Her skin . . . Jesus Christ, her skin, like liquid sunlight. Then and even now, there was nothing wholesome in his wanting to see her, he could admit this much to himself. One of his friends had walked up to him after she'd left.

"Stop looking at her like that," he'd said to Ahmed with an amused laugh. "They say she's not only exclusive but she's also bloody expensive."

Ahmed had stared at her ass under the silk sundress she was wearing. "What does she do?"

His friend laughed again. "She's a . . . personal stylist."

Ahmed heard him. "I can afford her," he answered, as if it was nothing—because it was.

His friend acquiesced with a tilt of his head. "You have the money, yes. But she has other criteria for clients, and no one understands what the fuck they are exactly."

"Sounds complicated." Ahmed had looked over at his friend. "You tried, didn't you?" He watched the man's reaction, the brief angry bitterness that he quickly covered with a casual grin.

"All the best of us try," he said, raising his glass to Ahmed. "It's the most we can do."

"Preach."

They'd clinked glasses and didn't mention her again. She'd refused to give Ahmed her number when he'd asked but told him he could find her on Facebook. He did, but her profile was sparse; she clearly didn't use it much if at all. He'd left her alone at first—complicated wasn't something he had time for—but then other things had happened and they both had to leave Joburg, and it had taken him forever to stop thinking about her.

But now—now was different. She was here; she was reaching out to him. He was seeing her in an hour. A small voice in the back of his head reminded him that there was that whole situation with Okinosho and Kalu, but Ahmed brushed it aside. Nothing was confirmed. He could steal some time with Souraya, which felt like a fucking miracle, really. After Joburg, he'd spent night after night fighting the urge to reach out to her, only the fact that he'd promised her that he wouldn't holding him back, the desire to be—for her—a man of his word. Souraya was like a mirage, a ghost, and he had no idea how long she'd be in the city. He *had* to see her. Even after all these years, even after everything they'd been through together, he still wanted her as much as he had when she first walked into that braai. It had been shallow then, superficial, but it had aged into something else, something richer and deeper. Still unwholesome, like everything else about Ahmed's desires, but developed in that.

Ahmed stepped into the shower and let the heated waterfall drench him, thunder falling from the metal plate in the shower ceiling. He stroked himself, mildly surprised that the night hadn't been enough, that the thought of her could still coax a reaction from him. Part of it was not wanting to think about anything else, about Machi or Seun or Okinosho or Kalu, or what the fuck he was supposed to do next about that. He didn't have to think about it. Just a few hours of something else, then he would handle it. After Thursday confirmed.

Kalu would be fine for the next few hours at least; he lived in a secure complex. Ahmed would just have to text him and tell him to stay home, that he was coming to visit him later, or something. Keep him in his flat. Right now, what Ahmed needed was time, just a little more time to clear his head so he could make a plan. Figure out how to placate Okinosho without making an enemy of him, especially since he himself didn't seem to be in Okinosho's crosshairs, at least not for now. It was a little too early to head to the Signature and pick up Souraya, but he could drive along the water and just *think*.

Maybe Souraya could help. Maybe she'd let him touch her again, and he could disappear into her, seek that white space of pleasure, find clarity folded within it. They hadn't spoken in years, so this was definitely presumptuous, but it was nice to imagine. Ahmed just wanted to look at her, try to remember how her face moved when she couldn't control it anymore, when everything was too much of a flood. Flood of her over him, flood of him into her, on her. Ahmed stared down at his erection and wondered what to do with it. There wasn't time, he decided, and he could use it later. He tamped down his thoughts and stepped out of the shower, brushing his teeth before pulling on clean clothes. He grabbed his power bank from where it was charging beside the bed and headed downstairs. Thursday handed him a plate with an omelet and a cup of coffee.

"Ah, thank you." Ahmed took the plate and a fork but waved the coffee away. "Can you put that in one of those ceramic to-go cups? I forgot I have a lunch meeting."

Thursday frowned. "You're not going to sleep?"

Ahmed paused with a mouthful of egg. "You sound like my mother. No, I'm not going to sleep. I'll be fine with the coffee."

"Okay o. I'll get the car."

"No need." Ahmed shoved another mouthful of food down. "I'll drive myself. You go and get some rest."

Thursday paused. "What about Okinosho?"

Ahmed put his plate down. "Tell Kalu to stay in his house, that

I'm coming by soon. And call me as soon as you get a confirmation that this is really happening. I'll think of something by the time this meeting is over."

Thursday raised an eyebrow but took the empty plate. "No problem."

Five minutes later, Ahmed pulled out of his gate. The back of his neck was itchy, like a prophecy was stuck to it, that sense of the inevitable, that something very bad was coming and that no matter where or who he ran to, it was going to find him. What was that thing his father always used to say? *Chicken wey run from Borno go Ibadan go still enter inside pot of soup.* He grimaced at the memory. If he was the chicken, then all this was water boiling up to his chest, and his flesh was going to start floating apart any second now. If Okinosho hurt Kalu because of Ahmed and his parties, there was no way Ahmed would recover. Even if the pastor didn't turn his vengeance in Ahmed's direction, it wouldn't matter. He would be cut down all the same, because Kalu was—Kalu was supposed to be under his protection more than any guest, any client. Ahmed refused to allow himself to think of anything else Kalu could have been to him, ghosts of a teenage night that had drifted away with the years.

There hadn't been time for them to be anything other than what they were. Both of them had left, gone to other lives, other *straight* lives. When Kalu came to his parties and fucked women who weren't Aima, Ahmed had ignored the wicked little part of him that enjoyed owning a part of Kalu that Aima would never see. He'd watched those women ride the broad expanse of his friend's body, watched Kalu's wide mouth fall open, and sometimes Kalu's eyes would meet his as they came, and a surge of possessiveness would wash over Ahmed. Kalu was *his*. Afterward, it was nothing. His parties were worlds unto themselves, and they didn't exist afterward. They couldn't.

Ahmed gritted his teeth. He was not going to lose Kalu or himself over one stupid incident at a party. There had to be a way to keep it together. Until he figured out what that was going to be, he drove.

eight

Ola stared into her mirror, her hands careful as she painted a deep-plum lipstick over her full mouth.

Next to the deep glossy dark brown of her skin, her lips looked like a swollen flower, her face a hooded garden. Ola never chose bright colors like pink or coral even though she knew they'd stand out against her skin. That look was too garish for her; she preferred to be rich and matte and luxurious with her makeup, wines and nudes and occasional shimmering metal over her flawless skin. Taking a step back in the hotel bathroom, Ola tilted her face and studied her reflection, the way her eyes were black pools fringed in mink, the hint of cruelty in her bones. She'd never been interested in pretending to be something soft—she knew her beauty was stark and alarming, and she welcomed it. Her dark skin, the lush pillows of her lips, and even her flared nostrils all added up to a face people didn't always know how to look at. But Ola looked, because she'd taught herself how to.

Some things on her face she'd had to surgically change—her jaw, her chin—because she'd felt they were too masculine, like she couldn't find the woman she was in them, only what other people saw. But things that advertised her Blackness? Ola wasn't interested in cutting them away. She never cared when some of the girls challenged her on this, saying if she really felt that way, she wouldn't wear weave, she'd rock her natural hair.

"Don't be stupid," she'd say. "No one can look at this face and this skin and think I'm trying to be anything other than Black as fuck, Nigerian as fuck, African as *fuck*." She knew they were all jealous. Girls like her weren't supposed to look this way and still get to where she'd gotten to.

Ola smiled a petty smile at the mirror, her eyes glittering, and slipped her lipstick into her purse. She smoothed down the silk of her blouse, then ran both hands behind her neck, lifting and fluffing out the weight of black curls that dropped to her waist. It was good to be winning. She checked her teeth for lipstick and hoped that whoever Souraya's guy was would keep her entertained for the afternoon. With any luck, he'd even be a new client for the girl. Ola always worried that Souraya didn't work as much as she could, that she spent too much time in her flat doing God knows what. "But what do we work for?" Souraya would say in response. "Isn't it so we can enjoy ourselves, do what we like? That's what I'm doing now."

Ola frowned at the thought. There was no security in slowing down like that, not unless you had savings upon savings, property, things that meant that when you stopped you would never have to go back. Investments. One day she was going to disappear, use her money to reinvent herself, then pop back up with a different job, meet a different kind of man who knew nothing about her past—an artist, maybe—and settle down. On her own terms. Not like her clients' wives. Shit, her husband wouldn't even know about her assets; he would never find them or touch them.

Souraya didn't understand. Yes, she'd been through terrible things—hadn't they all?—but she had other things working for her that she didn't even see. The fact that she was cis, that she was mixed, light skinned with that loose hair. Ola scoffed to herself. The girl was literally the world's favorite type of Black woman. She had no idea how much more dangerous it was to move through the world like this, through a girlhood like theirs while being dark skinned and trans. She had no idea what it took to feel safe after that. Ola was proud, truly proud, of how hard she'd worked to create the world she lived in now, one where she was comfortable and protected. Where she'd made enough money to have all the gender-confirming surgeries she needed, the best recovery suites, how she'd literally built herself from the torn pieces people thought they'd left her in. The thought of her future was what pushed Ola now, and she had so much momentum, she was nearly flying.

A select few of her clients knew she was trans, and they paid exorbitant prices for that knowledge, for the privilege of being with and near her. This client was one of them, one of her most lucrative ones, in fact. Ola had been seeing him for about a year and a half now. The man was famous throughout Nigeria, his face looming on signboards and TV screens all over the country, his followers crooning his nickname until nearly everyone had forgotten what his real name was. Thomas Okinosho. Or as a few million people called him, Daddy O, the Overseer of the Rekindled Glory Church of God, which had branches in 175 countries in the world. His net worth was a rumor, perhaps fifteen million dollars, perhaps fifty. Ola was fairly sure it was much more than that—you always had to account for the hidden money, the secret assets. He was married, of course, with five children and a wife heavily involved in his church. Ola never asked about his family life because she didn't give a shit, and he didn't offer information because he didn't give a shit either. That wife wasn't going anywhere no matter what he did, but after a Snapchat scandal with some Canadian sex workers earlier that year, Thomas had become more guarded than before.

"I don't have time for the wahala," he'd told Ola when it happened. "There is too much of God's work to be done."

They had been in London then. She bent over to run her hands down the latex thigh highs she was wearing. "Amen, Daddy," she said, keeping her voice serious. He'd been talking as he unbuttoned his shirt, putting his diamond cuff links carefully down on the carved wooden dresser of the hotel they were staying in, his eyes fixed on her.

"This mantle is truly heavy," he had sighed. "But I do what I have been ordained to do."

"I know you do, Daddy," she'd agreed, through the fall of hair obscuring her face.

"Hmph," he had grunted. "That's enough of work talk." He'd arranged himself in a plush armchair. "Come here." She'd grinned then and obeyed. She always obeyed. Daddy O didn't like disobedience, and if his mantle was heavy, his hand was heavier. She'd received a deed to a property in South London the next day.

Ola smiled through her plum mouth at the memory. If she behaved like Souraya, she could have taken off work for months after each visit with Thomas. Maybe even for a year or two. Sell one of her places; it would be easy. But Ola was always worried that she didn't have enough, that if things were bad she would run out. It felt like she was always being chased, but one day, she knew that one day she would stop running and live. Live even better than she was living now.

She threw a lock of her curly hair over her shoulder and pouted at her reflection. Daddy O wanted to have lunch out instead of in one of his houses, and she was dressed reasonably conservatively for it, going for a bit more of a business look. Not that it really mattered what she wore, anyone seeing him out with a beautiful girl would wonder about his motives. She was surprised he was risking it after the scandal just a few months ago. He seemed to have changed his plans suddenly, texting her that one of his drivers would be coming to pick her up. It was a curt text, so Ola didn't ask any questions. When the car arrived, she threw a silk scarf around her shoulders and hurried down. She was driven to one of her favorite restaurants, an Italian place with lovely lighting.

Ola walked in, already arranging her face into her most welcoming smile for Okinosho, but she faltered when she saw there was already someone sitting at the table with him. A girl around her own age, with long highlighted hair and, even Ola had to admit, a gorgeously done nude lip. She was wearing glasses that had translucent pink frames, turning over a menu in her hands as she looked through it.

"You've brought me a surprise," Ola remarked as she came up to the table, and the girl's eyes darted up. The pastor levered the tall bulk of his frame out of his chair to welcome Ola, squeezing her arm with a little more pressure than was necessary.

"Ah, you've arrived, my dear," he said, brushing his cheek against hers. There was a subtle warning in his voice. "This is my god-daughter, Ijendu." He gestured to the girl and Ola extended her hand across the table.

"It's a pleasure," she lied. "I didn't know you were joining us for lunch."

Okinosho pulled her chair out for her and Ola sat down, leaving the faint quizzical smile on her face.

"That's my fault," he said. "Ijendu wanted to talk to me about some of her business ideas and I mentioned I had to run out to lunch with one of my mentees. Once she found out you work in fashion, well, I couldn't keep her away."

Ijendu smiled at Ola warmly. "You look every bit as glamorous as I thought you would. I'm so glad I get to meet you."

Ola didn't look at Okinosho in case he saw how irritated she was. "Glad to meet you too."

A waiter came up and she ordered some sparkling water. She wasn't sure if Okinosho would want her drinking in front of his goddaughter. Briefly, she wondered who the fuck would let him be godfather to their child, but then she reminded herself that the Thomas she knew was not the Daddy O everyone else did. Of course they would let him be a spiritual parent; he was the most powerful man of God on the continent. He probably had hundreds of godchildren all over the place. Shit, he probably had hundreds of children all over the place. You could do anything as *the* Daddy O, couldn't you?

Ola felt his hand squeeze her thigh under the table. *Behave*, his hand said, but it wasn't a rough squeeze, so she amended the translation. *Behave, please. For me.* Ola smiled and leaned her body slightly over the table to convey interest. It turned out that Ijendu was an aspiring designer who wanted to, as she put it, bring modern silhouettes to local fabrics. And by local fabrics, she meant ankara. Ola fought the urge to roll her eyes and dragged a vaguely interested smile on her face instead.

"That sounds lovely," she lied. Okinosho smiled.

Ijendu asked Ola questions about the industry through the course of the lunch, and Ola gritted her teeth as she answered them, trying not to let her irritation show. It was hard to put on a face for someone who wasn't a client, and while she could usually socialize with other people around her clients, she felt impatient this time. Maybe because all those other times, she was talking to people who had power and capital, not little girls who had dreams. Different worlds, and the latter was one she'd left a long time ago if she'd ever been in it at all. She resented Daddy O for putting her in this position—he'd have to make it up to her later. The thought of that, of what she could lever out of him, calmed her a bit, and she felt the coiled tension in her shoulders and neck loosen. He would pay for this. They always paid, and Ola always collected.

When lunch was over, the three of them entered Daddy O's car, looking like they were two of his daughters. The driver dropped Ijendu off at Mbano Estate then, finally, Ola was alone with the pastor. She smiled up at him, and his hand crawled over her thigh as he leaned over and kissed her roughly, his lips full and pressured against hers, his tongue a swollen snake in her mouth. When he pulled away, Ola let her hand caress his cheek.

"I'm so glad to be alone with you," she whispered, because drivers never counted. "It feels like it's been forever."

"I know," he said. "I've been fantasizing about you for weeks; I missed you so much. Missed this body."

Ola smiled before remembering he'd canceled on her the night before, then his anger earlier in the morning. "But you left me and went to that party last night," she said. "What happened there? Who vexed you?"

His face darkened instantly, and she noted how his eyes flickered toward the driver. *So, it's something he's actually embarrassed about*, she thought. *Interesting*.

"One small boy like that decided he would try me. So now I have to show him pepper. You cannot touch the anointed of God and expect that nothing will happen to you." Okinosho's voice had tightened with anger. "But it's all right. Things are moving against him. The justice of the righteous will fall on his head."

Ola was already regretting asking him about it, his grudges always killed the mood for her. "Nobody can try you, Daddy." She slid her hand over his chest. "I'm so happy I finally get to be next to you again."

He looked at her and some of the rage in his face faded. "It's good to see you, my daughter." He squeezed her thigh hard enough for it to hurt. "Let's go home."

Saturday, 2:15 PM

Daddy O had several houses on the island, many of them his own family didn't know about. He took Ola to the one in the deep highland, her favorite, the one she had helped design from the blueprints to the interior decor. He had offered to gift it to her several times, but she'd refused. "I like to think of it as ours," she told him. "A little love nest, you know? A nest you've built for me." It was a line for his ego. Ola already had a house in Section One that was being rented out by a management company, and honestly, she just didn't want another. There were other countries she was more interested in acquiring property in; this one was no longer high on the list.

In the bedroom, Okinosho dropped the calm face he wore outside, and she watched his mouth twist with desire as his thick fingers fumbled at the buttons of her blouse. She'd deliberately covered up for modesty since they were in public but also to tease him, keep him thinking about all the skin lying underneath, warm and pulsing. The silk under his large hands was butterfly yellow, like gold against her deep skin, diving into wide-leg patterned trousers that hugged her ass but drowned her legs. Ola knew how Daddy O loved her thighs, her calves, how not being able to even see the shape of them would arouse him as much as being able to see her ass did. She laughed low in her throat as he bit at her neck, still working on the buttons, clumsy with want and impatience.

"Are you hungry, Daddy?" she asked, her voice a drawl, and he growled, ripping her blouse open. Mother-of-pearl buttons exploded across the bedroom floor, muffled in the carpet. Ola remained passive, refusing to engage, her body pliant in his hands. "Why did you have to bring your goddaughter to lunch?" she complained. "And you didn't even warn me beforehand. It's not nice; I was looking forward to just being with you."

Daddy O had one hand cupping her ass, his palm full of firm flesh, pulling her hips in against his erection. The other hand was groping at her left breast outlined in strips of lilac satin, a piece from the Balogun sisters' line. His fingers found and twisted a nipple as he sucked on her collarbone and Ola gasped aloud.

"Can't I do something nice for my own goddaughter?" he said, then he ran his tongue up her neck into her ear. "Don't start acting like these small girls, always giving me trouble over nonsense things. I don't like that kind of behavior. You understand?"

Ola pouted and turned her head away from him, the length of her neck taut and gleaming. She left her arms dangling by her sides, like a doll he was manhandling, like she was unmoved by the swollen evidence of his arousal, the ardor of his mouth. It infuriated him, and he reached for the waist of her trousers, ignoring the zipper and tearing them open. The expensive material gave way with a hiss, fraying at the newly raw edges. Daddy O shoved the ruined trousers down her hips and pulled the rest of the broken yellow silk off her arms. He grabbed her waist and tossed her onto the bed, face down, then levered her legs open with his knee as he shoved three fingers into her past the pale satin of her thong. His other hand held her down by the back of her neck and Ola cried out, her voice swallowed by the duvet her face was pressed into.

"I said, do you understand?" he spat out. She was a long dark spill against the white of the bed, her mouth smearing a plum trail.

He couldn't see her face, but she smiled. "Yes, Daddy," she said, breathless. The pastor twisted his fingers inside her for good measure, then pulled them out roughly. Ola heard his belt unbuckle and the rasp of his zipper, then he was pulling her up by the back of her neck as she scrambled to keep her balance.

"Turn around," he ordered, not releasing her neck. She twisted her body as he pulled her close until she was sitting at the edge of the bed, her breasts spilling out of their satin cage, her chest heaving. Daddy O tugged at her neck and stepped back, dragging her off the bed. "Kneel down," he said, his face hungry. "Open your mouth."

Ola parted her lips and the pastor shoved himself past her teeth, down her throat, pulling the back of her head close as she gagged and swallowed him, her mouth flush with his body. His head fell back and he closed his eyes, sighing as if he had finally reached home.

Saturday, 3:38 PM

"I'm going to shower," Ola said, rolling off the bed naked, the pastor's semen trailing down her cheek and neck.

He replied with a grunt, sprawled on his back and already dozing off, cleaned off by her mouth. She pushed her damp hair off her neck and grabbed her phone as she stepped into the bathroom, the tile cool under her feet. Large mirrors lined the walls and Ola stared at herself in them, the smudged mascara, her lips rubbed bare, a welt on her hip from where he'd hit her too hard with his belt. The pastor's semen was mixed with her saliva and smeared over her hands. She rinsed them off, then turned on the shower before pulling out one of the drawers by the sink and rummaging around until she found a hair clip. She twisted her hair and clipped it up, then stepped into the shower and let the hot water pulse off her skin, rinsing away both the fluids and his touch.

She was in a strange mood, in a hurry to leave instead of cuddling with him and playing house some more like she usually did. Maybe it had been the lunch that threw her off; maybe she just wasn't in the mood to play that character today, the tender one. She felt off her game. It had been easier to provoke him into roughness, which was a familiar buffer, something she could get off on. But today, she just didn't want him pawing over her afterward, smiling at her. She wanted to be alone in her hotel room. *Oh God*, Ola thought, *I'm hanging out too much with Souraya, she's rubbing off on me.* She washed her face and got out of the shower, drying herself off quickly so she could hunt through the walk-in closet for a change of clothes and head back out. Maybe she'd tell him she wasn't feeling well. Maybe she'd just sneak out and he would wake up annoyed that she wasn't there and fuck her this roughly again that night . . . that would be nice. His buttons were so easy sometimes, stretching into almost puppet strings.

Ola smiled at her reflection, stretching her lips wider and wider until they became a caricature, like when he'd hooked his fingers into the corners of her mouth as he thrust into it. She turned it into a snarl, a grimace, then exhaled and reached for the moisturizer that was always on the bathroom counter. Everything in that house was always left the way it was from whenever she'd last been there, like a customized hotel. It was one of the reasons she liked the pastor; he understood and supported her need for regular comfort. She was dabbing little dots of moisturizer on her face when her phone started vibrating. Ola looked down and saw it was Souraya calling. She frowned; it was unlike Sou to call when she knew Ola was with a client. She accepted the call and whispered into the phone, "Hold on one second, let me get my earbuds."

Leaving the phone in the bathroom, she quickly stepped into the bedroom and grabbed her earbuds from the bedside table. Daddy O was snoring gently in the bed, but still, Ola closed the bathroom door firmly behind her before slipping the buds into her ears. She adjusted them as they beeped awake and stepped away from the door, sitting on the toilet.

"What's up, Sou? Is everything okay?"

"Babes, sorry to call you while you're at work, but I have a strange favor to ask."

Ola listened with growing incredulity as her friend spoke; even more so when Souraya passed the phone to her lunch companion and he continued explaining what they needed. When they were done, she was silent for a minute. "Are you people serious?" she finally said. "Why the fuck should I get involved in all of this?"

"Ola, come on. The girl was a teenager." Souraya's voice lowered, as if she'd turned aside. "You remember how it was for us. Is trying to protect her something someone should go and die for?"

Ola flinched. She hated it when Souraya tried to flatten their lives into one thing. She had no idea what Ola had gone through; it wasn't the same. They'd had this conversation before. "Really, Sou?"

A pause on the other end. "I'm sorry. I didn't mean it like that. I just meant the girl's doing what she has to do to survive. We were like her once—who ever bothered to try and protect us?"

"First of all, fuck you." Ola was still angry.

"I said sorry, na."

"Second of all, that guy was an idiot to get involved, I don't care how old she was. It's common sense to mind your own fucking business."

"I'm not saying he wasn't an idiot. We're just saying maybe he shouldn't die because of it."

Ola rolled her eyes. "People die for less all the time, Sou."

Her friend sighed. "I know."

"You shouldn't be getting involved either."

An exhale. "Trust me, I know."

Ola rubbed her forehead, feeling a headache creep in already. "Wait, am I on speakerphone?"

"No, of course not."

"Okay. Are you doing this because of him? You don't know him. You don't owe him anything."

A pause. "I know, Ola. We can talk about that one later. Just tell me if you're going to help."

Ola groaned. "You don't know Daddy O, Souraya. It's not that easy."

"But you do. You know him better than most people. Just try, Ola."

Fuck. She shouldn't have brought Souraya with her. The girl couldn't handle New Lagos; she was already trying to save people. Her and her useless soft heart. "Okay, fine. But I can't promise anything."

"Thank you! I really—"

"I have to go." Ola cut off the call and fought the urge to throw the phone across the bathroom.

What a bloody mess.

She took a deep breath and went back into the bedroom, climbing up next to Daddy O's body. Kneeling back on her heels, she looked down at him and thought about when she'd been a teenager too, when she'd first met men like him. The things they had done. The things they had done to her. There was a time when she'd been angry about it, but then she'd become rich instead and the anger had set into something cold and untouched. She had made it, made it out, made her life into what she wanted it to look like. Being able to do that, *that* was power. That was freedom. Justice wasn't something she looked for or believed in, and how useful would it be anyway? People didn't understand that. They wanted revenge; they wanted people to be held accountable in a world where that just didn't happen. It was like expecting a rotten tree to bear edible fruit. It was never going to give you that.

It could give you other things, though, if you knew how to work the rot, if you weren't afraid to touch it or use it. The rot could give you power. Souraya only played with the edges of that world nowadays, she didn't enter it anymore the way Ola did, she didn't remember that the thing she was asking for was ridiculous.

Ola stared at Daddy O and shrugged to herself. She'd told Souraya she would help, and she would the way that she could. The way that was real, not the way Souraya thought was possible. At least the boy would be alive at the end of it. She reached down and cupped the pastor's balls in her hand, rolling them gently around as she drew him into her mouth and started to apply suction. When he started to moan as he woke up, she pulled him deeper and used her other hand to stroke him as he began to get hard.

Daddy O opened his eyes and looked down at her, her back arched and ass in the air as she worked on him. "Ah, you this girl. You neva tire?"

Ola pulled her mouth off and smiled at him. "I was thinking about that small boy you told me about in the car. I think I have a better idea of how you can deal with him." She put her lips to his ear and whispered, her voice secret and suggestive as her hand kept stroking him. She felt his erection turn to burning iron as he listened to her. "What do you think?" she asked. He turned his head to stare at her as if he was just seeing her for the first time. They looked at each other for a moment, then the pastor grabbed her and flipped her on her back, rising over her like a wave. Ola shrieked and giggled, then cried out with pleasure as he drove into her.

"I always knew you were wicked," he gasped. "I had no idea you were *that* wicked."

"Always happy to surprise you, Daddy," she replied between pants. He laughed and bent his head to bite her nipple. Ola smiled to herself and reached a hand up to brace herself against the headboard. She was going to have to charge him later for going raw, but it didn't seem like he'd care. She closed her eyes and wrapped her legs around him. At least she'd done Souraya the favor she'd asked for. By the end of everything, the boy might still be alive.

nine

Souraya danced in her hotel room to an Asake song as she put things into her purse—a tube of lipstick, a compact, a condom. It was just lunch, but you never knew, especially with Ahmed. The thought of being close to him again made her pulse stutter.

She opened a small vial of perfume, a gift from a client in Cairo, and dabbed it on her wrists, behind her ears, in the hollow of her throat. It smelled strange and decadent, bitter and full, something that pulled people in even as they tried to decide if they liked it. She'd worn it one night in SA, just the scent and nothing else. She wondered if Ahmed would remember. Souraya looked at her thigh harness lying on the bed, the delicate leather straps sprawled against the cover.

Maybe she didn't need to wear it. It was only Ahmed, after all.

"Don't be stupid," she muttered to herself. "You know what it's like here. You have to be ready." She put her foot up on the bed and rucked her dress up, buckling the sheath against her upper thigh, the slim knife cold on the soft flesh of her inner thigh. It was better to be safe, to assume the worst. Her phone buzzed and Souraya snatched it up.

It was him. I'm downstairs.

She dismissed the notification, surprised at how nervous she was. It had been what—a few years since Joburg? Surely that was enough time to stop being haunted. Worse things had happened to her when she was young enough for them to be an atrocity—these recent memories didn't even compare. They should've been neatly processed and tucked away in their appropriate files, but instead of smelling the fragrance she'd just put on her skin, Souraya's lungs were filled with a cologne that couldn't possibly exist, not in this hotel room. It had existed in that other one, yes, that horrible one in Joburg, but it shouldn't be *here*. Damp hands grabbed at her thighs and she choked back a scream, pinching the skin of her wrist to bring herself back.

"Stop it," she hissed. "You're free. You're free."

She said it over and over, until it felt like her tongue swelled with the words. How would Ahmed look at her when he saw her? With the same stunned desire he'd had when they first met at the braai? Or would his eyes hold more complication, like by the time they'd fled from Joburg? Souraya could still remember his face at the airport, the cloaked pity that had knifed her in her gut. She'd made him promise to never reach out to her again, just so she never had to see him look at her that way, like she was a beautiful thing irretrievably broken.

If she came downstairs and saw pity on his face again, would she be able to stand it? But she had reached out and he had reached back. Her past was waiting downstairs for her even as nightmares nipped around her thighs.

Souraya turned off her music and grabbed her hotel key, slipping it into her purse as she closed the door behind her. In the mirrored lift, she reviewed her reflection, adjusting the cuffs of her dress. Thin gold bands wrapped around her upper arms, glinting under the sheer sleeves of the dress. She slid on a pair of large sunglasses as the lift reached the lobby, the last piece of her shield clicking into place. Souraya stepped out and walked into the hotel foyer, looking around for Ahmed. For a moment, she felt lost and scared, like a child in a crowd in the city she'd all but sworn never to return to, with its heat licking at her skin. Strange men turned at her entrance and slid their eyes over her, uncouth and hungry. If it wasn't Ahmed she was waiting for, Souraya wouldn't have cared, but she felt vulnerable because it *was* him. As always, he lured out a softness in her that Souraya usually kept closer to her chest.

Souraya adjusted her glasses, kept her spine straight and looked around the lobby, reminding herself of who she was. Men destroyed their families for a chance to touch her skin. Women wanted her and wanted to be her. She hadn't been a trembling little girl in years.

Her shoes clicked on the polished floors as she strode forward. When she saw Ahmed leaning next to a large palm with his skin still as dark as a secret, looking down at his phone, her heart jumped a little. He glanced up as if he could feel her gaze, and their eyes locked. Souraya gave him a small smile and watched his almond eyes crinkle with pleasure as his mouth split into a wide grin. He was wearing a white tunic buttoned to the throat, dark mustard trousers, and white sneakers. A silver bangle rattled against his left wrist, and sunlight reflected off the signet ring on his right hand as he pocketed his phone and stalked toward her, his movements sleek and feline. There was no pity anywhere in his face.

He stopped directly in front of her. "Hey."

His voice was exactly as gentle as she remembered it. Souraya stared up at him. Had she forgotten he was this tall, this attractive? Years ago, she had tasted his sweat on his throat as he gasped into her.

"Hey," she said back.

Ahmed touched her elbow and leaned in, softly kissing her on one cheek then the other. Souraya let him, glad that he wasn't wrapping her in his arms, that he was being cautious. One of them had to be. If she turned her head, would he taste the same?

"Should we go?" he asked, his hand still warm against her elbow.

She nodded, fighting the urge to sway toward him. As they walked out, Souraya took a few deep breaths, grateful that the hallucination of cologne from the hotel room had faded. Instead, Ahmed was wafting something cool and sharply fresh; a clean cut through the air. He smelled different than he had before, slightly more edged.

The sun spilled over them as they walked to where his car was idling by the curb of the hotel's entrance. He tipped the uniformed man standing by the car and opened the passenger door for Souraya. She climbed in, the blue silk of her dress riding up her thighs and watched through the filter of her sunglasses as Ahmed's eyes followed the hem dragging up her skin. When he got behind the wheel and reversed out of the parking spot, he stretched one arm behind her headrest and twisted his body to look out of the back windshield, ignoring the rearview mirror. Souraya traced the length of his long arm, the sliding bones underneath the lean muscle. The car merged into the traffic outside the hotel and Ahmed turned to look at her. She immediately glanced down, her eyes hidden by her sunglasses.

"It feels like it's been forever," he said.

There was a short and slightly awkward pause.

"I know," she finally said, taking off her sunglasses and folding them into her purse. "I don't want to talk about Joburg, Ahmed."

"Of course," he replied quickly. "We're here now. *You're* here. Never thought I'd see the day." He threw her a wink and Souraya's mouth tugged into an involuntary smile.

"How have you been?" she asked.

"Happy to see you."

She cut a look at him. "Do better than the easy answer, Ahmed."

His laugh was rough, snagging at the edges. "Darling, let's leave it at the easy answer."

Souraya frowned. There was a shadow around him, loud enough to be perceptible, and a tightness in the corner of his eyes that spoke of worry. She'd seen it before, and it made her want to cup his jaw in her palm until he exhaled.

"I'm asking," she pointed out.

Ahmed switched lanes and a muscle in his jaw jumped. When he glanced back at her, both hesitation and hunger showed in his face.

"Today is not great." His voice was too controlled.

"Do you want to talk about it?"

He shook his head almost immediately. "I just want to forget for a little bit. Tell me something, anything."

It should have been fine. It was a normal thing to say, and maybe someone else would've indulged his request, given him the empty chatter he wanted, but Souraya felt herself bristle at his words. She bit her cheek and looked out the window, trying to calm the jump of anger in her chest. When she stayed silent, Ahmed craned his neck, trying to see her expression.

"Sou? You all right?"

"Don't call me that." It came out sharp and Souraya dug her nails into her palm. It did nothing for her anger. "Not if you're going to do this evasive bullshit."

"What bullshit?"

She rolled her eyes. "I'm not an escape, Ahmed. You'd have to pay me for that."

He winced. "Shit. Sorry."

Souraya nodded in acceptance and they drove in silence for a while.

"You just got in," Ahmed finally said while making a left turn. "I didn't want to off-load this shit on you when I haven't seen you in years."

"Do you think the years matter?" Souraya countered. "Or that I ask questions I don't want real answers to?"

"I know. I'm sorry."

Souraya was still irritated, still painfully attracted to him, and that annoyed her even more. "Whatever, Ahmed. Keep your fucking secrets."

Why did it *hurt*? Because he'd seen her at her lowest and she wanted a chance to see him vulnerable for once? It was exhausting feeling this raw, running away from the memories.

"Souraya." His tone was coaxing, but she refused to look at him.

The car swerved slightly as he pulled over. Souraya heard the click of his seat belt as he unbuckled it and then his hand slid behind her neck as he leaned toward her.

"Darling, look at me."

The anger jumped again, and she lashed a hand out at him. "Don't *call* me that!"

Ahmed caught her hand in his and Souraya gasped as she felt the warm heat of his mouth press to her palm. Her head whipped around to stare at him in shock and Ahmed looked back at her with inky eyes.

"I'm sorry, Sou." He folded her hand to his chest and pulled her closer, burying his face in her neck. Souraya's skin trembled as he inhaled harshly, his breath stroking her skin. "Fuck, this might sound crazy, but I *missed* you. Been needing to hold you since you stepped out of that damn elevator."

"Ahmed." Her voice was unstable even as she sank her fingers into his hair. He couldn't have missed her. Never mind if she sat out on her balcony at home sometimes and fought the urge to find him again, wondered what they could be like if they hadn't crashed together the way they had, wondered what could have been in another time line.

He leaned his forehead against her cheek. "Should I let you go?"

Souraya slid an arm around him. "No," she whispered. "Don't let go." Her heart felt like it was swelling behind her ribs. She could never tell Ola this, how this man was both a stranger and an old friend. "You didn't really miss me. We don't know each other, not really."

"Fuck off." Ahmed nuzzled against her skin. "I know you shut me away too. Like this thing between us would go away if we tried to forget it. Soon as I saw you, it hit me right in the fucking chest." He pulled back so he could look at her, their faces a breath away. "Where the hell have you *been*?"

Souraya gave a half-shrug. "I went home."

"Why did you come here? You told me you'd never come back here."

Souraya tilted her head in thought. Had there been a moment when a reason had solidified in her mind? Not when she'd said yes to Ola, not even on the plane over when she'd looked out at the lights of New Lagos as they pulled closer. It had all been an odd blankness, an acceptance of her decision without prying into what had swayed it in the first place.

"I don't know why I came," she admitted. The sun slanted a ray through her window and angled heat across her thigh. "My friend has a client here, but I think maybe I just wanted to look at the city one last time and show it that I wasn't afraid anymore."

"So, like a goodbye."

"Maybe."

A hawker carrying a tray of groundnuts walked across the road in front of them, and Souraya watched her walk to a bus window and lift the tray down from her head, talking to a customer whose arm dangled out. "I missed it too," she admitted. "I never wanted to miss this place."

"Did you miss me?" Ahmed had a small smile as he asked it, like it was a joke, but his eyes were searching hers.

"You were right," she replied. "I shut you away. I almost forgot you were based here."

He pulled back into his seat but kept hold of her hand. "I'm glad you remembered."

As he turned the car back into the flow of traffic with his free hand, Souraya looked down at his fingers lacing through hers. This man had worried her when they first met in Joburg—enough that she'd accepted a dinner date with him just to face down the fear. Their chemistry had been scorching, and she'd been horrified to discover that she wanted him for himself, not as a client. It was a dangerous thing to want, but Ahmed Soyoye was a dangerous man. He had leaned across the table at their date and looked deep into her eyes, power threatening to burst out from under his skin.

"If you ever need *anything*," he'd said, "let me know immediately."

At that point in her life, Souraya had met enough dangerous men to know when they would spill real blood for her, and Ahmed looked like he couldn't wait to get his hands wet.

The next time she'd seen him was a week after their date. Souraya had been lying on the floor of a penthouse suite in Joburg. Ahmed had been kneeling beside her, cupping her face in his hands and speaking to her in soft, soothing tones, his words blurred. Behind him, the white man who'd intruded on her nightmares since then, the man who'd locked her in the penthouse suite for five days before she'd managed to sneak a message to Ahmed, that man stood behind Ahmed, crying with anger.

"So, I'm the bad guy," he said, in between sobs. "I try to help the girl, give her a better life, and I'm the wicked one. She's a fucking slut, a whore! I can take her out of this gutter; I was trying to get her out, and now you come here and act as if I'm some monster, as if I kidnapped her. I just wanted to show her something better!"

Ahmed had ignored the man, slipping one arm under Souraya's neck and the other under her knees. "Put your arms around my neck, darling," he whispered.

Half her face had been swollen and bruised, an insistent ringing circling through her ears. The man had seen her put down the phone as he came out from the bathroom, but he hadn't been able to figure out what she'd done on it. He'd been furious at his own carelessness, and had taken great pains to communicate that anger against her flesh, then had left her on the floor afterward and watched a cricket match on TV until Ahmed had knocked on the door. Souraya never knew what Ahmed had said, only heard snippets of the low leashed rage in his voice as he spoke to the man, the man's voice spiking to a high pitch in response, angling into a whine until he started crying. She hadn't opened her eyes until she felt the warmth of Ahmed's hands against her face.

"Look at me, darling," he'd said. "We're leaving now."

She'd managed to drape her arms around his neck as he lifted her up, her bare legs dangling over his forearm, the chiffon robe she was wearing falling slightly open and trailing its belt like a ghost down Ahmed's body as he stood and walked out of the suite. The man shouted after them, but Ahmed had kept talking to Souraya, his voice a steady and sure thrum that wiped out anything else.

"It's okay; I've got you. You're safe. We're leaving right now."

Souraya had slipped into darkness then, tears falling into her ears. When she woke up, she was in a different hotel, a suite where Ahmed had been staying, and he was asleep in a chair next to her bed. It took a long time before she was healed enough to walk or move around, and Ahmed never left her side. Not through the nightmares, the times when she would sit in the shower and scream under the raining steam, or when she threw glasses across the room to watch them shatter against the wall because the rage was boiling too high in her chest. Ahmed wrapped her in towels, held her as she shook with fury, and slept next to her instead of in his room when she requested his company.

One night, Souraya turned to him, her hands folded under her cheek, and asked him what had happened to the man who had taken her. Ahmed's eyes had gone flat and cold, but he had met her gaze steadily and slid his hand behind her neck.

"I killed him for you," he said, and Souraya's heart had pounded wildly.

"Yourself?" she asked.

Ahmed had smiled at the worry in her voice, and he touched his

forehead to hers, his eyes coming alive again. "Don't worry, darling. It was just an accident."

She had wriggled into his arms and wrapped herself around him.
"No one's ever hurt the people who hurt me," she'd whispered, feeling horribly young. Ahmed had held her tightly.

"Give me their names," he'd said. She'd burst into tears then and
he murmured sounds until she cried herself to sleep. Souraya never
gave him the names.

They had slipped into a strange and intimate friendship, yet
Ahmed never made a move on her. He'd washed her body when
she was injured and he slept next to her some nights, but always
with clothes over his skin and he never so much as kissed her cheek
or forehead. One evening, Souraya made a decision. She walked
out of the bathroom after a shower, her towel already hung neatly
on a hook, her skin bare to the air of their suite. Ahmed had looked
up from the couch and gone as still as ice.

"What are you doing?" he'd asked.

Souraya had been nervous, but she knew she needed to be touched
and that it needed to be someone safe, someone whose hands she
could trust. Ahmed was keeping his eyes firmly fixed on her face,
as if she hadn't oiled every inch of her skin, as if it didn't gleam and
call out to him. Souraya had slid into his lap, and he had made a
twisted sound deep in his throat.

"Darling, please." He sounded like he was begging, and his hands
were pressed against the leather of the couch. "I just want you to be
okay."

She'd laughed. "You think I won't be if you touch me?"

Ahmed had looked at her then, allowed her to see the corralled
wildness in his eyes. "I mark the things I touch," he'd said.

"Good thing I'm not a thing." Souraya had kissed his cheek, slipping her arms around his neck. "Good thing I'm your friend."

He'd hitched out a breath. "If I start touching you, darling, I'm afraid I won't stop."

"That's okay," she'd replied, unconcerned. "I need my flesh back, Ahmed. Do you understand? It's mine, not a dead man's."

"I get it." He let one hand slide up her leg and electricity sizzled along her skin. Souraya bit back a whimper and cupped his jaw in her hand.

"You've done so much for me already," she whispered, her voice sultry. "But I need you to do more. Can you do more for me, Ahmed?"

She saw the moment his restraint broke, like power snapping darkly in his eyes. He'd lifted Souraya in his arms with a growl, then carried her to his bedroom, slamming her on the mattress. Pure clean relief had washed through her then. He already knew not to be too gentle, and as that night passed, Ahmed showed her many of the other things he knew. Worship, for one. In the days that followed, Souraya had been happy.

But their suite was a transient world and as the time slid by, Souraya could feel their clock begin to run out. Maybe Ahmed would have kept being who he had been, but she had lived too many lives and she didn't want to see the real-world version of Ahmed seep into this one and inevitably disappoint her. She no longer knew who she was if she wasn't the broken girl he had rescued—there hadn't been enough time for him to see who she had been before, and she couldn't keep using him to cobble her pieces back together. She needed to go home.

So Souraya had left and made him promise not to contact her. Ahmed had inhaled a sharp shattered breath when she told him, but he'd given her his promise anyway. When he took her to the airport, he'd laced his fingers in hers just like he was doing now. Souraya scraped a nail lightly across his skin.

"I'm sorry I made you make that promise," she said.

Ahmed turned the car into a quiet street and pulled into a compound overgrown with bougainvillea. He parked the car and turned off the ignition, then lifted her hand to his mouth and kissed it.

"You did what you needed to do." His eyes crinkled with amusement. "And I don't think you're really sorry, are you?"

"No, I mean it." Souraya smiled at him, but it felt a little sad on her face. "Maybe you would've come to find me otherwise."

Ahmed's face went serious. "Darling, I would have hunted you down."

She blushed and tried to change the subject. "We're at the restaurant, no? Tell me what's going on with you over lunch."

He frowned, glancing around the parking lot. "It might be better to tell you in here."

Souraya shrugged. She liked sitting in the car with him. They'd done that a few times in Joburg, parked somewhere with Nando's takeout and just sat and talked for hours while the bruises on her face healed. "So just turn up the AC and we can talk about it here."

Ahmed smiled at her and she knew he'd entered the same memories. The engine purred back to life and cool air threw itself out of the vents, hitting Souraya's skin in welcome gusts. She unbuckled her seat belt and curled up a little on her side as Ahmed told her about his party, about the pastor and the girl, and Kalu. When he was done, she gave a low whistle.

"Oh, your friend is *fucked*."

He gave her a look. "Thanks, love. I'd figured that part out on my own."

Souraya stroked a hand over his arm. "What are you going to do?"

"I can't pay him off—he doesn't care about the money."

"Yeah. I know the type."

Ahmed wiped a hand over his face. The sun angled through the tall bougainvillea and streaked through the windshield, bathing both of them in heat. "I got a text from Thursday earlier confirming that the hit is real. I don't know how to stop this."

"This pastor has more power than you."

Souraya didn't realize she'd said the words out loud until she heard them and saw the answering grimace on Ahmed's face.

"I hate hearing it that way, but you're not wrong." His jaw clenched. *"Fuck."*

Her heart wrenched a little. Ahmed looked a little lost and it was so different from the version of him she knew, the one who had all the answers.

"Everyone wants something," she said. "We just have to figure out what else he wants."

Ahmed laughed sourly and tried to pull his hand away from hers. "Please. You don't have to enter this with me."

Souraya held fast. "Shut up. What's this pastor's name?"

"Okinosho. Thomas Okinosho."

Her eyes widened. "Wait, as in Daddy O?"

Ahmed raised a surprised eyebrow. "How do you know him?"

"Who *doesn't* know him?" Souraya tapped her finger against his knuckles. "He's my friend's client, the one who flew us in. Ola didn't even tell me his name at the start."

Ahmed's eyes sharpened. "Ola Roberts?"

Alarm rang through Souraya's skin. "How do you know her name?"

It wasn't Ola's birth name, of course; it wasn't even the name on her passports or deeds, but it was the one she used as a loose mask and there was still no reason why Ahmed should know it.

Souraya pulled her hand out of his. "How do you know her?"

"I don't." Ahmed's voice was careful. "I know a few things about Okinosho. That he has a favorite girl. That she's trans and Nigerian."

She stared at him, but his gaze was open and clear.

"They say no matter where in the world she is, he sends his private jet for her. That he's given her houses from here to London." A corner of his mouth tugged upward. "There aren't *that* many famous Naija escorts with a reputation like that, and Ola Roberts is the only trans one I know."

Souraya tried to force her hackles down, unclenching her hands and fanning out her fingers. "What, you have an international directory of sex workers?"

Ahmed laughed. "It *is* my job, you know."

She smiled despite herself, because he was right. He had blood on his hands and his finger on the darkest pulses on the continent.

"Maybe Ola can help," she found herself saying. "I could ask her."

Ahmed raised an eyebrow. "Now why would she want to get involved?"

Souraya shrugged. "Because we were all girls in New Lagos once? Because I asked?"

He didn't respond, his gaze drifting sideways into nothing. It was easy to read the calculations on his face—if asking a favor from Ola would put him at any disadvantage, running the risk permutations. Souraya didn't get the hesitation. If Ola was in danger, she would have leapt at any offer for help.

"Who is Kalu to you?" she asked.

Ahmed drew back slightly, just a fraction. Souraya waited. He'd spoken of Kalu during their time in Joburg, always with a fondness that had something edged folded underneath. She'd wondered if they'd been lovers, but somehow, she thought Ahmed would have cared less if that had been the case. Still, it was obvious that there was an old and deep bond there.

"He's my best friend," Ahmed replied, but his voice was knotted as he said it.

"You want to protect him," she offered, and Ahmed nodded.

That was fair enough. Privately, Souraya thought Kalu sounded like a rich and careless man who probably didn't deserve the help. New Lagos had so many girls who needed it more, who probably needed help precisely *because* of men like him.

Still. Ahmed wanted to protect him and Souraya remembered what the city was like, why she'd left, how easy it was to wipe a hand and take a life with it. Especially with men like Okinosho.

"I'll ask Ola," she said. "But I do think your friend is a bloody fool, just so we're clear."

Ahmed gave a flat smile. "True. I just don't think he should die for it."

Souraya started dialing, pretending she couldn't feel the heat of Ahmed's gaze on the side of her face.

Saturday, 2:53 PM

After Ola hung up on them, Ahmed took Souraya's hands in his and kissed her knuckles.

"Thank you," he said solemnly. "I owe you and Ola a debt."

Souraya smiled sadly. "I'm sure she'll collect."

He kept her hands in his and she let herself linger in the warmth from his skin. Back then, she hadn't been able to tell if the feelings she'd had for him were real or engineered, and she knew even now that she had made the right decision in leaving. Removing Ahmed had been necessary so she could build a world where she was the one who could make herself okay. But now, those feelings were still there, simmering low and insistent. Souraya wasn't sure what to do with them.

The corner of Ahmed's mouth twisted up. "I owe *you* a debt," he clarified.

"Let's call it even for Joburg."

He flinched—he actually *flinched* when she said that. Souraya stared at him, fascinated. Did he not know she was in his debt from back then?

"You owe me nothing," he replied, his voice raspy. "Do you hear? *Nothing.*"

She didn't believe him. The debt was something she'd carried in her bones ever since he'd lifted her off that floor and out of hell.

"You killed a man for me," she reminded him softly. "There is nothing you can say to undo or erase that, Ahmed."

A low snarl. "He deserved to die."

"But would you have killed him if he'd done it to someone else? Some girl off the street?" She watched Ahmed closely as the question sank into his skin, and she saw the shame rise up in response. "Of course you wouldn't, Ahmed. Men like that are your clients. It happens all the time."

"Souraya." His face was twisted and she stroked his cheek.

"I'm not judging you. Men like that have been my clients too. I'm just saying, you did it for *me*. Not because it was the right thing to do."

Ahmed blew out a long stream of air. "So much for trying to sound noble," he joked, but his eyes were disturbed. Maybe he hadn't expected her to hold up such an accurate mirror to his face. She didn't regret it—he needed to know that she saw who he was, not who he pretended to be.

"Maybe we should actually enter the restaurant and get lunch," he was saying.

Souraya laughed and glanced through of the window into the heat shimmering outside. The restaurant's security guards were lounging on plastic chairs under a bower of flowers, their boots pushed into the sand, their eyes watching the car with an easy curiosity.

"I like being in small worlds with you," she said, her voice thoughtful.

Ahmed's eyes softened, and he started to lean in, perhaps to kiss her. Souraya held her breath, her eyes on his, but then his phone buzzed. Ahmed pulled back, apologetic, and took it out of his pocket, swiping the screen open. Souraya watched as blood left his face and all the light drained from his eyes, leaving them as flat as a snake's. He kept holding the phone even as the screen faded to black. Incoherent chatter from the security guards trickled across the yard and through the glass of the window, over the air-conditioning. Ahmed looked like he'd forgotten how to breathe, like the air around him was about to shatter.

Souraya reached out and touched his shoulder. "Is everything okay?" she asked.

He turned his head toward her, his face blank. "I have to go," he said.

"*What?*"

"I have to go." He looked down on his phone before shoving it into his pocket. "I can't tell you what happened, but it's an emergency. I'm so sorry, Souraya. Can I drop you back at your hotel?"

Disappointment coursed sharply through her. "Whatever you need to do."

She turned and buckled her seat belt again, not caring if the insincerity of her words was fucking obvious. This was exactly why she'd left him behind in Joburg. It was easy to be open in their small worlds, but the minute something real intruded, he had shut down and shut her out.

Ahmed slid his hand over hers as her seat belt clicked into place. "I mean it. I'm so sorry. I just have to go take care of this, but I'll call you immediately after it's handled, okay?" His hand was still warm and gentle but his eyes didn't match his words. His pupils were freezing, arctic and distant.

She tried one last time. "Are you sure you don't want to tell me?"

Ahmed stroked her cheek with a knuckle. "Some things I really do have to keep to myself," he said apologetically. "Trust me, darling, it's better this way."

He leaned in and kissed her cheek before buckling his seat belt and pulling out of the compound. Souraya fought the urge to wipe his kiss off her skin, to slap him for thinking his charm would make the apology stick. Suddenly, she was thoroughly sick of the city and the way it always let her down. She couldn't wait for her hotel room.

Ahmed was silent as they pulled out into the road, and the bougainvillea retreated behind them like a thousand small and colorful fires.

ten

Ahmed had tried to kiss Souraya while he was dropping her off at her hotel, but she'd ducked away from him, her eyes cool and unreadable.

"Focus on your friend," she'd said, right before closing the car door with a damning click.

Shame had heated up under Ahmed's skin. Ever since the text message from Seun had interrupted them, Ahmed had felt insane, like incompatible worlds were happening around him at the same time again. In one of them, he was on a halfway date with Souraya, a beautiful ghost sitting in his passenger seat, saying ghost things, and telling ghost stories except for when she spoke to Ola and stitched hope into his chest. Kalu filled the second world, his tears and his rage and the threat on his life that felt too surreal to process. In the last world, there was the blue of Ruqaiyyah's party and Seun's body, then the text message Ahmed had received from him, a screenshot of a video of the two of them fucking at that party,

Seun's face out of frame, the play button an incriminating triangle stuck in the middle.

If you don't want to see this all over the internet, better send me your address now now, let's discuss.

It had taken every fragment of self-control that Ahmed could summon to not lose his temper immediately after he'd read that. He'd suddenly understood why Okinosho wanted to remove Kalu, eliminate him for having the audacity, the insolence, to overstep the lines that marked his place. In the grainy image, his hips were slotted neatly against Seun's, his torso gleaming in the blue light, his face contorted into a snarl. There had been no fear in Ahmed when he saw the screenshot. There had only been a cold and instant rage. Who did this small boy think he was? Because Ahmed had allowed him to suck his dick, this boy thought he could come and play with fire?

Ahmed had pushed the rage aside, locking it into a neat compartment while he dropped off Souraya. It was only when he pulled out of the hotel compound that he allowed the rage to return; it curled through his veins with a heady heat, singing up his nerves and humming in the back of his skull. He texted Seun his address and nothing else—he knew he couldn't feign the fear Seun was hoping for, the fear the actor wanted to harvest, reap it into some blackmail profit. The boy was moving too predictably. He probably thought Ahmed kept a stash of money at home, that he could get a pile of quick cash or something. Or maybe he just didn't want to show the video in a public place, and he was going to ask for an account transfer. Perhaps a monthly transfer. Ahmed's temper enjoyed going through all the possible scenarios Seun might attempt. Each of them felt like a fresh insult, even just their possibility, reasons to stoke the anger Ahmed was barely keeping a lid on.

Some of it was directed at himself. It had been so many years of ignoring those wants, of diverting them into other places—a roughness with women, for example, but only those who liked it. Sometimes he'd imagined that these women were someone else, that the cheek under his palm was textured with stubble, that he could reach around their hip and wrap his hand around a penis like he had that night when Kalu had panted next to him with such inviting desperation. How foolish was it, to have a desire from so long ago follow you in a haunting?

Ahmed wiped a hand over his face, dispelling the shame that threatened to enter. No, those wants hadn't been that loud, that articulated. They had been fleeting—quick images that scattered into fog almost as soon as they formed. It was Kalu who had condensed them into something that wouldn't leave Ahmed alone, something that had started in the office when they were touching. Desire had shown up and wriggled its way under Ahmed's skin, an itch that he couldn't flay off with Timi, a hunger that had sighed in relief when he'd fucked Seun in the whispering veils—to have another man's body finally so close to his own, to be inside him, to hear him cry out. Ahmed had, inevitably, Kalu in his mind, pictured Kalu looking up at him with those I-just-want-to-please-you eyes, Kalu reaching back to hold on to his thighs, to pull him closer.

In short, it was Kalu's fault that after how many years of dismissing those insignificant flares of want, Ahmed had finally given in and fucked a man. And not just that, but done it in the city, at a party, with some narcissistic child who now thought that he could come and look for Ahmed's trouble. A muscle flexed in Ahmed's jaw as he merged into a roundabout. He was still driving slowly, in no rush to reach his house, taking his time. If that meant that Seun would have to wait, then fine. If he arrived before Seun, also fine.

No wahala. He didn't have a plan of how to handle the situation; he was waiting to hear what Seun had to say first.

Clear visuals of breaking his smug face entered Ahmed's mind. It would be so easy. The boy was a bloody idiot to want to come to Ahmed's house, but when an insect invites itself into the spider's web, who is going to argue with it? Certainly not the spider. Idly, Ahmed wondered how Seun's blood would look arcing against the white of his walls if he smashed the idiot's face with enough impact. It was like a film scene, thick red saliva spooling out in slow motion from Seun's mouth as his head spun to the side, Ahmed's fist continuing past his flesh with leftover momentum. It made Ahmed smile as he turned into his street.

Seun was outside his gate, leaning against a parked candy-red convertible with his arms folded. He was wearing ankara trousers and a linen singlet, his biceps gleaming—*he was the type who probably moisturized with baby oil*, Ahmed thought with a sneer. He ignored Seun as he opened his gate, driving past as if the boy was nothing (he was), parking his car inside the yard. Thursday wasn't around, which was just as well. Ahmed didn't have a plan, but none of this was something he wanted Thursday involved in. Just in case, he shot him a text.

Where are you?

The gate began to slide shut and Seun, realizing that he was about to get locked out, jumped up and hurried into the compound, his casual facade slipping. Ahmed's phone buzzed with Thursday's response.

In the lowland. Running an errand. Do you need anything?

Seun was standing awkwardly, unsure of whether to walk to Ahmed's car or wait where he was. Ahmed smiled at his discomfort.

No, it's fine. Ping me after. He slid his phone into his pocket and stepped out of the car.

Seun rearranged his body, dragging on some confidence and an irritating smirk. "Did you miss me, baby?" he said, grinning at Ahmed.

Ahmed glanced at him, then let his eyes drift off with indifference. He said nothing as he walked to his front door, unlocking it and leaving it open, not bothering to look behind to see if Seun was following. After a pause, he heard him walk into the house and close the door behind him.

"You're being very rude," Seun complained. "I think you should start behaving better toward me. After all, we both know why we're here."

Ahmed walked into his parlor. The anger was motionless, white-hot in his chest. He could almost feel Seun's frustration and annoyance boiling in the air, but it was too easy to continue baiting him with silence. He tossed his keys on the table just as Seun grabbed his arm, pulling him around and shoving his phone in Ahmed's face. It took a moment for Ahmed's senses to catch up, for the grainy moving image on the screen to make sense, for the sounds he and Seun were making in the video to filter into his ears, grunts and flesh slapping eagerly against flesh.

"Are you paying attention now?" Seun asked, his voice slippery and triumphant. "Or are you going to continue pretending as if I'm not here?"

Ahmed stared at the video. It was strange, fascinating even, to see himself like this. He wondered where Seun had hidden the camera in that room. It had to be something he did often; no wonder he'd picked that room specifically. Ahmed watched himself pull out from Seun, watched him spin around and wrap his lips around Ahmed.

Seun leaned over to look at the screen as well. "Oh, don't worry, I'll edit out that part before I put it online, of course." He smiled at Ahmed. "We can't have my face out there with this; it would ruin my brand."

Ahmed looked at Seun and wondered how this game had worked out in the past. It was amazing that no one had made him disappear yet over nonsense like this.

"What do you want?" he asked, and Seun's face lit up.

"Oho, now you know how to talk! I was wondering." He took the phone away and put it in his pocket. "Let's sit down and discuss our options."

Ahmed took a step forward, deliberately invading Seun's space. He stood a few inches taller than him and when Ahmed bent his head, his words fell into Seun's face. "I don't feel like sitting down," he said, his voice slick. "What. Do. You. Want."

Seun's pupils dilated, a buried fear flickering up for a moment. Combined with the rage inside him, seeing that flicker started to make Ahmed hard—it was too perfect, the urge he had to punish this small boy, the way Seun was forming as if he was strong, as if he didn't want to be broken into whimpering grateful pieces. Ahmed slid his hand up Seun's chest, wrapping his fingers lightly around his throat, a frisson of delight coating his anger as he felt Seun swallow nervously, his gullet rippling. "Or is this why you wanted to come to my house? You wanted to look for my trouble, ehn?"

Seun's eyes flitted from side to side. He looked confused, torn between whatever his original intention had been and this unexpected arousal.

"Is it that you wanted to make me angry?" Ahmed asked, tightening his grip by a fraction. "Because of how I left this morning? Did it hurt your feelings? Or you just wanted some more; I didn't give you enough before I left?" He watched Seun's lips part, as if by reflex, and lowered his voice so it thrummed in the tight air between them. "Is that why you came? To get some more?"

Seun reached up to grasp Ahmed's wrist, his eyes widening as they met Ahmed's. He didn't try to pull his hand off and they stood like that, locked at two points, staring. Ahmed could see Seun's bravado melting away, eroded by the force of Ahmed's aura pushing out into the air, everywhere. Nothing could stand before it. Seun made a last effort, one defiant glare, a curled lip.

Ahmed smiled like a shark and tilted his head as if he was thinking, then stroked a thumb against Seun's throat. He did it gently, with an easy tenderness, and it was too simple—the way Seun's eyelashes fluttered involuntarily, the goose bumps that skittered across his skin. Seun broke their gaze and looked away, his body slacking imperceptibly, his hand releasing Ahmed's wrist and falling instead on his chest, his fingertips grazing the cotton of Ahmed's shirt. The surrender was a pleasure to watch. Ahmed growled approval deep in his throat and put his hand on Seun's head, pushing him down. Seun sunk to his knees easily, his hunger obvious now as he reached for Ahmed's zipper.

It was child's play to break weak men, small boys like these who didn't know what actual power was, who tried projections of it on for size but it never fit, as if they were drowning in their fathers' clothes.

Ahmed hit him across the face and Seun moaned, his eyes watering as he looked up at Ahmed. "See your face," Ahmed said, contempt curling out from under his lip. "This is where you belong, ba?" He hit him again on the other cheek. "Answer me!"

Seun moaned and nodded, his fingers digging desperately into Ahmed's thighs.

"Stand up."

Seun obeyed, wiping his mouth with the back of his hand.

Ahmed gestured to his sofa. "Arrange yourself"

Seun pulled off his trousers, his genitals swinging free. He made to lie on his stomach, but Ahmed grunted his disapproval and Seun looked back at him.

"Not like that. I want to see your face."

Seun was breathing fast, his movements quick, wanting to please. He took off his singlet and lay on his back, pulling his legs up and locking his elbows behind his knees. He looked up at Ahmed silently and Ahmed almost smiled—he never liked hearing them talk, it was nice that Seun remembered. He didn't bother taking off his clothes as they continued; he didn't want his skin against Seun's. When Seun tried to pull him in for a kiss, Ahmed slammed his head back into the sofa. All the rage he was feeling, at how Seun had dared to try him, interrupting his time with Souraya, all his frustration over the situation with Kalu and Okinosho, he channeled it into Seun's body, lubricated by saliva, and to his surprise, Seun not only took it but enjoyed it. He came while stroking himself frantically, then smiled up at Ahmed as Ahmed kept going.

"Don't think we don't still have business to discuss," he gasped, his body jerking under Ahmed's thrusts.

Ahmed frowned and put a hand over Seun's mouth. *Who told him he could talk?*

Seun kept smiling with his eyes as if he'd already won, as if none of this had anything to do with his inevitable victory.

"Shut up," Ahmed said, quietly at first. He moved both hands to Seun's throat and started choking him. "Shut up. Shut up. *Shut up*."

His grip had doubled, tripled in force, driving the smile right out of Seun's eyes, replacing it with alarm. Seun tried to talk but all that came out was a coughing grunt. He began to struggle, and Ahmed slipped out of him, pinning his lower body down with his legs, leaning heavier into his arms, putting his weight against Seun's throat.

"Shut up," he kept saying calmly, a chant, a mantra. Everyone talked too much, said too much, like Kalu, like Machi, saying things he wasn't in the mood to hear, not caring, just talking, talking, all the time talking. They didn't learn. They wouldn't just shut the fuck up and give him some peace, some fucking *quiet*. Ahmed leaned forward some more and looked up in concentration, trying to find a silent place in his head. Everyone was trying to box him into a corner, put him somewhere impossible. His client trying to kill his best friend. This idiot here scratching his arms after threatening to release the video. It was too much of a headache—imagine if the video made it to those gossip sites, those clickbait Instagram accounts. It would go unbelievably viral. The amount of damage control he would have to do. He didn't have time for that, not with this Okinosho shit happening, not with Souraya coming back into his life. There was so much going on.

He just needed some quiet so he could focus.

Saturday, 3:59 PM

The body had stopped moving.

Ahmed gradually loosened his hands from around its throat, sweat cooling on his forehead. A faint voice in his head noted how quickly you could go from being a person, a Seun, to a nothing, a body. He stood up from the sofa and tucked himself back into his trousers, zipping up. Seun—he had to force himself to return to that name; this was, had been, a person—was strewn over the sofa cushions, his eyes wide and glassed open, his mouth ajar. Ahmed looked down at his hands. The tremor had taken over completely; both hands were visibly trembling now. He tried to curl his fingers, control the shaking by forming fists, but it was useless; it did nothing. He glanced from his hands to Seun's discolored neck. How was it possible that they had been strong enough to do that? They were just hands, just palms and fingers and skin and bone. It wasn't possible.

Ahmed shuddered in disbelief and grabbed Seun's shoulders. "Wake up!" he ordered. "It's not funny."

When had any of this been a joke?

He didn't even remember deciding to do this. Seun's eyes had just been so loud, he'd wanted the laughter in them to go away, but now . . . now they were even louder. He shook Seun again, slapping his cheek lightly. The split insanity had returned. On one track, Seun had just passed out and would wake up soon. On the other, no one wants a dead person staring at them. It's unholy. His skin was still warm. Ahmed looked around, then ran to the kitchen and slammed open the refrigerator door, his shaking hands skimming the contents until he found a bottle of water. He ran back to the parlor, untwisting the cap as he stumbled against the sofa, dropping to his knees and pouring the water over Seun's face. "Oya, wake up now! It's enough."

You're going mad, a small voice in his head observed. *You've known he was dead from since.*

"Shut up!" Ahmed yelled into the lonesome air. How was he now the only person in the house? It didn't make sense. "Come on," he whispered. "Wake up; do it for me."

He sat back on his heels and pressed Seun's hand to his forehead. The skin was warm. It was warm. He had to be alive. Ahmed fumbled his fingers till they were pressing against the inside of Seun's wrist, angry with himself for not doing that sooner, not doing that first—looking for a pulse. His searching fingertips found nothing, so he pressed them to Seun's neck with an uncommon gentleness, and when that returned empty as well, Ahmed pressed his ear to Seun's naked chest, willing the heart to kick back in like a recalcitrant generator. He felt slow, like his thinking and reactions were warped into a delay. CPR? Chest compressions? He'd never been trained for any of that, only seen it on TV.

He layered his hands on top of each other and started pressing down on Seun's chest as hard as he could. "One, two, three," he counted aloud, then paused before starting again. He had no idea if the count was correct. Was it ridiculous to look it up? Kneeling at an angle to keep his weight on one hand, he kept pressing on Seun's chest with that arm while pulling his phone out and trying to type with the other hand.

Stop lying to yourself, the small voice said. *You haven't even tried to get help. All this is to make you feel like you tried to do something.*

His hand was trembling too much to hold the phone steady, let alone type. Ahmed let it tumble out of his fingers, the leather phone case bouncing off the carpet. Why was he pretending? He wasn't actually trying to bring Seun back. He already knew Seun was gone, had been gone in one of those terrible blurred moments he was deliberately not remembering, as if the act of pushing the memory away was going to overwrite it, perhaps with a grayness or a piercing white or just the nothingness of a blackout. He had kept strangling him after he was gone, why? To make sure? To be careful?

None of this was an accident. Blurring the moment of a decision didn't change the fact that he'd made one and that the consequence of this was lying on his sofa with one leg dragging on the floor and limp genitals. Ahmed crossed his arms, tucking his hands into his armpits to try and stop them from shaking. He began to rock back and forth, staring at Seun's face, at Seun's dead face. *What the fuck have I done? What am I going to do now?*

He pushed himself back against the coffee table and drew his knees into his chest, and Ahmed began to cry.

eleven

When Aima woke up, she was alone in Ijendu's room, only rumpled sheets marking where her friend had been sleeping next to her. Her head hurt and her eyes ached in their sockets. She rubbed them and rolled over, patting the nightstand clumsily as she looked for her phone. The bedsheets were tangled in her bare legs, the cloth smothering her skin. Aima kicked free and stretched her legs over the bed, sighing as the room's air-conditioning cooled her off. She tapped her phone's screen to check the time, and there was a text from Ijendu.

Hey sleeping beauty. I went to have lunch with Daddy O. See you when I get back.

Aima's immediate reaction was relief. She hadn't been sure how she was going to look at Ijendu after what they had done last night. It had been so hard to slide back into that same bed with her after she'd been crying in the bathroom, to position herself in such a way that none of her was touching any of Ijendu. She'd prayed quietly and desperately, curled up at the edge of the bed, until she fell asleep.

Lying there now, Aima stared up at the ceiling and wondered what to do next. How to move on, how to redeem herself. She'd hoped that the guilt would've gone away by the time she woke up, that she would've felt lighter, like God had forgiven her while she slept, but it was still there, a brooding weight on her chest. Aima looked down and realized she was still wearing Dike's T-shirt. Revulsion crawled over her skin as she remembered how he'd fed himself last night, spooning her into his eyes, breathing close to her. Aima sat up quickly and pulled the T-shirt off her body, balling it up in her hands and throwing it into a corner of the room. She pressed her hands to her eyes and took deep trembling breaths. She had invited it, how he looked at her, how he'd propositioned her so blatantly—she'd always thought he saw her as a sister; they'd grown up together after all. But when someone sees how you behave—and she had acted like a slut last night—who can blame them for treating you as such? Aima fought back tears and climbed off the bed, padding naked across the bedroom floor to take a bubu out of Ijendu's closet, pulling it over her head, the cotton falling and draping over her body, covering her entirely.

She knelt at the side of the bed like she used to when she was a child doing her bedtime prayers, interlocking her fingers and propping her elbows on the mattress. She pressed her knuckles to her forehead and squeezed her eyes shut.

"Please, Father Lord," she whispered. "Please forgive me for the wicked things I did last night. You know my heart, You know that's not me, that's not how I want to move in the world, against Your favor. I wasn't in my right mind, I wasn't sober, and I should have been. I should have kept my body pure, kept my mind clean, and I wouldn't have fallen down that path. I'm so ashamed of myself, but please, please forgive me. I swear I won't ever do it again. I will stay in Your Light; I will live a life worthy of being Your child, worthy of Your Love. I want to find my way back to You, please show me, please help me, please, Father Lord . . ."

Warm tears dripped off her hands onto the bedsheets. She kept praying and whispering, letting the words turn into a semiconscious stream pouring out of her mouth while her mind spun in multiple directions, looking for a sign, a clue that could lead her back to some form of righteousness. There had to be a point to what she had just gone through, what she had put herself through. This had to be rock bottom. It tasted like it, rich with despair and shame and hopelessness, like a cloak she was dragging over herself.

When she'd been doing all the things she did last night, it hadn't felt wrong. It had felt wild and delicious and right, albeit with that small thread of Kalu-sadness running underneath. For a brief and blasphemous moment, Aima wondered why she was beating herself up so hard—like, what if it had been nothing more than what it was, a night of simple distracting pleasure? Did she actually feel guilty or was she performing it because that was the only world she knew, where these things weren't allowed, where pleasure in those forms wasn't allowed? She blinked with wet eyelashes and frowned, confused and suddenly reluctant to keep praying. She had a few lesbian friends, some of whom were Christian, and she'd reassured them several times that it was okay, that God still loved them, that God was, in fact, Love so their love couldn't be wrong. So, what did she actually believe? Was it the words she said to them or the ones she was lashing herself with?

Aima sat back on her heels and chewed at the cuticle of her thumb. Was it that she'd slept with Ijendu or that she'd had casual sex at all in the first place? Or that she'd been drunk or high? Or that she'd done sexual things in front of other people? Where exactly was the guilt coming from; where exactly was the sin?

She was beginning to feel that a vague and generalized repentance wasn't good enough, that there had to be specificity for any of this to count. Would sleeping with Ijendu have been different if she loved her? But it wasn't as if she didn't love Ijendu; of course she did. Everything felt muddled and mixed up, odd and guilty. Aima wanted to figure out how to leave it behind, how to just start over without having all these questions haunting her, wearing last night's clothes and smelling like a hangover. She dropped her hands into her lap and stared at them. Her nails were shaped into peach ovals, decorated with small crystals. There used to be a time when she'd try different manicures, imagining each of them with the diamond ring she was sure—had been sure—Kalu would propose to her with. Aima had been following several engagement and wedding accounts on Instagram, trying to pick out which stone shapes she wanted, which style of ring. She'd send her favorites to Kalu, but his responses were always careful, approving but never enthusiastic.

At the side of Ijendu's bed, Aima stretched out her left hand and imagined a ring on it one more time. Two rings. A platinum wedding band that nestled into the engagement ring. The image was clear, and with it, a sudden revelation swept across Aima's mind. This thing, this hitting rock bottom, maybe it was meant to give her perspective, to show her that perhaps she was running away from the very thing she thought she was running to. Kalu loved her. He'd always loved her. They were always meant to get married; they'd both talked about it, agreed on it. The only reason he hadn't proposed yet was because they'd gotten into those terrible fights, the ones where he'd shouted that they should get married when they both wanted to, not because everyone else was deciding for them.

He'd been so hurt that she didn't trust him, that she'd started treating him like an enemy who only wanted to take advantage of her. That love—the one she shared with him—that was the true and clear thing. This confusion she was feeling, this other life she'd tried so hard to spiral into in just one night, it was all optional; it was all just a choice. There was a fork in the road, and she'd tried to leave the path that ended in Kalu. She'd tried to go down the other one, and this result, this harsh guilt, had sprung up to block, to show her the correct way to go, to save her. Kalu still loved her. All she had to do was find him, and she could return to the road she'd been on, one that ended clearly, with her and Kalu taking their vows in God's presence. What better way to ensure that she stayed in God's Light? Matrimony was holy; everyone knew that. Aima could see now that she'd been wrong to listen to other people—her relationship with Kalu should have been just between the two of them and God. That was it; she could tell Kalu that when she talked to him.

Aima exhaled with a small smile, but it faded at the thought of talking to Kalu. Would he even want to see her? Her relief at the decision she'd made was eaten up by anxiety moving in a greedy path through her, whispering that there was no way she could hope to just waltz back into Kalu's life as if she hadn't broken his heart and expect him to take her back. And if he didn't take her back, then where would that leave her? She couldn't stay with Ijendu forever, especially after last night. Aima stood up and dusted the front of her bubu, dragging resolve from deep inside her. She wasn't going to continue in this direction, not when she knew that there was peace and love and clarity down the road with Kalu. She had to know whether he'd want her back, find out what he was thinking, if he'd be open to that or if he was angry and needed some time to cool off.

The bedroom door opened and Aima turned, startled. Ijendu entered the room, tossing her glasses and purse on the bed, a cloud of perfume wafting in with her.

"Bebi gehl!" she said. "You're awake!" She talked as if nothing had happened, as if everything was exactly the same. Aima seized on it gratefully. She wanted nothing more than to start over, reset her life, and erase the last several hours.

"You woke up early," Aima replied.

Ijendu looked in the mirror and ruffled her hair. "Yes o. Daddy wanted an early lunch so he could introduce me to one designer friend of his visiting from Malaysia."

"Ah, how was that?"

Ijendu shrugged. "It was okay. How about you? How are you feeling?" She turned and looked at Aima, concern creasing her forehead.

Aima groaned. "Hungover."

"Ei-yah. Have you been drinking water?"

Aima struggled to control her face at the memory of the conversation she'd had with Dike outside the kitchen. "Not enough," she managed to say.

Ijendu frowned and put her hands on her hips. "Wait, have you eaten anything?" Aima gave her a guilty smile and Ijendu rolled her eyes. "Oya, get dressed. We're going to get you some food."

"Ah-ahn, but you just ate!"

"And so? I'll just watch you. Hurry up, you can't go out in that old bubu."

Aima gave in and rummaged through her suitcase for something to wear. She found a sea-green cotton dress and held it up against herself, smoothing out the wrinkles.

"Ooh, I like that one," Ijendu said.

Aima smiled. "Thanks."

They looked at each other for a moment, then it stretched out to an uncomfortable length. Usually, Aima would change in front of Ijendu, but this time she felt self-conscious. She bit her lip and looked away, and Ijendu blushed.

"I'm going to get you some water from the kitchen," she said, and Aima nodded. She watched Ijendu leave, shutting the door behind her, and Aima felt a twinge of sadness pass through her. She changed her clothes, her movements heavy, wondering how much of their friendship the night before had ruined.

Saturday, 2:54 PM

They'd driven for a while, all the way to the other end of the highland, to Ijendu's favorite health bistro. She only wanted a cold-pressed green juice but insisted that Aima eat. It was easier to order food than argue that she had no appetite, so Aima picked at a salmon salad while Ijendu chattered away easily, gossiping about her godfather and how she suspected there was more to the story between him and that designer friend of his. After a while, she put down her juice and put her hand on Aima's.

"How are you feeling about Kalu?" she asked. She said it gently, like she was afraid that it would be a hard question for Aima to hear.

Aima tried not to show her relief at the subject being brought up. She'd been worried that Ijendu would want to talk about them (how strange that there was a "them" to talk about now). "I prayed about it this morning," she answered. "And . . . I think I want to give it another chance."

"Yes!" Ijendu clapped in delight. She looked genuinely happy to hear it. "I was hoping that you'd come to that decision, but I know it's not been easy between the two of you."

Aima sighed. "Love never is."

"Amen, my sister." Ijendu wriggled in her chair as she sipped on her juice, doing a small dance. "You're getting back together!"

"I don't know o. He's probably angry with me right now; I don't know if he'll even want to see me."

Ijendu scoffed. "Are you mad? That man's been in love with you for years. He'll be overjoyed that you're giving him another chance."

Aima moved some spinach around on her plate. "I don't know. He doesn't even know I'm in the city."

Ijendu flapped her hand. "It doesn't matter. Just call him and say you want to see him."

"No." Aima bit her lip. "I'm not ready yet."

Her friend gave her a soft look. "It's okay. Take your time."

Aima nodded, but she wasn't sure Ijendu was right. The longer she delayed in reconciling with Kalu, the further he might drift away from her. It had barely been a day, but still.

Ijendu changed the subject smoothly, telling some small story about one of the girls they'd gone out with last night, and Aima half listened, interjecting with the appropriate murmurs and laughs. Despite Ijendu's confidence, she was still terrified that Kalu wouldn't want her back, that the road she wanted so badly to be back on was closed to her, and it would be all her fault.

After they paid the bill, the two girls walked back to Ijendu's car and Aima climbed into the passenger seat. Ijendu often liked to drive around the city herself without a driver. It drove her parents wild with worry, but she was stubborn and insisted. There was an edge to her that Aima wondered about, some hardness that Ijendu usually took care not to show to her. Even in everything last night, even while drunk and high, Ijendu had been laughing tenderness and teasing softness. Aima looked over at her in the car and on impulse reached out and touched her cheek. Ijendu stopped mid-sentence, surprised. Aima smiled a little sadly to see it. She'd been keeping some distance from her all day, and clearly her best friend had noticed but understood and said nothing.

"Thank you," Aima said. "For everything."

Ijendu leaned her face into Aima's hand for a moment and smiled back. "Of course."

Aima withdrew her hand and Ijendu turned her attention back to the road, continuing her story. They ran into traffic on the expressway that stretched across the highland and Ijendu sighed.

"Every day," she said. "This country will not kill me." She turned up the volume of the radio and sang along to the Lady Donli song that was playing. "You can rest if you want," she told Aima in between, and Aima gave her a small grateful look before reclining her seat and leaning back into it. The radio slid from song into song for the next twenty minutes, and Ijendu sang along to all of them until the traffic eased up. They were getting closer to the estate when Ijendu turned the car into a residential street and broke off her singing. "Wait," she said. "Doesn't Ahmed live around here?"

Aima looked out of the window. "Oh yeah, his house is just down the road." She and Kalu spent—used to spend—as much time there as they did in their own place. Ahmed loved to barbecue, and even

Ijendu had spent many balmy evenings in his garden, all four of them sitting and laughing together. It suddenly hit her that her entire life in the city would be completely different without Kalu, a cataclysmic shift, one world ripped apart and an unrecognizable one left behind.

"That's perfect!" Ijendu's face lit up, excited. "We should stop by and see him."

Aima was confused. "Why, what for?"

Ijendu rolled her eyes. "Look, you're scared to tell Kalu that you're still around and you want him back because you're not sure how he feels. If you want to find out, we can just ask Ahmed. He'll tell you, won't he?"

She was right, Ahmed would. He'd tried to talk Aima out of breaking up with Kalu quite a few times before she'd finally left. "I want to see you two together," he'd said. "I know Kalu's made mistakes, but I just don't want this city to be the thing that tears you apart."

"Yeah," she replied. "He'll tell me."

"Good. Let's see if he's home."

They pulled up in front of Ahmed's compound and Aima tried to call his phone, but it rang through to voice mail.

"Ugh, that's annoying." Ijendu tapped her nails against the steering wheel.

"No, he's probably home. That's someone's car parked there, so he has a visitor." Aima opened her door and started climbing out of the car. "It's okay; we have keys to each other's houses. Let's just ring the doorbell." She unlocked the small pedestrian door set within the gate and they entered the compound.

"You're right, he's home," Ijendu said, pointing to Ahmed's car. She smiled at Aima. "Let's get some answers so you can have your happy reunion and I can continue looking forward to my maid of honor duties."

When they got to the front door, it was already cracked. Aima pushed it open more as they entered.

"Ahmed?" she called out. "Are you home?"

There was no answer, and she and Ijendu walked deeper into the sterile silence of Ahmed's house.

twelve

Kalu woke up feeling like his eyes were full of sand. His cheek was damp from where he'd drooled onto his pillow, a wet patch of cotton blossoming under his mouth. He groaned and rolled over on his back, swiping a hand over his face. Even with his eyes closed, Kalu winced at the sunlight filling his room.

For the first several minutes, he didn't remember—that Aima was gone, everything from Ahmed's party, the warning on the train. He opened his eyes and reached out to the other side of the bed, the one she used to sleep on, and his hand met emptiness, blank sheets, a smooth pillow. Kalu was wondering if she was in the bathroom when memory caught up to him and with it an immense surge of grief that dragged up tears. He covered the surge with anger, grabbing her pillow and throwing it across the room with a shout. Just opening his mouth broke a dam, however, and sobs burst out, loud and ugly. Kalu bent over, muffling the sounds against his palms. There were other hurts buried in there; he could feel them. They looked like a little girl gagged on a bed, like Ahmed's hands on his skin, like a laugh over a telephone line, like a terrible aloneness wandering the city. Accumulated, they were so heavy, the bartender's warning didn't even seem real. So much of the night felt like a dream now anyway. The story was just part of it, an unreal message being filtered through the lowest points of the city.

The grief made way for the warning nonetheless—the bartender's face, his fear when Kalu had said the pastor's name. Was it even possible that the man at the party was Okinosho? The man's face was splashed over signboards across the city and in full pages of newspapers. He was in television advertisements, his voice booming out from the radio, his sermons online—wouldn't Kalu have recognized him? It was with a little shame that Kalu remembered the frenzy he'd been in when he burst into that room, the fury that had burst in his eyes and hands when he'd seen that girl. Hers was the only face in that room he could remember, not even the bouncer who he'd spoken to at the door. It made complete sense that he wouldn't recognize the man he'd thrown to the floor even if he was someone as famous as Okinosho. The import of what he'd done slowly filtered in, turning his hands numb.

He'd attacked the most powerful religious leader in the country.

He'd thrown him to the ground, naked. If that bouncer hadn't intervened, Kalu would have tried to crush the man's testicles.

He'd humiliated Okinosho in a room full of his peers.

Terror crept up Kalu's spine. He'd had no choice—would he have turned and walked away from the girl if he knew that it was the pastor on top of her? No, it had been inevitable and he would do it all over again, but part of his head was frantically begging, praying that he was wrong, that the bartender was wrong, that it wasn't Okinosho he'd attacked. He had to ask Ahmed.

If Ahmed had been with a man when Kalu called him, so what? It was too many emotions making a storm inside him—grief, this irrational jealousy, the developing terror. The jealousy was easier to ignore. He'd been ignoring it for years, after all, telling himself that he was just possessive of Ahmed's time because they'd been friends for so long. Whatever ran underneath was something Kalu didn't want to dig up, so he left it alone. As for Aima, Kalu couldn't help but be grateful that she'd left the city when she did. If Okinosho wanted revenge for the scene at the party, Aima could be a target. All this was an ugliness he didn't want to bring her into. It was better to not tell her anything about it. She'd be safe in London with her parents by now.

There was even a chance that Okinosho would blame Ahmed for what Kalu had done. It was his party after all, and Kalu was not just his guest but his friend. Kalu looked around the bed for his phone, leaning over the edge to reach underneath where it had fallen. The phone was dead again. He growled in annoyance and plugged it in, then went to the bathroom to splash water on his face and rinse his mouth. He was too anxious to do anything else more than swipe on some deodorant. Aima had left things on the counter—a nearly empty bottle of perfume, a rattail comb, a broken earring. Kalu picked up the bottle and sprayed some of the scent in the air. The intercom to the apartment rang, a short and obnoxiously cheery tune. He put the bottle down and went into the parlor, answering the call.

"Yes?"

The voice of the security guard at the gate came through, edged in static. "Oga, delivery pessin dey here for you."

Kalu frowned. "I didn't order anything."

"Na your name dey for the receipt. Dem no get correct apartment number, so I say make I call and check."

The terror reared up again, a primal warning scattering up the back of his neck. *Run*, it said. *Run now.* Kalu fought the urge to take his hand off the intercom and run out of the door, down the corridor, down the stairs, whirling out into the naked outdoors. It was only the possibility of running into the person at the gate (the *assassin*, the warning hissed) that held him in place. He had to do something, he had to get somewhere safe, he had to leave this apartment. They knew where he lived, the gates of the estate could only protect him for so long, and Kalu wasn't sure if he was in a safe house or in a trap, a hole dug into the ground with hunters gathering at the mouth of it, eager to flay him and take his pelt to Okinosho.

"Oga?"

Kalu collected himself, his hand trembling. "Don't allow him inside. Don't allow anyone inside who says they're looking for me. If someone else comes, tell them I'm not around, that I traveled."

"Okay, sah."

Kalu took his hand off the button and the static bled into silence. He looked over at his windows, the glass stretching from the floor to the ceiling, a dark linen curtain blocking out the light. His apartment was at the front of the building; you could see the parking lot and the gate from his balcony. Kalu stepped over to the edge of the window, leaning over the potted lilies Aima had kept blooming on a table behind the sofa. The air there dragged sweet from the blossoms. He stood to the side and gently pulled the curtain back just a few centimeters, hoping it wouldn't be noticed by someone outside looking up at a seventh-floor window. Peeking out, he could see the front gate, wrought black iron, and the security guard in his ironed blue shirt, talking to another man, someone short and lean, wearing a red T-shirt and khaki shorts, holding a small brown package. The conversation got animated as the man with the package gestured toward the building, jerking his arms in sharp, aggressive darts, clearly demanding entry. The security guard squared his stance and puffed out his chest, hooking his thumbs into his belt loops, and Kalu could just imagine the bass that had entered his voice. He watched as the man with the package threw up an arm, then turned away. Kalu let the curtain fall back and exhaled in relief. Some more time, perhaps just enough to figure out where he could go, where would be safe. He had to call Ahmed.

He went back to the bedroom and picked up his phone, pressing the power button and tapping on the screen, frowning when glitched lines appeared underneath the cracked glass.

"What's this? It was working this morning."

Fear began to bubble up in his chest as the phone warbled nonsense colors at him. He needed to call Ahmed and figure out what to do. Maybe he was being dramatic to think people were out to get him. Maybe the man outside was simply trying to do his job and deliver a package. Maybe he was overreacting, but Ahmed would know. Ahmed would know exactly how all this worked and what to do. Kalu put the phone back down. If he left it to charge a little longer, perhaps it would work then. It *had* to work then.

Wiping his hands on his thighs, he went back to the window and looked out. It took him a moment to locate the man in the red shirt, but he found him standing next to a small battered white car. As Kalu watched, the man tossed the package from hand to hand, thinking, then he tapped on the window of the car. Someone inside wound the glass down and reached out to take the package. They conferred for a moment, then the man in the red shirt walked away from the car but not toward the gate. Kalu frowned. Why wasn't he entering the car to leave? He angled himself to see the man better, then felt his stomach drop as he realized the man was heading for the fence, casting surreptitious glances toward the gate to make sure security wasn't watching him. There was a row of flame of the forest trees right at the fence, their branches draping over the wrought iron, drowning a section of the fence in green and blooms of yellow and orange. With one step, the man was hidden by the trees, but Kalu could catch glimpses of his red shirt, loud flashes in the green. He was climbing the fence.

The warning bell in Kalu's head started screaming again in full siren sounds. *RUN*, it said. *RUN NOW.*

This time, Kalu didn't argue. He grabbed his phone, shoved it into his pocket with his wallet, then took his keys, slamming the door behind him. Out on the landing, he jabbed at the elevator button, his heart pounding in his ears. It was only a floor above, thank goodness, and once the doors opened, Kalu threw himself inside, hitting the button to close them again. He hadn't had time to put on shoes, only slide his feet into leather slippers on his way out. They made it a little harder to run, but he was using his car so it didn't matter; he could get away from this red-chested assassin hunting him down; he could disappear into the roads of the city. He beeped the car open and sat inside to collect himself for a few seconds. There was no need to rush; it would only draw attention if he sped out of the estate with his wheels burning. It was better to stay calm, ignore the panic shouting in his head. He pulled out of the parking space up to the gate and waved to the security guards. They smiled and nodded and opened the gate, and Kalu started to turn left to connect to the main road, tentatively relieved. He glanced in his rearview mirror at the trees and the fence, and the man was still hidden, still climbing. For a moment, Kalu felt safe.

The feeling was shattered by the white car blasting its horn behind him, the window lowering to show another man leaning out to shout at the man climbing the fence, gesturing toward Kalu's car with frantic arms. They knew what his car looked like, Kalu realized; they knew he was getting away. The man in the red shirt emerged from the trees, brushing leaves and twigs off his clothes. He looked between his companion and Kalu's car, then broke into a dead run. Kalu didn't wait for him to enter the white car; he simply smashed his foot against the accelerator and shot out, swerving wildly into traffic and shifting across three lanes while the other drivers shouted and pressed on their horns. Kalu didn't care, his car was a large Jeep, it would cause more damage to these smaller cars than they could inflict on him. He sped through two intersections before looking back in his mirror and was horrified to see the white car weaving through the other cars, bearing down on him.

"Fuck, fuck, fuck!" A sharp right turn, spinning through a roundabout, barely missing the side of a bus as he careened down a side road. The bus conductor swore at him and slammed a hand against the side of his car as it passed, but Kalu couldn't spare a breath to even attempt an apology. He was frantically hoping that no traffic policemen would stop him; there was no bribe he could give that would be worth the time that would cost.

Ditch the car, the voice in his head told him. *It's too easy to find you with it.*

"I don't have time!" he shouted back at himself, his voice shaking, his hands clenched on the steering wheel. The panic was filling his car, choking him. His face was wet. When had he started crying? He slid tightly in and out of traffic lanes, his fear tightening into a slick knot, but then he swallowed it down, calculating. No one was going to save him except himself. He couldn't afford to scatter, not right now. He could save that for later. For now, he had to think.

There was an intersection coming up, with traffic police and a light that was about to change. There was a market on the right, pyramids of tomatoes catching the sunlight, and a bus stop close to it filled with loud danfos and a fleet of okadas. Kalu fumbled with his right hand at the radio while accelerating to overtake the tanker in front of him, cutting dangerously across two lanes as horns blared and people shouted at him through their open windows. The radio popped loose, thanks to Ahmed—Kalu hadn't thought he was serious when his friend told him to have the mechanic put a secret compartment behind the radio, but as usual, Ahmed was right. "You never know when you'll need money on the go," he'd said. "Whether it's for a bribe or something else." Kalu drove even faster as the light turned orange, steering with his left hand as he pulled out wads of cash from the compartment, his radio dangling heavily by its wires. He glanced in the rearview mirror, and he could see that the white car was a few lengths behind. He had time, just a sliver of it, but it would be enough; it had to be enough. And he was going to lose this car. Fuck.

The light turned red and the cars in the other direction started moving. Kalu sped through the intersection, swerving to avoid a small sedan but clipping its bumper. The traffic police yelled and started to walk over. The bundles of money were in his lap as Kalu pulled over right in front of the market between two buses, blocking one of them. Everyone was shouting and he knew he only had moments before someone would start grabbing his shirt. He threw the car into park, shoved some money into his pockets, and ripped the worn yellow rubber band that was holding the other bundles together. Jumping out of the car, Kalu threw the money into the air with as much strength as he had, and the sky exploded with thousand-naira notes. People screamed and rushed, and Kalu ran for the okadas, dodging the bodies pushing and jumping, their hands outstretched. He was living in split seconds—the ones before the traffic police reached him, before the men pursuing him spotted him through the crowd he'd created, before the okada driver who was sitting astride his motorcycle and turning his head toward the noise realized what was going on. Kalu jumped on the back of the motorbike, pulled a wad of money from his pocket, and reached around to slap it to the man's chest. "No questions," he said. "I need to disappear now now."

The driver looked at Kalu, and it was a boy, a teenager with yellowed eyes and a scar on his bottom lip. He glanced down at the money and his eyes narrowed, then he kicked off and started his engine, throwing a smile that was almost a snarl back at Kalu.

"Oya, let's go," he said, his voice like gravel, and they shot off, the bike leaning wildly as the boy slipped it between buses and other bikes, then sped down a narrow side road with potholes and red mud kicking up at their ankles. Kalu didn't dare look back. He didn't want anyone to see his face; he needed to be a back vanishing into the city.

"Continue going," he urged the boy. "Dey go, dey go."

The boy drove madly, like he was in a video game, like he'd been waiting for a chance to drive as if he was in a video game. The wheels dug up the ground and splattered it as they turned off the side road onto another main road, then the boy jumped the curb, sped across a stretch of concrete under a highway, bumped down on the other side, and cut across four lanes of traffic. Kalu had stopped breathing—it was entirely possible that this escape was going to kill him before the hunters got their chance, but he said nothing because at this point there was no way those men could still be following them. Even Kalu didn't know where exactly he was. They sped down a narrow road lined by video shops, turned left at a food stand, then the bike pulled into a mechanic's yard and parked behind a wrecked lorry, the engine turning off. The driver turned around and took the money Kalu had been clutching the whole ride.

"You have officially disappeared," he said to Kalu, licking his thumb as he started to count the money. His fingernails were thick and square.

Kalu swung his leg over and got off the bike, his knees liquid with terror. "Where are we?" he asked.

"My brother's yard. He does car repair."

Kalu looked at the boy, still on the bike but with his feet planted on the ground and his torso leaning back, totally relaxed as he counted his money. "What's your name?" Kalu asked.

The boy didn't look up. "Felix."

Kalu leaned against the lorry and his panic climbed back up his throat, dissolving into shaky relief. "You just saved my life, Felix."

Felix side-eyed him. "Nobody was even shooting at you."

"What?"

The boy shrugged. "It's not that serious." He unzipped a red running bag that was buckled around his waist and carefully put the money in there.

Kalu blinked and decided to ignore the easy dismissal of his running for his life. "You drive very well."

Felix brought out a cigarette from apparently nowhere and lit it.

"I'm the best," he said casually, and hissed a plume of smoke out from the gap between his two front teeth. "Who were you running from?"

For a moment, Kalu thought about telling him the truth. Everyone knew Okinosho; it was almost impressive to have someone like that take such a personal, if homicidal, interest in you. He squashed the idea almost as quickly as it came up—it was too dangerous. "My business rival is trying to get rid of me," he lied.

Felix tapped some ash off his handlebar. "So, what are you going to do?"

"I need somewhere to hide." Just being under the sky made Kalu feel too exposed; he needed to be tucked away somewhere safe, somewhere they wouldn't know to look for him. He needed to charge his phone, pray it was working, and call Ahmed.

"For how long?" Felix asked. "You get more cash?"

"I don't know how long, a few hours? I need to charge my phone." He didn't answer about the money even though Felix could probably see it right there in his pocket. They were alone in a place Kalu knew nothing about; the boy could decide to just rob him.

Felix took a drag of his cigarette and flared the smoke out from his nostrils, watching Kalu's discomfort rise. "Not all of us are thieves even if we're poor," he said, and there was a cutting judgment in the look he gave Kalu. "I don't need to steal your money; are you not going to just give it to me if I continue to help you?"

Kalu deflated with shame. "You're going to help me?" he asked.

The boy dropped his cigarette and ground it into the sand with his sneaker. "Are you going to pay me?"

Kalu nodded, the money distorting his pocket.

Felix shrugged. "Okay now." He sat upright and started the bike again. "Let's be going."

Kalu climbed on uncertainly. "To where?"

Felix grinned, feral. "I know a place nobody will look for you." He gunned the engine and sand spun up in a dust as he wheeled around, and they shot back onto the road.

thirteen

I t was the sound of shoes against the tile of his floor that got through to Ahmed first. He raised his head slowly, the coffee table cutting into his back, his hands locked together with laced fingers. He had been praying . . . he thought he had been praying, maybe, after he'd wept, or during. His name rang against the walls of his house.

"Ahmed?"

He frowned. He'd expected Thursday's voice, but that wasn't him—it was a woman's voice. Instead, Aima walked into the large parlor, concern rippling over her face as soon as she saw him sitting like that.

"Ahmed?" She rushed to his side, crouching to put her hand on his shoulder. "What's going on? What happened?"

Her palm felt warm through his shirt, heating the chilled flesh underneath. Seun was on the sofa behind her, but Aima hadn't even noticed him yet. All her attention was fixed on Ahmed. He let his eyes travel dully over her shoulder to where Ijendu was standing by the doorway behind the sofa, the large cushions blocking Seun's sprawled and horrifically still body from her view. Ahmed said nothing, and Aima put her hand to his face.

"Ahmed." Her eyes searched his. "Are you okay?"

He couldn't look away from Seun. It seemed wrong, to have left him like that, naked and with dried semen splattered on his stomach. He should have covered him.

"What's going on with him?" Ijendu asked, confused. "I've never seen Ahmed like this. Is he high?"

"I don't know," Aima replied. She tried to turn his face toward her, and while he didn't stop her, Ahmed's eyes remained fixed on Seun. Aima turned to see what he was looking at. When she saw Seun, Aima screamed.

"Blood of Jesus!" She scrambled back, losing her balance and falling over.

"What? What is it?" Ijendu rushed over and looked around the sofa, then gasped at the sight of Seun's body. "Holy shit." Ahmed watched her struggle with her shock and listened to Aima hyperventilating on the floor beside him, whispering prayers and pleas. Seun looked entirely too dead for them to think for a moment that he was asleep or unconscious. His eyes were open and glassed, his head fallen to the side.

"I should have covered him," he said aloud. "I shouldn't have left him like that." He had made so many mistakes. He should have called Ruqaiyyah as soon as he received the text from Seun instead of trying to handle it by himself when he was so consumed by rage. It was her party that had been compromised, and she would have come with him to confront Seun and the boy would still be alive. He shouldn't have moved alone, unleashed. Was the shame of Ruqaiyyah's knowing worse than the shame he felt now?

"Father God, Father God," Aima said, her voice trembling. "What happened, Ahmed? *What did you do?*"

For a foolish moment, he wondered why she didn't assume something else—a heart attack, an embolism—but then Ahmed saw how the girls were looking at the purple mottling on Seun's neck, the clear signature of Ahmed's hands, and he knew he was damned completely. Aima had nothing to be surprised about. She had always seen him, perhaps never trusted him entirely because of that, and clearly, she had been right not to. Belatedly, Ahmed looked over at her and registered her actual presence with some confusion.

"Aren't you supposed to be in London?" he said.

She turned a horrified stare at him. "What?"

"Kalu said you left last night."

She continued staring at him, her eyes wide and incredulous. "There's a dead man in your parlor and you're asking me about London?"

Ijendu leaned forward a little and looked at Seun's face properly. "Wait," she said. "Isn't this that actor? The one who just did a documentary on himself?" She clicked her tongue rapidly as she tried to remember his name. "Seun! Eh hehn. That's his name. It's him."

That pulled Ahmed's attention back to the body. "I should have covered him," he said again.

Aima looked as well, then covered her mouth with her hand, stifling a sob. Ijendu reached down and closed Seun's eyes. Ahmed sighed as she did so, spared finally from the emptiness of that lost gaze. She looked at him, then at Aima's shaking form, then seemed to come to a decision. She left the parlor, returning with a heap of fleeced fabric in her arms. Ijendu flapped out the blanket, the pattern unfurling into the air before it settled slowly over Seun, covering him. She turned to Ahmed and Aima, putting her hands on her hips.

"Both of you need to get your shit together," she said. "We need to take care of this."

Aima looked up at her. "*We?* No, no." She shook her head, her braids swinging. "Me, I don't want to be a part of this." She stood quickly and made to leave the parlor, but Ijendu grabbed her arm and pulled her close.

"We're already part of this," Ahmed heard her whisper. "Besides, look at him." They both turned and he looked away, not wanting to see whatever was in their eyes when they shifted from seeing him as their friend to seeing him as the murderer he was. "He can't handle this," Ijendu said.

"What makes you think *we* can handle this?" Aima hissed.

Ijendu didn't answer right away. She came over to Ahmed and knelt next to him. "What was he doing here, Ahmed?" she asked, her voice gentle.

He looked at her and said nothing, simply let her see all that was tearing through him, allowed it to swirl up into his eyes and into the air between them. Ijendu nodded, her own eyes heavy with understanding. "It was an accident," she said. "You didn't mean to."

Ahmed was numb. "No. I didn't." He wasn't sure if he was lying or not, but she was giving him an option he seized with both hands. A terrible accident. Manslaughter instead of murder. He'd paid to have this done so many times before, but he'd never done it himself, ended a life with his own hands. He'd been such a coward, a fraud. "I don't know what to do," he whispered to her.

"Please, let's leave this place," Aima said, raising her voice to catch Ijendu's attention.

"You want to just leave him like this?" Ijendu answered, an edge entering her words.

"Why do you keep talking as if there's something we can do? That man is dead! What are we supposed to do about it?"

Ahmed watched Ijendu's face shift in calculation. She glanced at Aima with some hesitation, then at Ahmed, then bit her lip and stood up, dusting her knees off. Her face slid into a calm surety. "I can help you handle this," she said. "But that's only if you want, Ahmed."

Aima stepped forward, confused. "Ijendu. What are you even saying?"

"Yes," Ahmed said. "Just tell me what to do."

"Oh my God, Ahmed, shut up!" Aima spun on him, furious now. "Stop trying to drag her into this mess you've made!"

"No one's dragging me anywhere, Aima, relax." Ijendu remained unruffled as she looked around the room. "We have to move the body, first of all. Ahmed, stand up." He obeyed quickly, holding his hands close to his thighs, trying to hide the way they were palsying. He saw Aima's eyes dart to his trembling fingers, and he curled them into fists. She folded her arms and glared at both him and Ijendu. "Wrap that blanket around him properly," Ijendu said. "I think it's big enough that we won't need to tie it with anything."

Ahmed faltered and Ijendu touched his arm lightly. "It's going to be all right," she said. "Just be doing what I'm saying and we'll take care of this."

Aima threw her hands up. "I don't know what you people are

planning to do," she said. "But this is a bad idea. This is a very bad idea."

Ahmed started to wrap the blanket more securely around Seun's body, and Ijendu stepped in to help as Aima looked on with her arms wrapped around herself. Seun was heavy, heavy in a way that seemed particularly inanimate, like a horribly realistic dummy made from someone else's flesh. The blanket was green, with a pattern of yellow flowers, small and bunched into sprays. It was soft in Ahmed's hands yet strong enough to hold the weight of Seun's errant limbs. Ijendu gave instructions, coordinating the way they heaved his body about, and Ahmed followed them obediently, shrouding his victim in a woven garden, guilt chewing away at him like an army of termites let loose on his heart.

Saturday, 4:51 PM

They'd carried the body outside and fitted it into the boot of Ahmed's car, folding it at the knees. Ijendu had forced Aima to help even though she'd objected at first, then had to vomit in a corner of the compound.

"We'll be done soon," Ijendu had said, rubbing her back before giving her some water.

"I can't believe you're making me do this," Aima replied. "We didn't have to get involved!"

"We got involved as soon as we walked into a house with a dead body in it, Aima." Ijendu had closed the boot of the car and entered the driver's seat. "Ahmed, get in the back."

He had no idea where her calm was coming from or why she felt she knew what to do with a corpse, but Ahmed was spinning wildly inside and her surety was a compass, so he was following it blindly, spared the effort of thinking. The girls continued to argue in low-ered voices from the front of the car while Ahmed looked down at his hands, still trembling in his lap as the highland swept past. The car slowed down, and Ijendu's window whirred as she opened it to speak into an intercom.

"Yes, good evening. It's Ijendu, Dr. Okoye's daughter."

Ahmed raised his head, and the whorled metal of the towering gate they had pulled up in front of filled his eyes. He frowned. "Isn't this Okinosho's compound?" he asked, looking around. How had they driven all the way to Cassava Hill without him noticing? He would have been panicking if he didn't feel so numb and now, so utterly confused. Why would Ijendu bring him here? Did she know what had happened last night?

A staticky voice came back over the intercom, then the gate slid open. Ijendu put up her window and drove forward.

"Wait," said Aima. "You brought us to your godfather's house? With a body in the trunk? Are you mad?"

"Relax." Ijendu turned into the courtyard and pulled up in front of a large white house with faceted columns. It reeked of money carelessly flung around. "I know what I'm doing."

Ahmed sat up, horror stinging its way through his shock. "He's your godfather?"

Ijendu rolled her eyes. "I'm surprised you didn't know." She opened her car door and stepped out. "Come on."

Ahmed exchanged an anxious look with Aima, both of them un-moving in their seats.

"What the *fuck* is going on?" he said. His shock wasn't so much about Okinosho being her godfather—her parents attended the church, after all—but for Ijendu to show up so casually with Seun cooling in the trunk? Ahmed had always just thought of her as Aima's friend, far removed from the slinking dark world he and Okinosho truly moved in. How close was she to Okinosho for her to come here? How many other things had he missed?

Aima just shook her head, her eyes frantic. "I don't know, mehn. This is too much. This is insane."

Ijendu banged on the glass of the window. "Are you people coming or what?" she asked.

"Is she about to tell the pastor that you killed somebody?" Aima asked, her face twisting in disbelief.

Ahmed couldn't even reply. Aima and Ijendu *couldn't* know anything about last night, about Kalu or Machi or the hit that was out. Unless Okinosho had told Ijendu? But then Ijendu would have told Aima, and if that had happened, Aima would have been panicking long before she saw Seun's body. For God's sake, Aima wasn't even supposed to *be* here. He looked at the fear marking lines in her face and pulled up some sense in himself.

"Why don't you wait in the car?" he suggested. Okinosho would have undoubtedly looked into Kalu and he would know who Aima was to him. It was better to keep her away, keep her safe. Besides, she wasn't designed for things like this, stories like this. She already looked like she was breaking. "Stay here," he said. "I don't know what Ijendu is doing, but I've already dragged you into too much of this."

She looked at him and wiped her eyes, trying not to cry. "I'm scared, Ahmed." Her voice broke and he leaned over to hug her, the seats of the car cutting into them.

"It's going to be okay," he whispered against her braids. "It was an accident. I'll take care of it. Just stay here."

"Where's Kalu?" she asked.

He hid a wince and cupped her face in his hands. "I don't know. We'll go and find him as soon as this is over." It was true, but his mouth felt swollen with all the things he wasn't telling her.

Ijendu banged on the window again, looking annoyed now.

"I'm coming, okay?" Ahmed kissed Aima's cheek. "Stay here," he said, and she nodded. He stepped out of the car, and Ijendu folded her arms.

"What were the two of you talking about?"

"Doesn't matter. She's going to wait for us in the car."

"Why? What did you say to her?" She stepped toward the car door, but Ahmed grabbed her arm.

"I don't know what we're doing here or why you came to Okinosho," he said, his voice low. "But if the place you go with a dead celebrity's body is *here*, then you know Okinosho in a way that Aima doesn't. We know what he is. She doesn't need to find out." He bent his head to look directly into her eyes. "You know that's not safe information to have. Leave her out of it."

Ijendu narrowed her eyes at him for a few moments, then nodded and shook her arm free. "Let's go, then," she said.

Ahmed walked a few steps behind her as she went down a gravel path that curved beside the mansion, winding through small gardens filled with hibiscus and cattails. They came to a set of double doors on the side of the house and Ijendu rang the doorbell there. A steward opened the door and greeted them, standing aside to let them in.

"Hello, Cletus," Ijendu said. "How's the family?"

"They're doing well, madam, thank you. Pastor said you should wait for him in the study."

"Okay, thank you."

He led them down a few corridors before opening the door to a large room lined with books, a large desk sprawling over a Persian rug. Ijendu smiled politely as Cletus left, her face falling back to neutral as soon as the door closed behind him.

"Do I want to ask how well you know your godfather?" Ahmed asked.

Ijendu paced the room slowly, trailing her hand over the books, light reflecting off her manicure. "Mind your business," she said lightly.

Ahmed raised his eyebrows. "Okay o." He sat down in one of the armchairs. "I want to say thank you, but I really don't know what the fuck we're doing here so I'm not sure what to thank you for yet."

Ijendu laughed. "It's okay," she said. "It's been a strange day." She glanced over at him. "So, you've been fucking Seun."

Ahmed put his head in his hands. "Guy, I just met him last night."

"Wow." Ijendu stopped pacing. "Shit."

"Yeah. Exactly."

She grimaced. "I'm sorry it got out of hand."

Ahmed didn't reply, simply pressed his fingers into his temples. He wondered if he should've mentioned the blackmail but was interrupted by an errant yet urgent thought—what had he done with Seun's phone? He sat up and patted his pockets, not finding it. Probably still in the house. *Fuck.* He was trying to remember where exactly it could be when the study door swung open and Okinosho walked into the room wearing a gold caftan and leather slippers, rings studding his fingers. Ahmed shot to his feet nervously and Ijendu gave him an amused look.

"Good afternoon, Daddy," she said to the pastor, walking into his embrace and accepting his kiss on her cheek.

"Is it not just this afternoon that I saw you?" he joked, smiling at her. "You missed me like that?"

She laughed, a ripple of sound snaking around the study. "Always," she joked back, linking her arm with his. "I wanted to ask you for a favor." Her voice lowered and he bent his head to listen as she whispered into his ear, her eyes flickering over to Ahmed, who was standing by the armchair, waiting awkwardly. Okinosho hadn't even acknowledged his presence since he'd entered the room. Ahmed was having trouble believing Thursday's assertion that the pastor wasn't holding the fiasco of last night's party against him. He watched Okinosho concentrate on whatever Ijendu was telling him, the man's face still and deceptively amiable until a sharpness rose in his features and he tilted his head slightly to look at Ahmed, interest entering his eyes. When Ijendu was done, the pastor straightened and patted her shoulder.

"You are a good friend," he said. "Ahmed and I can take it from here."

Confusion flitted over Ijendu's face. "Wait," she said to her godfather. "You know him?"

Okinosho grinned like an oil spill. "Oh, Alhaji Soyoye and I have done business a few times before, isn't that right?"

Ahmed nodded and said nothing. He wasn't sure how much Ijendu had told the man, but she obviously hadn't even mentioned his name yet.

"Now, why don't you head back home?" the pastor said to her. "The driver will take you and I'll see you in service tomorrow, yes?"

Ijendu looked like she wanted to argue but then thought better of it. "Okay, Daddy," she said.

"Go with God." They hugged again, and she gave Ahmed a complicated glance as she left—curious yet sympathetic.

Once she left, Okinosho walked slowly around his desk and settled into his chair with a sigh, gesturing for Ahmed to sit back down. Ahmed obeyed, his pulse racing. He couldn't gauge what the pastor was thinking or feeling, and it was strange to look at the man's fleshy face and think this was the same man who had put out the order for Kalu to be killed. None of that rage was showing—Okinosho looked at ease, relaxed, unhurried. As if lives weren't orbiting around the snap of his ringed fingers.

The pastor stared at Ahmed across the gleaming stretch of his desk. His face carved itself into a dark smile.

"So, Alhaji," he said. "My daughter tells me you need my help."

Ahmed hoped he didn't look as scattered as he felt. "Yes," he said. *Keep it simple, don't talk too much, don't show how weak you are right now.* It would be such a mistake in the face of this kind of casual ruthlessness.

"You know, the first time Ijendu came to me asking for a favor like this, I wasn't sure. She wasn't even supposed to know that I was capable of helping with these matters." Okinosho cracked his knuckles and rested his elbows on his desk. "As it turns out, that little girl had been using her ears to hear more than she was supposed to. But I'm not annoyed by it. She has kept her mouth shut for many years, and that kind of discretion is rare. She can be useful to me. I feel as if I can trust her, and in this life, there are not many people you can trust, especially as a man of God. Snakes lie in wait in the grass."

Ahmed said nothing, just waited, clenching his hands around each other to keep them still.

"But this time, because it's you, I am particularly interested. You see, you're an interesting man, Alhaji. You mind your business, you run your parties, you don't really have an attitude about them.

Many men would be power drunk in your position. Feeling as if they're gatekeepers when the only real gate anyone should be worrying about is that to the Kingdom of Heaven. You have a humility that I like. That's why I didn't do anything to you when your friend had the temerity to lay his hands on me even though it happened under your roof." Here, the pastor's mouth twisted, his canines showing. "I decided to keep my problem with him separate. God works his grace through me. But in this favor my daughter is asking, I saw an opportunity. You are someone who can do many things for me, both now and in the future. So, yes"—he leaned back in his velvet chair—"I can help you dispose of this, this *actor.*" Okinosho made a dismissive gesture with his hand at the thought of Seun, as if the boy was smoke already dissipating from the world.

Ahmed's eyes flickered up, surprised. He'd been expecting—he wasn't sure what he'd been expecting.

Okinosho noted his surprise. "What is it?" He chuckled. "You thought I wouldn't help you?" A shrug. "Life is a fleeting thing, a brief gift from God. It is far, far more fragile than people are led to believe. Sometimes, it evaporates from right under our hands. Who are we to question the timing of the Almighty when He calls the young ones home?"

That was . . . one way of describing killing someone, Ahmed thought. He wondered how often the pastor had done it himself. The man's eyes were shiny and slick as they slid up to look at Ahmed. It was surprising how penetrating they were.

"Or did you think I would judge you?" Okinosho straightened up. "That is not my place in life, my child. Whether it's for the circumstances in which the incident occurred or the incident itself. We are all just humans, flawed and ugly."

Ahmed couldn't stay silent anymore. "Is that why you're helping me?" he asked, skepticism heavy in his voice. "Because we're all just humans?"

The pastor tilted his head. "Because we are all here to help one another. There are many things you can help me with later on. But for this, for right now"—he made a moue with his mouth—"I will only ask for one thing."

Ahmed's heart thudded. *Who knows what this madman will ask for?* "And what is it?"

Okinosho regarded him seriously. "I want the girl from that night. From your party."

It took Ahmed a few minutes to register what he was saying. "Wait . . . Machi?"

A dismissive wave. "If that's her name. The young one."

A chill threaded through Ahmed. "What do you want her for?"

"Oh, don't worry. It's not like last night. In fact, I won't even touch her. I want to hire her for something else—it won't take long. An hour, maybe two. It depends." His gaze stroked over Ahmed, assessing. "And since you seem to be the conscientious type, I will be paying her well, so don't worry about that."

"And . . . this is what you want in exchange for helping me?"

"Yes. You bring the girl here. You can even take her back afterward, I don't care."

Ahmed felt an odd surge of protection toward Machi. "You don't want another girl? I'm sure I can get you one."

Okinosho gave him a small and patient smile. "No, Ahmed. I want that exact girl. You got her before; you can get her again and bring her here. I am a generous man; I will give you some time."

"Will . . . will she be hurt?" He felt like an idiot asking, but he had to.

A laugh. "You are so upstanding, Alhaji. It surprises me, in your line of work. But no, nothing will happen to her. This is just another assignment, another job for her, you get?" The pastor folded his arms, the gold fabric stretching across his biceps. "Bring her to me and I can take care of your problem for you."

Ahmed's skin felt clammy. "I know I asked before, but what do you want her for?"

The pastor smiled then, and it was like a knife sliding slowly out of its sheath. "Wait and see," he said. "It's not something I want you to miss anyway." He looked down at his watch, thick gold choking his wrist. "Why don't we say by nine tonight. I have service early in the morning."

Ahmed tried to think, but his mind was tangled. It would be easy to get Machi; he could just send Thursday. But there was still a hit out on Kalu, and this silken monster of a man sitting across from him was responsible.

"About my friend—" he began, but his voice dried out in his mouth as Okinosho's eyes snapped up with a look so cold and razored, Ahmed almost felt the skin on his face begin to bleed.

"You dare open your mouth to ask me for something else?" Okinosho's voice was soft, a wire gently looping around Ahmed's throat. "Alhaji, don't try my patience."

Ahmed swallowed hard. "Please. I don't want him to die." Would he beg? Would he tell this man how Kalu held parts of him that Ahmed had never given to anyone else? Would he give Okinosho *that* much of a weapon over him? Ahmed feared that even this plea had exposed more than he would have ever wanted to show to this man.

The pastor stared at him flatly for several long moments. "You are a fool, Alhaji," he finally said. "I will forgive the way you are asking me to ignore the attack committed against a man of God, but I warn you, if you bring it up again, I cannot guarantee further mercy. Do you understand?" There was power in the air, a hovering guillotine, and Ahmed could do nothing but nod in agreement. Okinosho let the corner of his mouth rise up.

"Bring me the girl," he repeated. "And there may yet be salvation in unexpected places."

Ahmed had no idea what he meant, but there was nothing more he could do at this point. Seun's folded body in the trunk of his car was becoming more and more of a problem with each hour that passed. "Can I leave my car here?" he asked. "I will bring the girl."

Okinosho nodded and stood up from his chair, ending the meeting. "We won't touch your car until you've fulfilled your side of this bargain but, yes, you can leave it. I'm sure driving around with it is a little . . . strenuous on you."

"Thank you."

The pastor paused and swung his head slowly toward Ahmed, his eyes glittering. "I beg your pardon?"

Ahmed cringed.

"Thank you, Daddy," he said, his throat thick around the words, his hand shaking.

The pastor unsheathed his smile again.

"Go in peace, my child. We will see you tonight."

fourteen

Thursday walked into Ahmed's house and called out his name. Empty sound echoed back from the white walls. He tapped his fingers against his thigh as he surveyed the parlor, pausing when he saw a phone lying on the floor in a red leather case. He picked it up and turned it over in his hands—it wasn't one of theirs. As if on cue, his own phone vibrated from his pocket and he put his hand up to the Bluetooth device clipped to his ear.

"Ahmed," he said.

"Where are you?" His boss's voice was rough, panic like a deep-set bass thumping through it.

"At the house. I thought you were here. Whose cars are parked outside?"

Ahmed's laugh was shaky. "I'll tell you about that later."

"Looks like they left their phone."

A sharp breath. "Collect the phone. And get rid of the convertible outside the gate."

Thursday immediately became curious but didn't ask any questions. That wasn't his job. "No wahala. What about the G-Wagon inside?"

"Leave it, that one belongs to Ijendu Okoye." Ahmed hesitated. "I need you to go and find the girl."

He already knew who Ahmed was talking about. Since Kalu had left the party, there had been something shaken loose in Ahmed and it was rattling loudly. It was annoying. That's why Thursday hadn't allowed Machi to spend the night at the house; he wanted to get her away from Ahmed before he did anything stupid, like fuck her.

"Find her for what?"

There was silence on the other end of the phone for a while. "I cut a deal with Okinosho," Ahmed finally said.

"Oh, for Kalu?" That was impressive.

Ahmed's silence suddenly filled with guilt. "No, I couldn't—I couldn't sway him on that matter."

Thursday slid the red phone into his pocket and folded his arms. "What could you have made a deal for that's more important than Kalu's life?" he asked, censure thick in his voice.

"Thursday . . . a lot has happened."

"It has," his second agreed. "I spoke to my guys and people are moving on Kalu. I put one of them to watch him, he's supposed to be texting me updates. But you had a chance to deal with Okinosho and you couldn't resolve this? What does he want with the girl?"

"He just wants her for a job." Ahmed sighed on the other end of the line. "If I had tried to push the issue, I might not have made it out of that man's house alive. You know how he is."

Thursday exhaled. Ahmed was right; Okinosho had made bigger men than Ahmed disappear and no one in New Lagos had blinked. "What do you want me to do about Kalu?"

"Check on him at his house on your way to collect the girl. I've tried to call him but his phone seems to be off. I'm going to stop by the garage and pick up another car."

"Okay. I'll get rid of the convertible and the phone, check his house, then find the girl."

"No, keep the phone." Ahmed paused on the other end of the line, then seemed to make a decision. "It has content that could compromise me. I need you to get access to the files and wipe everything, including whatever's on the cloud. If something was sent out, find the people it was sent to."

Thursday raised an eyebrow. "Something?"

Ahmed barked out a harsh laugh. "Oh, you'll know it when you see it, Thursday. Try not to enjoy it too much."

The call ended and Thursday stood quietly for a moment. The red phone was a weight in his pocket, but he would handle it for Ahmed, eat as many secrets as Ahmed needed him to. They had followed each other into unspeakable darkness; they had spilled blood and done cruel, inhumane things for and with each other, and they would do those things again and again if it was necessary. Today felt like one of those days—something really fucked was going on if Okinosho wanted that little girl. Thursday headed back out the door and called Jackson on his way out.

"Bros, how far?"

"I have a job for you."

"I salute."

"Alhaji's house. The red convertible wey park outside. Make am disappear."

Jackson laughed. "Ọ dị egwu," he said. "Two hours. Usual price."

"I'll transfer it into your account."

"All right, oga. Take am easy."

Thursday beeped off his earpiece and headed back to his car.

fifteen

Aima had sat in the back seat of Ahmed's car for all of five minutes before realizing that she was alone there except for the corpse folded into the boot.

She'd reached frantically for the door then, her fingers scrabbling at the handle until she pushed it open and stumbled out onto the driveway. Okinosho's compound was lush and tropical, and Aima felt utterly mad standing there, knowing that Seun was just a few feet away in a metal compartment. She dragged in desperate gulps of air and braced her hands on her knees, her braids falling forward. A security guard gave her an assessing look, then apparently decided she was unimportant as he looked away.

Aima straightened up and wrapped her arms around her stomach, forcing deep breaths. Why had Ijendu brought them here? What could a man of God like Okinosho possibly do to help Ahmed? Sure, there were rumors of him being a womanizer, but no one was perfect and this was Nigeria and he had too much power to fall to temptation now and again—but disposing of a dead body?

She started pacing up and down, trying to forget what Seun had looked like in Ahmed's parlor. How Ijendu could call that an accident was beyond her—unless it was something else, like a BDSM scene gone wrong. There was entirely too much information for Aima to process. That Ahmed was kinky, fine. That he was gay? That was a whole different thing. Kalu would have mentioned it before, would have said something. How could he not have known?

A sharp suspicion ran through her, and Aima stopped dead in her tracks. The only person who took up as much space in Kalu's life as she had . . . was Ahmed. Had always been Ahmed. He had been a part of Kalu's life long before Aima had ever met Kalu. Even when she'd lived with Kalu in Houston, he had spoken of Ahmed as if the man lived down the road from them, his name constantly in Kalu's mouth. Aima had always just seen them as best friends, as close as brothers, and after she and Kalu had moved to New Lagos, Ahmed's presence in their lives had felt not just inevitable but even comfortable.

He'd hugged her tightly the first time they met, like she was being welcomed into a family. He'd toured apartments with them to help them pick out where they would live, commenting on the views from the windows and the security of the estates. Aima had become comfortable calling him when she needed help, a connection, the answer to a question. He had met Ijendu several times and they had gotten along wonderfully—having both her and Kalu's best friends living there had helped Aima so much in adjusting to a new city. In short, Ahmed had been nothing but a friend to her even as he knew she didn't like what he did with his parties. He'd kept that part of himself away and it had felt respectful, like he was bringing the best of himself into the room whenever he was with her and Kalu, whenever they went out for dinner or to an event, whenever he stepped out of his shadows to be respectable in the light.

Had she ever realized that she didn't actually know who Ahmed was when he was alone with Kalu? Or even who Kalu was when Aima left the room and he was there with this man built out of dark secrets? This whole time . . . could they—no, it was impossible. She would have seen something—a stray touch, a longing look between them. Ahmed never reacted when Kalu kissed her in front of him, certainly not with anything close to jealousy. Aima could see his face easily, the fond smile whenever he looked at her and Kalu together. Still, doubt crowded her and elbowed certainty out of the way. Had that been fondness or amusement? Maybe an indulgence because he knew something she didn't. Had she been the third wheel this whole time? Was this why Kalu didn't want to marry her? Because his heart belonged to someone else?

Aima's rambling thoughts were interrupted by Ijendu striding toward her, long legs gleaming in the sun. Her friend looked deeply irritated, and Aima grabbed her arm as soon as Ijendu was close.

"What's going on?" she asked. "Where's Ahmed?"

Ijendu's lips pressed together for a moment. "He's fine, he's with Daddy O. The driver's going to take us home." She groaned in annoyance. "Wait, my car is still at Ahmed's."

"I can't go back there," Aima said immediately. "Please, Ijendu. I take God beg you."

Her friend glanced at her and softened out of her mood. "Fine, I'll send someone to pick it up later." Aima sighed in relief and Ijendu put an arm around her. They both looked at the boot of Ahmed's car and Ijendu shuddered.

"Gross," she said. Aima turned an incredulous stare her way and Ijendu grimaced. "I'm sorry, but it is! You think I wanted to be touching a dead body today? I'm going to need about five hot showers before I feel clean again."

A chauffeured car was pulling up from around the back of the house, and Aima lowered her voice as she and Ijendu started walking toward it. "Ahmed murdered him," she whispered. "I know we can't tell the police, but how am I going to tell Kalu?"

Ijendu stopped in her tracks and grabbed Aima's shoulder. "Babes. You can't tell *anyone*."

"Oh, come on. It's Kalu."

Aima winced as Ijendu's grip tightened.

"I'm so fucking serious right now, Aima. We were never at Ahmed's house and, more important, we were never *here*. Do you get? This is Okinosho we're talking about. You can't say anything, *ever*." Ijendu's eyes were hard and glittering, her mouth set. Aima could barely recognize her.

"But he's your godfather," was all she could manage, her voice confused. "You don't trust him or what?"

Ijendu stared at her blankly, then let go of her shoulder. "Oh my God, Ahmed was right."

That just annoyed Aima. Ever since she and Kalu had moved back, there had been moments when she felt like Ijendu and Ahmed saw them as naïve, as if there was a secret in New Lagos that those two knew but that Aima and Kalu were excluded from. There was never anything said explicitly, just certain hesitations, small smiles wiped away quickly, enough to raise Aima's hackles once in a while. And, yes, it was true that she was more sheltered than they were, especially given Ahmed's work and Ijendu's friends, but it had felt condescending then and it felt condescending now.

"Right about what?" she snapped.

"It doesn't matter. I shouldn't have brought you here in the first place." Ijendu ran a hand over her face. "I'm sorry I dragged you into this, Aima. I should have listened when you said you didn't want to be involved."

Aima growled in the back of her throat. "It's a little too late for that now, isn't it?" she snapped. *"What aren't you telling me?"*

Ijendu stepped in close and spoke in a low harsh whisper. "My godfather isn't the man you think he is and that's all you need to know. We shouldn't even be talking like this in his compound. Like I said, forget everything today, for your own fucking good." The car pulled up by them, and the driver stepped out and opened the back door. Ijendu gave him a brief smile and ducked her head as she entered the back seat. "Get in the car, Aima."

"Wait, but—"

Ijendu stuck her head out and this time her face was unmistakably tense, her voice lashing. *"Get in the fucking car."*

Aima bit down her words and obeyed, too aware of the body sharing the driveway with them and the edged strangeness of the world she had entered when they had crossed Okinosho's gates.

"We can't speak about this again," Ijendu said. "I can't explain anymore, okay? It's enough."

She was afraid, Aima realized, and she had never seen Ijendu afraid. That immediately silenced the arguments she had been about to make.

"Okay," she replied, taking her friend's hand. "I understand. None of it happened. It's okay."

Ijendu nodded and looked out of the window but kept her hand in Aima's. The driver took them back out through the gates, and Aima sat there, reeling from all the worlds she was ricocheting through. Ijendu had never shouted at her before, talk less of swearing at her.

Their sinful night seemed irrelevant now, after the horror of Seun, after Aima had made her peace with God. *This was what salvation could look like*, she thought, being reminded that she didn't really know the woman whose hand was in hers, that secrets were filling up the back seat of the car they sat in. Sometimes God showed you which paths to turn away from no matter how much love was there, showed you how a little darkness could lead to being swallowed by a devouring night. Aima knew with every fiber of her being that she didn't want this—bodies and death, lies and men terrible enough to make or hide corpses. One day, maybe, she would be able to tell Kalu what had happened today, make him see that they could make a life in the light together, a *cleaner* life. They would stand in front of God and make everything all right again. And it would be worth it.

It would have to be.

sixteen

Kalu wondered if he was getting kidnapped.

Felix wasn't driving as wildly as he had before, but he was still reckless on the road and over South-South Bridge, as if neither of them could die. Kalu had tried asking where they were going, but his words were torn away by the wind ripping past them and Felix couldn't hear him. Eventually, the motorcycle pulled up in front of an unassuming gated compound deep in the lowland.

A short gateman stuck his head out, a chewing stick rotating in a corner of his mouth. His eyes sharpened with recognition when he saw Felix, and he grunted and began opening the gate. Felix gunned the engine and the bike lazily pulled into the compound. Kalu and the gateman exchanged wary unfamiliar glances. Kalu could feel paranoia crawling over his skin like a thousand cockroaches, skittering tiny legs of panic. Okinosho's reach was beyond anything he could imagine. Kalu had no idea if it extended here, this quiet yard with ixora bushes lining a gray house, sand underfoot as they dismounted the bike. Felix slipped the gateman some naira notes from the bundle that Kalu had given him, then jerked his head toward the door. "Let's go," he said to Kalu.

They walked through the door into a lobby that was empty except for a large mirror hanging on the wall in an old frame with chipped edges. Kalu flinched at his reflection. His eyes looked haunted, ringed with shadows, dull with fear. Sweat stained his shirt and his shoulders were drawn tight. Felix looked feline in comparison, relaxed and sharp as he walked with easy strides to a staircase that spiraled downstairs. "This way," he said.

Kalu hesitated. "We're going into a basement?"

Felix grinned. "Something like that." He started disappearing into the floor, one step at a time, not waiting to see if Kalu would follow him, not bothering to reassure or explain. Kalu looked around the lobby and pulled his phone out of his pocket, pressing the power button as if that would resurrect it. The screen glitched brightly back at him and died again.

"Are you coming?" Felix's voice called out from the bottom of the staircase.

Kalu took a deep breath and went down the stairs, his eyes adjusting as the light moved from a basic fluorescence to a simmering sinuous red, as if filtered through bloody glass. Felix was waiting in front of a door blocked out by a curtain of crystal beads, shimmering unholy, lengths and lengths of them singing against one another. His eyes were bright and excited, as if he was bringing Kalu a present.

"This is the place where no one is going to look for me?" Kalu asked, arching an eyebrow. "What's in there? Ritualists?" He kept his voice dry and level, hiding the fear wrapped around his ribs.

Felix barked out a short laugh. "Better," he said, and reached through the crystals, opening the door. A wave of bass-heavy music poured out, a wall of sound slamming into them, Yoruba drums and Lagbaja's voice singing. The sound of strikes against goatskin pulled at Kalu's chest, beat by beat, ricocheting inside his head. Colored strobe lights pierced the smoky room and Kalu squinted as he walked in behind Felix. Silver poles stretched from the ceiling to the floor on velvet platforms scattered around the place. Naked girls in obscenely high platform heels were spinning on them, legs flung open or curled around the poles, vibrating into a pointed foot, thigh meat jiggling under glistening skin.

"You brought me to a fucking strip club?" Kalu hissed, but Felix didn't hear him. The boy was slapping palms with some other man, bumping shoulders, all grins and welcome. A dark-skinned dancer flipped a head of bubblegum-pink hair and fluttered neon-green eyelashes as she bent over then snapped back up, her legs an impossible length as she ran long sparkly nails over them. Kalu caught her eye and lowered his as soon as she gave him a knowing, feral smile. He kept following Felix as they wound through the club, the smell of shisha and perfume heavy in the air.

Kalu thought he'd been to every strip club in the city, Ahmed made sure of that, but he'd never known about this place, never even heard rumors or whispers. And there was money here, messy heaps of five-thousand-naira notes lying on the dancers' stages even as their assistants tried to scoop them up into bags as fast as the customers were spraying them. Surprisingly, there were no foreigners—no Lebanese men with slick shiny hair, no sunburned Europeans ogling the deep rich skin of the dancers like they did at every other strip club Kalu had been to. It was only Nigerian music playing, no trap, no rock 'n' roll, just a Lagbaja song sliding into

Asake. One of the seating areas was filled with Northerners in embroidered robes and covered heads, holding gold money guns that spat out currency notes in clouds of expensive paper. Felix leaned over their table to bump knuckles with a thin amber-colored man with a hooked nose. Kalu watched as the boy slipped a bag of fine white powder to them, then a waitress with long braids led him and Felix to empty seats, brushing a kiss against Felix's cheek before she left. Felix plopped into the leather seat and Kalu slid in next to him, leaning over to yell in his ear.

"What is this place?"

A corner of Felix's mouth tugged up as he leaned toward Kalu. "Somewhere for those people who don't want to be found." His eyes dragged away as two dancers came over to them, limbs snaking to the music, eyes hooded and promising. Felix reached out to one of them, pulling her hand till she tumbled into his lap, her red mouth open and laughing. The second dancer leaned into Kalu, her breasts oiled and golden in a copper demi bra. "What do you want, Daddy?" she whispered into his ear, and Kalu winced.

"One second," he said to her apologetically, turning away to get Felix's attention. The boy gave him an impatient look as the dancer in his lap nuzzled at his neck.

"Bros, what is it? You're safe here."

"I need to borrow your phone."

Felix rolled his eyes and pulled an iPhone from his pocket. "That's extra."

Kalu paused, a frown pulling into his face as he stared at the keypad. "I . . . I don't know the number off head."

The boy gave him an incredulous stare. "Are you serious?"

Kalu couldn't believe it himself. He spoke to Ahmed several times a week, but the man changed his number often and always called Kalu from the new one, so Kalu had never kept track of the morphing digits. "Who knows anyone's number these days?" he said weakly.

The dancer in Felix's lap giggled and gave Kalu a pitying look, as if he was the biggest mugu she'd ever seen but he just didn't know it yet. "Email them," she suggested. "Shey you know their email at least?"

Kalu could have kissed her for the suggestion. The other dancer slid her hands up his back and started kneading his shoulders. He was too stressed to even try and stop her, his head buzzing and his hands numb. How often did Ahmed check his email? Pretty frequently, and if his notifications were turned on, he'd see it immediately. "Thank you," he said, and Felix rolled his eyes, sipping on his drink.

"You owe me *so* much money, bros," he said, before turning back to the girl who was now straddling him, her hips wining in slow circles.

Kalu pulled up an incognito browser page and logged into his email, tilting the screen away from the girl working on his shoulders. He started to write a quick note to Ahmed, but then he realized that the only way he had to get out of here was on Felix's bike, and from the look of things, Felix wasn't planning on leaving anytime soon. He tapped the boy on the shoulder. "I need the address here."

Felix laughed and didn't even look at him, his gaze fixated on the dancer, who was unhooking her jeweled bra in exaggerated slow motion. "It's a private club," he said. "Members only."

"Someone needs to come and collect me," Kalu explained.

"Well, then, he needs to be a member."

Kalu took a deep breath and reminded himself that this boy just saved his life. "How does someone become a member?"

This time, both the dancers laughed with Felix. "It's five million naira," Felix said, leaning back as the girl planted her hand in his chest, her back arching as she pushed him.

"As if you paid that kind of money," Kalu replied. "Be serious."

"I'm being serious. My own was a . . . special case."

"A drug dealer discount, abi?"

Felix shrugged and pinched the girl's nipple, grinning as she hissed in air. "Whatever you want to call it. But your friend must sha show up with money if he wants the address. Otherwise, if he comes here without it . . ." He left the end of the sentence as empty as a noose, a bullet casing.

"Money is not his problem. What's the address?"

The boy told it to him and Kalu typed it into the email, keeping it brief, not wanting to mention Okinosho's name in case the girl saw it. The man from last night put out a hit on me. They came to my house. My phone died. You need to come and collect me. 54A Ubancheleke Avenue. Hurry up, please. You'll need to pay 5m to enter. Long story. I'll pay you back. Send me your number so I can call you. There was a whistle as the message was sent, and Kalu tried to return the phone to Felix but the boy waved him off.

"Keep it for when they reply. And stop disturbing me!"

Kalu slid the phone into his pocket and exhaled a shaky breath. Ahmed would see it. Ahmed would come, and everything would be fine. The girl behind him casually slung her leg over his shoulder, the point of her stiletto striking the leather of the seat between his thighs. "Do you have time for me now?" she purred. Her skin smelled like rose oil. "We can play while you wait," she added, and Kalu almost toppled into the smudge of her voice.

Everything else hurt with an insistent throbbing that started in his heart and radiated outward. There was nothing else he could do until Ahmed came, and as she slid over him, flinging off her bra, her breasts swaying in front of his eyes, Kalu found himself wanting so desperately to just forget everything else for a moment. She slid her long fingers to her chest and cupped her breasts, presenting them to him, straight black hair falling to her waist, dark brown eyes watching his. Kalu grabbed her hips and her flesh was warm, flooding his palms with fullness. She ground her pelvis into his and threw her neck back, her throat a dark skim of glory before him. He could feel an erection start and his throat thickened. It would be so easy to forget. She pressed her body to his as if he was everything she'd been waiting for. "Shey you have time?" she whispered.

"Yes," he answered, his voice raspy. "I have time."

seventeen

S ouraya didn't want to pick up the phone when she saw it was Ahmed calling. He'd dropped her off at her hotel just hours before, still apologetic but without an explanation, and still with those iced off eyes.

It didn't matter. She had ordered room service and the hotel staff had set it up at the foot of her king-size bed, metal domes covering the plates and cutlery wrapped in linen. After they left, she opened the domes, putting them aside in a rough stack. The plates were filled with fried yam and plantain, pepper stew, snails and gizzards, skewers of suya, two bowls of crème brûlée. Souraya turned on the television and watched a reality show while picking at the plates, the blue silk of her dress crumpled around her in the bed. When Ahmed called, she stared at her phone until it stopped ringing. He called again, and after a few moments, Souraya answered.

"What do you want?" she snapped.

"Tell me your room number," he said. "I'm here."

"What?"

"I'm at the elevators. Tell me where you are."

Souraya told him her room number out of shock more than anything.

"See you in a bit," he said, then he hung up. Souraya looked down at her phone, her brain moving slowly in confusion. Why had he come back? Why did she let him come up? Was she going to let him in or would she just yell at him in the corridor and send him away?

She reached for a spoon and cracked the bubbled sugar in her bowl of crème brûlée, sinking the metal curve into the soft pale yellow below. It melted on her tongue, a smooth ephemeral, crystals of sharp sweetness breaking between her teeth. On the TV screen, an enthusiastic girl was jerking her shoulders around as she gave a horrible audition, the judges staring aghast. She was moving like someone who didn't worry about the faces around her. Souraya thought she had a point.

There was a knock on her door, and she paused the reality show, putting down the bowl before sliding off the bed and padding barefoot across the room. She peered through the spyhole and Ahmed's jawline fell into view, his head turning as he looked down the corridor. He knocked again, calling her name softly this time. Souraya leaned her forehead against the wood, sighing as she unlocked the door, the latch clicking under her fingers. She pulled the door open, and Ahmed looked at her. His eyes were alive again, if a little shattered. They stared at each other without speaking for a few moments.

"May I come in?" he finally asked.

Souraya stepped aside so he could pass, then closed the door and folded her arms across her chest. Ahmed looked at the plates of food heaped on the tray.

"I'm sorry about lunch," he said, trailing his fingers against the edge of her bed.

"It's fine," Souraya said, finally hunting down her voice. "You didn't eat either. Help yourself."

Ahmed inclined his head in gratitude but didn't touch the food. He stalked through her suite, his eyes cataloging everything. It felt a little proprietary and it annoyed her, even as she noted the tightness of his shoulders and the way his hands intermittently shook.

"Why did you come back?"

He looked surprised at her question. "Why wouldn't I?"

Souraya growled softly. "If you leave, maybe you should stay gone."

Ahmed stopped pacing and narrowed his eyes, sliding his hands into his pockets.

"Are you going to ask another promise of me?"

This time, she was the one surprised. Was she going to shove him away again? It would be the smart thing to do. Ola would scream at her to do it.

"I don't like inconsistency," she replied.

Sorrow crossed his face, so naked and clear that it shocked Souraya to her core.

"Ahmed?" She took a step toward him, but he stepped away.

"What can I even offer you?" he asked, almost to himself. His shoulders bowed forward.

Warning crept over the back of her neck. "What happened, Ahmed?"

He shook his head and when he looked at her, his eyes vacillated between wild and cold. "First things first," he said. "I'll always come back for you, Souraya. Unless bound by a promise that stops me."

She waved a hand dismissively. "Something happened after you dropped me off. Tell me, Ahmed."

A raw laugh spilled from his mouth, and he leaned against her bathroom door. "You know, after Joburg, I thought about this city when I thought about us."

Souraya frowned. "Why?"

"Because you hate this place. Because I *am* this place. You did the right thing forcing me away." He pushed off the door and came toward her. "Otherwise I would have tracked you down, darling. I *know* I'll corrupt you and still, here I am."

Ahmed stopped right in front of her and raised his hands to cup her face in his palms. Souraya sighed at the contact, the sound slipping out of her mouth unbidden. He bent his head to brush his mouth against hers and she swayed into him, her hands finding his biceps.

"Ahmed," she whispered. "Stop trying to distract me."

He kissed her deeper and backed her up against the wall, his hips pressing against hers. "I did something terrible," he said against her lips. "That's what happened after I left."

"You've done many terrible things."

"And you don't care?"

"I didn't say that." She kissed down the column of his throat and her body thrilled as he slid a hand up her thigh, under her dress. It had been so long since she'd felt his touch and Souraya was surprised at how badly she craved it, how much she wanted to hear the sounds of wonder and gratitude that he made each time he was inside her. *"Ahmed."*

His hand dipped between her legs and her back arched, a hungry cry crawling out of her mouth.

"Yes," he crooned. "I missed you, darling."

Souraya fought to gather her mind as he stroked her. "Tell me what you did."

Ahmed's hand stilled and his breath passed over her hair.

"Why do you always try to see me?" he murmured. "Why won't you look away?"

"I'm not afraid of you. I'll never be afraid of you." He leaned back slightly to look at her properly, his fingers sliding again beneath her panties. Souraya could feel how slick and ready she was, how her hips were writhing against him. "Tell me," she insisted, gasping.

His jaw tightened and he placed his mouth next to her ear, thrusting two fingers into her as he spoke. "I killed someone today, darling."

Souraya cried out as he slammed his fingers in and out, exactly as rough as she liked it. Pleasure stretched taut over her body even as her mind fought to understand what he'd said. Ahmed was still talking.

"He was trying to blackmail me. I fucked him in my living room and I choked him till he stopped breathing. Is that what you wanted to hear, Sou? Are you happy now?" Ahmed was holding her up as he finger fucked her; Souraya's legs had gone weak as his wrist worked. She moaned as the images Ahmed laid out for her came to life in her head.

"You choked him . . . while fucking him?" Her voice was ragged, her mouth scraping against his neck.

Ahmed swore violently and pulled her tighter to him. "How are you so *goddamn* wet, darling? Didn't you hear what I just said?"

She'd heard him perfectly well. Souraya dropped a hand to the front of his trousers and pulled down his zipper. He was, as she expected, hard as iron in her hand. Ahmed hissed out a desperate breath.

"Sou, for fuck's sake. Make me stop. *Tell me to stop.*"

She let out a small laugh. "Don't put that on me. Stop if you want."

He stared at her like she'd lost her mind. "I killed a man, Sou."

"It wasn't the first time."

Ahmed shook his head, his face solemn. "It's the first time I've done it with my bare hands."

"Hmm." She stroked his erection, and he made a tangled sound. "Does that make a difference? Dead is dead."

"*Sou.*"

"Or is it because you were fucking him while you did it?" His erection jumped in her hand and Souraya gave him a sharp grin. Ahmed slid his fingers out of her and lifted them to her mouth, watching with hooded eyes as she licked them clean.

"How can you ask me that?" He leaned his forehead against hers.

Souraya reached into his pocket with her free hand, finding the condom he always kept there. Ahmed's mouth softened as she tore off the wrapper, and he dragged in rough breaths when she rolled the latex over him.

"What are you doing?"

She ignored his questions. "How did it feel?" He was pushing her dress up past her hips, skimming past her sheathed blade like it was nothing, shoving her legs open with his knee. Something close to anger pulled at his face. Souraya kept pushing because it felt *good*. "You liked it, didn't you, baby? It made you feel like a god? To hurt him like that?"

Ahmed grabbed her hair and entered her in one hard stroke, cutting her question short as she screamed. He slid out and pushed in again and Souraya let her head fall back, her body supported by his greedy hands, her mouth cracked open in a laugh.

"Just like that," she gasped out. "Fuck me like you fucked him, baby."

"Fuck you," he bit out. *"Fuck you, Sou."*

She laughed again and felt him lose control, something he'd never done with her before. He thrust into her so roughly that her head slammed against the wall, over and over again, his fingers bruising her skin, his teeth scoring her shoulder. A warped victory filled her chest. Ahmed wasn't fucking the broken girl he'd found in a penthouse. He was fucking the woman who'd looked at him, who hadn't looked away, and finally, it felt *real*. When he circled her throat with his long fingers, Souraya shuddered and came, her voice winging through the room. Ahmed called on the name of God as his orgasm hit, and they both collapsed to the floor.

There was nothing but the sound of both of them panting for a few moments, then Ahmed slid out of her and gathered her in his arms, dropping kisses on her head. Souraya could feel him trembling.

"Who are you?" he murmured. "Who the fuck are you?"

She let herself be held, inhaling the scent of his sweat, and she didn't answer. Neither of them brought up what he'd confessed to.

Finally, Souraya lifted her face to look at him. "What about your friend?"

"I'm not sure yet. My calls aren't going through." He reached down to his pocket and pulled out his phone to check it. Souraya trailed a finger across his chest, her mind scattered in a few directions, only returning to him when he swore softly.

"What is it?"

"Messages from Kalu and Okinosho." Tight lines pulled at his lips. "Kalu's somewhere in the lowland, apparently."

"And Okinosho?"

"Hasn't been able to find Kalu so he wants me to deliver him myself. Tonight."

Souraya grimaced. "Will you?"

Ahmed sighed. "I have to. Okinosho's now claiming Kalu won't be harmed. I have to keep him safe."

"Can you trust the pastor?"

"Not sure there's a choice here." He smiled sadly at her. "Maybe your friend came through."

Souraya sat up on an elbow. "That would explain it. That's good, right?"

Ahmed nodded, his eyes eating in her face. "Come with me," he said. "To pick up Kalu."

"I don't know, Ahmed." It was a bad idea. Souraya had no business flirting with this world, no business with a man as dangerous as Ahmed Soyoye, not if she wanted to keep the life she'd built for herself. But she'd already fucked him against the wall and said unthinkable things in his ear and none of it had felt unfamiliar. God help her, but maybe she was more of this city than she wanted to admit. She should run. She should get on a plane and get out while she still could, before this man wrapped more of his shadowed tendrils around her with such terrible tenderness.

"Darling. *Please*."

Souraya closed her eyes as her resolve crumbled.

"Fine," she said. "I'll go with you."

Saturday, 7:31 PM

The drive down to the lowland had been quiet, just the two of them in another of Ahmed's cars, listening to Aşa sing over the speakers. Halfway down, Ahmed reached out his hand across the space between them, and Souraya took it in hers. They held hands as the city draped past their windows, Ahmed's palm wrapped warmly around hers.

When they pulled up to the address Kalu had emailed them, Ahmed raised Souraya's hand to his mouth, kissing the tendons that ran along the back of it into her fingers.

"Stay inside the car," he said. "I'll be right back."

He stepped out before she could say anything, and the door slammed shut. Souraya watched through the windshield as Ahmed walked up to the gate and spoke to the gateman, a short and aggressive figure with curled shoulders and gesticulating arms. They both took out their phones, and Ahmed typed on his for a while, tilting the screen toward the gateman, who peered through the iron bars, pointing and shaking his head. Ahmed nodded and typed some more, then showed it to the man again, who nodded this time, then waited and checked his own phone after a few moments. He nodded tersely and Ahmed slid a small bundle of cash through the gate. The man on the other side finally broke into a kola-nut-stained smile and started to open the gate. Ahmed saluted, smiling back, and returned to the car, climbing in beside Souraya.

"What was that?" she asked.

"It's a private club," Ahmed said, shaking his head. "The cost of the address is a five-million-naira membership. I had to transfer the money to their account immediately."

"Really? Just to pick up Kalu? You shouldn't have paid."

"Oh, they make sure you do once you're here. There's a squad of soldiers over there on the side." Ahmed gestured with his head as they drove into the compound and Souraya looked. There were about ten soldiers lounging on benches against the wall, their machine guns leaning against their legs, bottles of beer at their feet.

"Ah," she said.

"Exactly." He parked the car next to a small motorcycle and killed the engine. "So now we go get Kalu. The gateman said to go downstairs from the ground floor."

Souraya frowned. "A basement?"

"Looks like someone took the meaning of underground quite literally." They disembarked from the car and Ahmed took her hand in his again. "Thank you for coming with me."

She smiled up at him. "It's no problem."

A private club was nothing, certainly not the level of dangerous she'd expected. They walked in past the mirror, down the stairs, into the bleeding light, and past the crystal curtain. Souraya laughed when the music hit them and she realized where they were.

"Oh, it's *that* kind of club."

Ahmed sighed. "Only Kalu would be hiding out in a secret strip club. *Unbelievable.*"

They wound through the place together, Ahmed searching faces through the shifting lights and smoke. A few minutes in, he squeezed her hand.

"Found him!" he shouted above the music. He pointed to a broad man sitting with his legs spread open. A dancer was on the ground between the man's knees, sliding up his body as he stared down at her, his face round and his eyes hooded.

Souraya leaned closer to Ahmed. "That's Kalu?"

"That's the fucker."

Ahmed left her side, striding over to snap his fingers in front of Kalu's face. Kalu looked up, startled, then his face dissolved into such delighted relief and joy that something in Souraya's chest twinged to witness it. He leapt up, gently pushing the dancer aside, and embraced Ahmed with such force that the two of them staggered backward, both laughing. Ahmed grabbed Kalu's head in his hands and shouted something at him, something Souraya couldn't hear, but she could see the fire in Kalu's eyes, and the feeling in her chest resolved into clarity.

He loved Ahmed.

She felt her body still as she looked at them. Her heartbeat slowed and steadied, everything oozing with sticky time. The way Kalu's eyes searched Ahmed's, his hand coming up to grip the back of Ahmed's head, the way his eyes closed as they embraced again, the twisting of his face when Ahmed couldn't see it when it was pressed against Ahmed's shoulder and neck.

He was *in love* with Ahmed.

Ahmed hadn't said anything to her about this, not even when she asked. Maybe he didn't know. Maybe they had been together the whole time and Ahmed hadn't mentioned it because it was none of her business.

Someone tapped on her shoulder. Souraya turned, frowning, and a thin man with amber skin and a hooked nose smiled at her, crow's feet crowding at his eyes. His eyes were narrow almonds, black, cutting through her. An alarm rang very faintly in the back of her head.

"What is it?" she snapped, her spikes up. His smile grew wider when he heard her voice.

"I thought it couldn't be you," he said, and for some reason, bile churned in her belly at the rolling melody of his voice. "After so many years."

"Do I know you?" She made the words as sharp and condescending as she could, pumping impossibility into the question.

The stranger tsked and made a sad face. "Ah," he said. "You don't remember?" He gave a sudden sharp smile. "Zainab, *Zainab*. You disappoint me."

Souraya lost all the air in her lungs. How could he—how did he know her name, the old name, the *lost* name? His words echoed in her head, their volume ballooning, and the club warped and collapsed around her, Souraya was spinning backward, backward, to a bedroom too long ago, blood on the back of her hand where she'd wiped her mouth, whimpers in her air, her twelve-year-old voice unfamiliar from dust and age, and in front of her, this man, this man whose name her brain had mercifully scrubbed clean; he had been one out of so many, but she had been choking, desperate for air, her nose smashed against his pubic hair while she flailed and struggled with his hand on the back of her head, and when he finally let her go, he'd hit her across the face and her mouth had bled and he'd said the same thing then, to little her. *Zainab, Zainab. You disappoint me.*

Souraya stumbled back in the strip club, vomit in the back of her mouth as he visibly shuddered with pleasure at her recognition. She reached out and grabbed Ahmed's arm. He turned, glancing from her to the man, already suspicious.

"We need to leave," Souraya hissed, her voice tight. "We need to leave now."

"Zainab," the man said. "You don't need to run away from me."

He seized her arm, and time slowed. From the corner of her eye, Souraya saw Ahmed coil swiftly, a snake about to strike, but she was faster now; she wasn't the same child they'd broken in. Her right hand slid up her thigh underneath the blue silk to the sheath buckled to her upper thigh. She drew the whisper-thin blade in the same breath as she stepped close to the man, sliding an arm around him. His breath smelled like rotting sin.

"*Shaitan*," she hissed. "May your soul burn in Jahannam."

She drove the blade into his side, into his kidney, she hoped. His eyes widened and his breath caught in his throat. Souraya twisted the blade, pushing it in to the hilt, then helped him into a seat, his shocked eyes following her, screams delayed in his throat. She turned to Ahmed.

"Walk out of here with me right now, don't run."

It would take a while for someone to notice the blood streaming down the leather underneath the man or the hilt of the knife that had been left in him. Ahmed's eyes were pits filled with storms and he was radiating with rage, but he didn't ask questions. He put his hand on Kalu's shoulder. Kalu tossed wads of cash to the girl who had been dancing on him and to a young yellow-eyed boy in the seat next to him, then the three of them walked out of the club, got into Ahmed's car, and drove out of the compound.

As soon as they reached a main road, Ahmed accelerated and the car hurtled along, leaping away from the club. It was only then that Souraya started sobbing, her hand cradled in her lap, the man's blood staining her silk dress. Kalu leaned forward from the back seat, and Ahmed reached a hand across the gear shift, cradling her face.

"It's okay, strange girl," Kalu said. He was drunk but worried about her. "Whatever happened, it's okay now."

"I have you," Ahmed said, taking his eyes off the road for her. "You're safe, darling. I have you."

"Take me to my hotel," she gasped between sobs.

"I'm not leaving you alone," Ahmed replied. "We have to take Kalu to the pastor's house."

Kalu jerked back. "Wait, what the fuck?"

"He's not going to hurt you. I cut a deal."

Souraya didn't care anymore. There was a screaming twelve-year-old inside her head. She jerked away from Ahmed's hand and screamed.

"Take me back to my hotel!"

Ahmed set his jaw. "I will not leave you alone." His voice was calm and firm, as if she wasn't a knife short of stabbing him as well if he didn't take her back.

"I'll call Ola. You save your friend." Souraya felt like her skin was boiling on her. She tried a different tactic. "Please, Ahmed. I need to take a shower."

Ahmed looked at her hands, noticing the blood for the first time. "Who was that man?"

Souraya turned flat eyes to him. "Someone who hurt me a long time ago."

He glanced away from the road again so he could look at her, then took her hand in his, ignoring the blood.

"Okay," he said. "You did the right thing, darling."

Her face crumpled and she knifed over in her seat, sobs tearing out of her. Her inner thigh felt abandoned without her blade. Kalu glanced between the two of them, sober now after the mention of the pastor.

"Pull over, Ahmed," he ordered. "I'll drive. You hold her in the back."

Souraya looked up at the suggestion. "I'm fine," she lied. "I'm fine; it's fine."

Ahmed swerved and the car's tires spun in the sand at the edge of the road. He unbuckled his seat belt and parked the car, he and Kalu opening their doors. Souraya couldn't stop shaking no matter how hard she tried, no matter how hard she ordered her body to get its shit together. When Ahmed opened her door and pulled her out, she didn't have the strength to fight him on it. He helped her into the back seat and closed the door behind them as Kalu buckled himself into the driver's seat. Ahmed wrapped his arms around

Souraya as the car pulled back onto the road, and she sobbed against his chest while he stroked her hair. "It's okay," he whispered. "I have you, darling. You did the right thing."

"You don't understand," she said, the words bubbling out between tears. "I hope I killed him."

Ahmed laughed and the sound was terrible and cold.

"I know," he said. "You did the right thing."

eighteen

Ola had just come out of the shower in her hotel room when Souraya called her.

"Hey, babe, where are you?" she asked, cradling the phone between her ear and shoulder. Static bled through the line, then a hiccup and a choked sob. Ola dropped the towel she was holding, her heart speeding up. "Souraya? What's wrong? Where are you?"

She pulled on a wrap dress as she spoke, slipping her feet into pony-hair slides and tying the dress closed against her damp body, then grabbing her purse. "I'll come and get you, just tell me where you are."

"Downstairs," Souraya said. Ola could barely hear her. "In Ahmed's car."

Ola took her hotel key and whirled out of the door. "What did he do to you? I'll fucking kill him."

"Not him . . . he didn't do anything . . . bring water. It's all over my hands."

Ola frowned in the elevator as it dropped her to the lobby floor. She had no idea what her friend was talking about, but she took a liter bottle of water from the reception desk and walked outside. "I'm outside, love. Where are you?"

A black Benz was parked haphazardly in one of the spots in front of the hotel, and a dark-skinned man in a white tunic was waving at her. Ola walked over quickly, and he stepped forward to meet her.

"I'm Ahmed," he said. "She's in the back." There was blood smeared on his clothes and his hands. Ola said nothing to him, bending instead to look inside the car. Her chest loosened the grip it'd had on her when she saw Souraya inside, her face streaked with tears, her hands covered in patchy blood. Ola put her phone away and reached her arms out.

"I'm here, habibti. I'm here."

Souraya recoiled. "I don't want to get it all over you."

"That's okay. Look, I brought the water. We can wash it off."

Ahmed was hovering, concern clouding off him. Ola couldn't look at him; she didn't trust her temper. One day. It had been only *one day* back here, and this man had taken Souraya somewhere, and this had happened. She held Souraya's hands gently over the edge of the car and helped her wash them clean. There were small bloodstains on her dress, but those were minor; they could get upstairs without drawing attention. Ola took Souraya's wet hands in hers.

"Let's go, habibti. We'll wash up and get you out of these clothes upstairs." Souraya let her guide her out of the car, and Ola put an arm around her. Some other guy was in the driver's seat, exchanging looks with Ahmed, but Ola didn't give a fuck about either of them.

"I have to go," Ahmed said. "Sou. I'll call you later, darling."

Ola glared at him. "You've done enough. Leave her alone."

He looked taken aback. "I—"

Ola bared her teeth, hissing at him, and Ahmed stepped back in the face of her anger. The man in the car leaned out of the window. "She's going to be fine, Ahmed. Come on."

"Listen to your friend," Ola snapped, throwing the words over her shoulder as she led Souraya away. "Don't you people have a date with the pastor to keep?"

She didn't look back to see how Ahmed reacted, but she heard the car drive away as she and Souraya walked into the hotel lobby. Ola took them straight to the elevators, then into Souraya's room. Once the door closed behind them, everything felt a little better. Souraya seemed to come alive a little, if only to rip the dress off her body and run the shower. Ola followed her into the bathroom and sat on the toilet lid as her friend finished undressing and started to wash whatever had happened off her. She didn't seem hurt—the blood must not have been hers. Ola looked down at the items strewn on the floor—the silk of the dress, gold armbands, lace underwear, the thigh harness. No. Wait. She did a double take. The *empty* thigh harness.

"Sou . . . where's your knife?"

Souraya laughed, but it was hollow. "Hopefully in some motherfucker's kidney," she said. It was as if the water was making her harder, scabbing up the soft pile of hurt she'd been in the car.

"Who was it?"

Her friend paused in the shower, soapy water running off her flanks. "Did you know I lived in New Lagos when I was a kid?"

"Yeah, you told me. After you left the East, before you left the country."

"Right. I was eleven, twelve. It was a man who . . . who knew me then. He did things to me for a long, long time before I got away."

"Ah."

Ola sighed and nodded. She knew that story intimately, that anger. Once, Okinosho had helped hunt one of those men as a gift for her. They'd found him and taken him to a riverbank near Calabar where he'd retired. Okinosho had given Ola a gun, and she'd wept as she pressed the barrel to the man's forehead, his little panicked animal grunts coming through the gag, but she hadn't been able to do it, squeeze the trigger. It was one of Okinosho's bodyguards who had taken it from her and blown a hole through the back of the man's skull just when his eyes were filling with hope that he might live. Ola had found that this part she could handle. That part she could watch, the warm spray against her clothes and skin, Okinosho's maniacal laughter. Their sex that night had been incredible.

"I'm sorry, Sou," she said. "We'll be going home soon. It's just one more day."

Souraya shook her head, looking hunted. "I'm flying back in the morning as soon as I can get a flight."

"Babe, I don't know if you should be traveling alone like this."

"*I can't be here anymore.*"

Ola pressed her fingertips to the bridge of her nose. "I'm going to kill that Ahmed guy."

"It's not his fault." Souraya turned off the water and reached for a towel. Her face was still now, smooth, detached. "I should never have listened to you."

Ola was confused. "To *me?*"

"You're the one who convinced me to come home." Souraya dried herself off quickly and pulled on a robe. Her voice sounded wooden. "I said I didn't want to. I said this place is *rotten* and I had no business entering my leg into it again."

"Oh, Sou."

Ola wasn't even angry at her. Poor thing. She'd had to stab a nightmare from her childhood, perhaps even kill him. If someone dragged Ola back to memories she'd worked a lifetime to forget, she would be unspooling too, probably even worse than her friend.

"This isn't my fault, and it isn't yours either," she said. "You were never supposed to get caught up in all this shit with Ahmed and Okinosho."

Souraya didn't seem to be listening to her.

"I should never have come back here," she was saying. "I need to pack."

She walked out of the bathroom and Ola stared after her, unsure of how to help. She could feel that Souraya was a beat away from turning on her and blaming her for everything. It was an expected reaction—sometimes it was hard to sit with the consequences of your choices.

Her purse vibrated, and Ola reached in for her phone. Okinosho was texting her, furious. Ahmed was late and the pastor was pissed that Ola wasn't there either.

"Fuck," she said softly. He was a terror when he was angry, and he might change his mind at any point about the agreement they'd made, the one Ola had set up because Souraya asked her to, for Ahmed and his stupid friend. Ola had no problem with that agreement collapsing. Ahmed's friend could die for all she cared, but Thomas was a client best kept happy. His pleasure was worth a *lot* of money.

She stepped into the bedroom where Souraya was pulling on sweats, airplane clothes.

"What are you doing?"

Souraya shrugged. "Might just go to the airport early and see if I can find a flight."

Ola nodded and glanced down at her phone. He was still texting angrily. "Okinosho wants me to come over. That thing to help your friend. But I can stay here, I don't mind."

Souraya flapped a hand, not looking up. "No, go. Save him. Your guy will still kill him if you don't help."

Ola didn't want to leave her, but it wouldn't take long. She could come right back. "Okay, but I'll make it quick, I promise." Souraya said nothing, just pulled out her suitcase and unzipped it. Ola walked over and grabbed her by the shoulders, forcing Souraya to look at her.

"You can be as mad at me or at everyone as you want. But *I love you*. Do not fucking leave for the airport before I come back or I will literally kill you. Got it?"

Souraya nodded sheepishly, her stance softening. Ola hugged her tightly.

"That motherfucker deserved it," she whispered. "It's going to be okay. You'll be home soon. I'll help you find a flight back."

Souraya sniffled. "Okay," she said, and hugged Ola back.

Saturday, 9:27 PM

When Ola reached the pastor's house, Okinosho had been in his office, seething loudly. He tried to get aggressive with her, but Ola had slapped him across the face, then shoved him into his chair, pulling up her dress. She rode him until he came, her nails cutting into his throat, then he calmed down. Ahmed had arrived shortly after. The pastor had him enter alone, and though Ahmed's eyes had flickered to Ola standing behind Okinosho's chair, he gave no sign that he recognized or knew her. Smart guy.

"Where's the girl?" Thomas asked, his tone harsh. He wasn't in the mood for pleasantries.

"She's outside, sir," Ahmed replied, and Ola felt Okinosho's shoulders relax under her hand.

"And your disrespectful friend?"

"He's also outside."

Okinosho leaned back in the chair and steepled his hands. "Good, good." He smirked at Ahmed, and Ola admired how unmoving Ahmed kept his face. "You know I wanted to kill your friend, yes?"

"Yes," Ahmed replied, deadpan. "I heard."

"It was God's will. You cannot violate the earthly vessel of God's anointed with such impudence and expect that there will be no repercussions. Our God is a jealous God."

Ahmed wisely kept his mouth shut. Ola hid a smile.

"I asked you here, to bring both your friend and the girl here, so that divine justice may be meted out. It would have been righteous to execute the boy, but the Holy Spirit spoke to me through none other than Ola here." Thomas reached up and caressed her hand, and Ola bent down to kiss his cheek. "The message was one of grace, Alhaji, one of mercy. The kind of mercy God showed Abraham on the mountain. Where a blood sacrifice was required, a proxy was accepted. And so, your friend's life will be spared."

Ahmed bowed his head. "Thank you, sir."

Okinosho raised a hand. "You have not heard what the proxy is, the extent of the grace I am proffering in my generosity, my God-given magnanimity."

"Of course. Please, continue."

"You see, your friend thinks he is . . . superior. Better than the rest of us when, really, he is nothing; he is dust as we are all dust. He needs to be reminded that we are, in God's eyes, all the same. Some of us might be anointed by the calling, but we will all return to dust. We are all flesh. Only God is God. Only God can judge." He stood up from his desk and smoothed out his agbada. "So. In exchange for your friend's life, he will do something else for me. For himself. To remind himself of who and what he is, what we all are. Weak subjects of the Most High."

Ola could see apprehension creeping into Ahmed's face. There was no need for it—not a drop of Kalu's blood would be shed. She was proud of herself for coming up with this alternative, something that would fulfill Okinosho's need for vengeance and keep everyone in this shitstorm alive. She'd even gotten Thomas to pay the girl so exorbitantly that the child would be able to retire after this job. Luckily, Okinosho was cruel enough to not care about how much money he threw away as long as Kalu suffered.

Suffering, Ola had learned, was quite often better than death. It left you space for a life afterward, a life you could bend into whatever you wanted. It left you a chance.

Okinosho leaned forward, planting his palms on his desk, his eyes boring into Ahmed's. "Your friend is going to fuck that girl in front of me, Alhaji. He's going to fuck her until he comes, and I want to see it, you understand? As proof, so to speak."

The blood had drained from Ahmed's face, but he remained silent. Okinosho cocked his head to the side, examining Ahmed's expression.

"I am being fair, Alhaji. Surely you can't have a problem with this. I am paying the girl far more than what you paid her for your party. You knew what she'd be doing there; I'm sure you don't mind your friend doing it as well." His voice tightened into a sliver of steel. "Be glad I am not requiring you to participate as well. It was under your roof that this unfortunate incident took place."

"I do not doubt your justice for a moment, sir."

Ola admired the skill with which Ahmed was lying to Okinosho's face. He was polite, courteous, hiding the horror he was feeling deep under layers of smooth facial muscles. She knew the pastor would appreciate it too.

"Good," Okinosho said, straightening up. "Good. You will be the one telling your friend what his punishment is. Ola will tell the girl. I will meet you both in the yellow parlor. Ola, you know the way." He gathered the folds of his agbada at his shoulders and swept out of the room, leaving Ola alone with Ahmed.

Ahmed's face distorted into rage. "This was *your* idea?" he spat out. "Are you mad? Why couldn't you leave the girl out of it?"

Ola stared at him. He couldn't be serious. "I did you a favor, you idiot. Do you know the kind of punishments Okinosho gives, the kind of shit he's capable of? What did you think he would accept as a substitute for your friend's life? Don't be so fucking naïve."

"But this? *This?*" His mouth twisted. "You're sick."

Ola laughed. "You're the one who put her in a room full of old perverts like Okinosho. Don't lecture me about who's sick. You should be fucking *thanking* me. I didn't need to do this, and I only did it for Souraya, who *you* exposed to all this rubbish." She eyed him up and down with contempt. "I should have let your friend die, you ungrateful piece of shit."

Ahmed's mouth opened and closed as Ola pushed past him out

into the grand corridors of Okinosho's house, uniformed staff standing discreetly at intervals. Ola snapped her fingers at one of them. "Where's the small girl they brought?" she asked.

"This way, madam." They led her into a dressing room where the girl was seated at a vanity, a woman applying kohl to her eyes. She *did* look young. The kohl wouldn't make her look any older, neither would the red lipstick they'd put on her. Ola knew from experience that this wasn't the point—in fact, it would only emphasize how young she looked.

"Can you people step outside for a few minutes? I need to talk to the girl." The servants melted away and Ola looked at the girl, whose head was bent, her hands folded loosely in her lap. "What's your name?"

"Machi." Her voice was clear and ringing, not wilting like Ola had expected. The demure thing was probably a mask, then; she was pretending to be good—quiet and well-behaved. What she thought they probably wanted her to be. She wasn't wrong. Okinosho liked them like that, the younger they were.

"Look at me when I'm talking to you," Ola said, and Machi raised her eyes to her. They were flickering between emotions almost faster than Ola could catch—admiration, a sullen defiance, nervousness. "Do you know why you're here?"

Machi shrugged. "A job," she said, and Ola had to bite back a smile. She sounded like a much younger Ola but with more manners and less sarcasm. Ola sat down next to her and told her what the job was, about Kalu, who he was, why Okinosho was paying so much for Machi to be there tonight, what he wanted from her and from Kalu. Machi gasped when Ola told her how much she was going to get paid.

"It's a lie," she said, tears springing to her eyes. "It's a lie."

"It's not," Ola replied. "That's how much you're getting." She watched as the girl threw her head back, trying to stop the tears from ruining her mascara. Ola wasn't the type of person to feel pity for anyone, but she did want this child to know that she had options. That you could have a chance after suffering. "You can do whatever you want with it. Get a passport. Leave this place. Go to another city. Go back to your family if you have one. Whatever you want."

"Why?" Machi asked. "Why is he giving me that much?"

Ola looked at her. "I told him to."

Machi's eyes widened and she dropped to her knees, throwing her arms around Ola's legs. "Thank you, ma! Thank you so much!"

"Oh, stand up, stand up!" Ola pulled her up and forced her back into her chair. "It's not that serious. You still have to do the job."

Much to her amusement, Machi pulled a dismissive face.

"I saw the man when he came in." She shrugged again. "It's nothing. The party was harder, that was many of them. This is only one and he doesn't even want to do anything."

She sounded like such a professional, it was—as much as Ola fought not to admit it—a fucking shame to hear how flippant she was about it. But Ola had been like that too. They had all been like that. You couldn't save people; this world was brutal. You did what you could where you could. At least Kalu would be alive and this child would be free afterward. Ahmed could call her sick if he liked, but he had changed nothing in anyone's lives for the better while Ola had saved two people in one day. It was enough even if no one else thought so. She stood up and looked down at Machi. "Let's go then."

Machi hesitated. "They were still doing my eyes."

"Let me see." Ola bent down and examined Machi's makeup.

"Oh, that's nothing. Here." She took the kohl and finished the swoop in the corner of Machi's left eye. "There you go," she murmured. "Perfect." She straightened up and Machi gazed adoringly at her. It made Ola uncomfortable. "Let's go before he gets angry again."

nineteen

I t was the most humiliating and devastating thing Kalu had ever done and would ever do in his life.

He knew it would follow him into his nightmares for years afterward—the feeling of taking his clothes off in a room full of people. Okinosho and his cruel smile, Ahmed's pained face, Ola's smooth one, Machi's expressionless mask of red mouth and lined eyes. She had taken off the robe they had put her in and was standing there naked, as if it was nothing. Her body was barely formed, a small chest, a body that was either shaved or—he was going to believe she'd been shaved. She was seventeen; Ahmed had told him she was seventeen. It didn't matter if she looked younger; he wasn't doing what it looked like, not like that. And he was being coerced. If he'd learned anything about consent, it was that if you weren't safe enough to say no, your yes couldn't count. This couldn't count. He would die if he didn't do it.

Kalu wondered if it was better to die rather than do it.

He had almost fought Ahmed when his friend told him what Okinosho had decided; he'd almost left, but Ahmed had caught him by the shoulders, those familiar grooves.

"He will kill you if you don't do it," Ahmed had cried out, his eyes shockingly wet. He had sounded so young, just a boy in secondary school clinging to his friend, terrified. "He will *kill* you, Kalu! You have no choice." Ahmed had pressed their foreheads together. *"You have no choice."*

Kalu had agreed, if you could call it agreeing. And now he was pulling off his T-shirt, the air-conditioning in the room goose-pimpling his skin.

Okinosho's eyes were greedy on him. "Lie on the floor," the pastor commanded the girl, and Kalu winced at her obedience. "Open your legs."

Ahmed looked away, which Kalu found rich. After all those parties, all those things he'd justified, this was the one he couldn't watch? What a fucking hypocrite. Ola was watching, though, her eyes unmoving except for an occasional blink. *Like a vulture*, Kalu thought, *waiting for me to rot.*

"Hurry up," the pastor said to him. "My wife is waiting for me and I have service in the morning."

Kalu took off his trousers and underwear. Okinosho grunted with satisfaction.

"Oya," he said, gesturing to Machi. "Start your penance. It will end when you spill your seed where we can see it."

Kalu knelt between the girl's legs and tried not to look at her face. He wished he'd never gone to Ahmed's party, never met that woman on the balcony, never heard what she'd said that led him barging into that room.

He'd saved no one, certainly not himself. Okinosho was laughing and telling Kalu he'd better do something to get hard unless he wanted to be paying penance till morning came. Ahmed, the coward, was still looking away. Kalu felt something in him curl and blacken as he reached down and began to stroke himself.

So, he thought, *this was what damnation felt like*—a corruption he would never recover from, a piece of his soul that would never come back to him, that would never be whole again. Machi didn't look at him, didn't move.

Kalu began to push himself inside her.

twenty

The car was silent as Ahmed drove Kalu home.

The air between them was heavy with things that simply couldn't be said, and Ahmed wasn't sure what to do. His hand tremored against the steering wheel, and the image of Kalu on the carpet of the pastor's house burned through his mind. Machi's bored face turned away beneath him, the expression on Kalu's face when he eventually came, the way he clutched at the girl's hips. He'd had no choice. Okinosho would've killed him. Ahmed hoped he'd been thinking of Aima while he did it. Souraya would have whispered something else, another possibility—what if Kalu had simply thought of the child beneath him and what if that had been enough?

Ahmed shuddered. Kalu would never admit that even if it was true and Aima was no Souraya. How could any relationship survive that? It was a blessing that Okinosho hadn't hunted down Aima and forced her to watch it as well. She could've easily been one of the people in that room, and Kalu would be even more shattered than he was now. Ahmed glanced over at Kalu, realizing that his best friend didn't even know Aima was still in the city. There hadn't been time to mention it, and Ahmed couldn't tell Kalu about Seun, about the specifics of how he'd been part of orchestrating this whole thing with Machi. How he'd asked Ola for help. How he'd been the one to bring Machi there. If Okinosho had cut Kalu to the bone with this thing, then Ahmed had been the one who forged the knife and handed it over. He might as well have wrapped his hand around Kalu's penis and guided it into the girl himself.

Kalu was curled up against the car door, unmoving. He'd been blank and numb ever since the pastor had waved them off with his shark's smile. Ahmed had had to buckle him into the passenger seat, murmuring the few lies of comfort he could come up with in that moment, that it would be fine, that it was over now. He'd plugged Kalu's phone into the car's charger. The screen was smashed and it glitched a few lines before turning on. Kalu had slumped against the door and hadn't moved since. It wasn't fine. It wasn't over at all—whatever personal hell Kalu was in was just beginning.

The guilt gnawed away inside Ahmed's chest, but he tried to push it down. Would he have done anything differently? Would he have refused Machi if he'd known that's what Okinosho meant to use her for? Wasn't it better than Kalu's dying, this bargain he and Ola and Okinosho had carved into existence? And then there was Seun's body—the heaviness of his limbs, the gape of his mouth. Hadn't this all been an impossible choice to make?

Ahmed was interrupted by Kalu's phone ringing. He glanced down and saw Aima's name jagged on the screen. Kalu hadn't moved his head or opened his eyes.

"Kalu," he said. "Kalu. You have to answer it. It's Aima."

A flicker crossed Kalu's face, a buried expression rippling under his skin, but he didn't move. The phone kept ringing. Ahmed swore under his breath. He could only pray that Aima would say nothing about Seun, that she would hold his secrets as well as he planned to hold Kalu's.

"She's here, Kalu. She never went to London."

That caught Kalu's attention. He raised his head slowly and tears filled his eyes.

"She's here?" His voice was broken and rusty.

"You should talk to her." The suggestion brought a panicked shame galloping through Kalu's face, and Ahmed rushed to reassure him. "Don't tell her anything about today or last night. It didn't happen. You hear me? *It didn't happen.*"

The phone stopped ringing, and Ahmed tapped on the compromised screen, calling her back. He handed the phone to Kalu. "You can still have a future with her; it's a good sign that she's calling you. Talk to her. Put all this behind you. Don't let what Okinosho did spoil your life."

Kalu nodded and took the phone, but when Aima's voice came through the line, Ahmed could see his resolve tremble.

"Kalu?" she said. "Are you there?"

"Yes," he said. "Where are you?"

"I'm here, but before you say anything, I just want to tell you something, okay?"

"Aima . . ."

Ahmed could hear her voice through the phone, faint but clear. "No, let me talk. It's important. I'm sorry, Kalu. You were right; it shouldn't have mattered about the proposal. We always said we'd do it in our own time, we were always on the same page, and we love each other. I shouldn't have listened to everyone else. I should've been on your team, on our team. I'm so sorry. I couldn't go to London. I'm not ready to give up on us. I want to try again, babe, do you? Can we try again? Please? I'm so sorry."

Kalu was crying with no sound, his cheeks wet. Ahmed knew it was all he'd been wanting, for Aima to come back, for them to have another chance. He smiled at Kalu encouragingly as the car wound up the highland roads, but when Kalu looked at him, there was a shadow in his eyes that was deeper, darker than Ahmed had ever seen.

"I'm sorry, Aima," he said, and Ahmed's heart sank. "I . . . I can't do this. I'm not . . . I'm not who you think I am."

His voice cracked apart and Ahmed looked away. In his head, the image of Kalu pulling out of Machi was playing, Okinosho's grin as he stared at Kalu, white ropes smearing along Machi's thighs.

"I'm so sorry, Aima," Kalu was saying.

"*No.*" Her voice was distraught. "No, you can't be serious. Kalu, please, I'm begging you! What happened? What changed?"

Kalu covered his mouth with his hand, as if the truth would leap out and shove itself into the phone, into Aima's ear, break her mind apart like it had broken Kalu's. "I can't . . . I can't tell you."

"Tell me what? You can tell me anything, love. Please."

Ahmed reached across the car and grabbed the phone, ending the call. Kalu exhaled in a ragged gasp. "You can't *ever* tell her," Ahmed said, keeping his voice harder than he wanted to. "Give it time and maybe you can try again. But you can't tell her any of it."

Kalu laughed, a hollow and dull sound. "What kind of relationship is that? What kind of love is that, keeping a secret like this?"

Seun's eyes going blank, Ahmed's hands clenched around his throat. He had almost let himself pretend it hadn't happened and even that twisted erotic moment with Souraya, that had been a mistake. He'd brought his darkness to her, fucked it into her. He'd taken her into the belly of the city she hated because that's who he was, and in the end, he had seen the hollowed look in her eyes when Ola led her away. He could chase her down, sure, but Ahmed knew he had already lost her. His throat was hoarse. "Everyone has secrets, Kalu. That's just how it is. You put it somewhere else in your head. You find a way."

Kalu gave him an unimaginably sorrowful look. "You pretend it never happened," he said, his voice plaintive, and for some reason, Ahmed felt like he was talking about two boys in a dark bedroom a lifetime ago. He forced himself to look at his best friend.

"It's how you survive," he said. "I don't . . . I don't know another way, Kalu. I don't know another way."

Kalu curled back toward the window. "I feel like he reached inside me, Ahmed. The pastor. I feel like he took a handful of dead things and he pushed his hand into my chest and dumped them there and now I'm decaying, like him. I'm rotting; I'm dying."

"He doesn't get to do that, Kalu. He doesn't get to change who you are."

"He already has."

Ahmed didn't know what to say to that. The night was thick and dark around them as they drove.

"The woman at the party warned me," Kalu said.

"Which woman?"

"Some woman on the balcony. She said this city changes us so slowly that we don't notice, little by little. Until it's too late. And we're part of everything we always hated."

Ahmed wanted to say something, anything, but there was Seun's weight in his arms, Machi's face against the carpet, Souraya sobbing over her bloody hands. He swallowed hard, a grief-colored stone falling endlessly inside him. Kalu fell silent, his broken phone lighting up with texts and missed calls from the woman he loved. Ahmed stopped the car at a red light. He wanted so badly to tell Kalu everything, everything that had happened, seek understanding, absolution, something. Anything that wasn't this silence, this horrific shame, this gutting despair carving both of them into pieces.

As if he could tell, Kalu suddenly spoke up. "It's too late," he said.

Ahmed's fingers dug into the steering wheel. The light turned green. "You're right," he said, as a fault line inside him yawned into something worse. "It's too late."

He put his foot on the accelerator, and looking straight out into nothing, he drove them both into the night.

Acknowledgments

This book has been a long time coming. It was originally a short story that was published in 2014 by *Sable Literary Magazine*, and I would like to thank Kadija George and Jacob Ross for their edits on that. You both helped develop my voice at such a nascent stage in my career, and I am deeply grateful for it. Jacob was the first editor to bluntly point out that I needed self-restraint and as a baby writer, that critique was such a gift. I took his advice and it has continued to serve me throughout my entire career. Thank you for not holding back.

Many thanks to my editor, Laura Perciasepe, and to everyone at Riverhead Books for your work in stitching this book together into a physical story that can now go out and touch the world. I hope you are as proud of it as I am.

As always, a deep well of thanks to my agents at the Wylie Agency, particularly Jacqueline Ko, Kristi Murray, and Jessica Bullock. What luck to have you all on my team!

To everyone who read drafts of this book over the years, who work-shopped it with me and gave me notes, thank you so much. These books are never made alone. To my family and my community, thank you for growing with me.

To my readers—I can't tell you how pleased I am to be sharing my *eighth* book with you! Thank you so much for supporting me and my stories, for telling your friends and family about them, for gifting my books to people you care about, for teaching my books in schools even while under threat, for understanding that disseminating the sto-ries is part of the work. I couldn't be in this service without you. This book might be difficult to witness but my hope is that it gives us some courage to witness the difficult things in our lives, to understand how close they can brush to our skin, and to move accordingly.